Also by Robin Cook in Pan B

Brain

Coma

Fever

Godplayer

Mindbend

Outbreak

Sphinx

ROBIN COOK

Mortal Fear

Pan Books
in association with Macmillan

First published in the United Kingdom in 1988 by
Macmillan London Ltd
This edition published 1988 by Pan Books Ltd,
Cavaye Place, London SW10 9PG
in association with Macmillan London Ltd
9 8 7 6 5 4

ISBN 0 330 30760 6

Printed and bound in Great Britain by
Richard Clay Ltd, Bungay, Suffolk

ACKNOWLEDGMENTS

This book could not have been written without the support and encouragement of all my friends who have helped me in a difficult time.
You all know who you are,
and you all have my heartfelt thanks.

For my older brother, Lee, and
my younger sister, Laurie.
I've never been between two nicer people.

PROLOGUE

OCTOBER 11, WEDNESDAY P.M.

The sudden appearance of the foreign proteins was the molecular equivalent of the Black Plague. It was a death sentence with no chance of reprieve, and Cedric Harring had no idea of the drama about to happen inside him.

In sharp contrast, the individual cells of Cedric Harring's body knew exactly what disastrous consequences awaited them. The mysterious new proteins that swept into their midst and through their membranes were overwhelming, and the small amounts of enzymes capable of dealing with the newcomers were totally inadequate. Within Cedric's pituitary gland, the deadly new proteins were able to bind themselves to the repressors that covered the genes for the death hormone. From that moment, with the fatal genes exposed, the outcome was inevitable. The death hormone began to be synthetized in unprecedented amounts. Entering the bloodstream, the hormone coursed out into Cedric's body. No cell was immune. The end was only a matter of time. Cedric Harring was about to disintegrate into his stellar elements.

1.

The pain was like a white-hot knife starting somewhere in his chest and quickly radiating upward in blinding paroxysms to paralyze his jaw and left arm. Instantly Cedric felt the terror of the mortal fear of death. Cedric Harring had never felt anything like it.

By reflex he gripped the steering wheel of his car more tightly and somehow managed to stay in control of the weaving vehicle as he gasped for breath. He'd just entered Storrow Drive from Berkeley Street in downtown Boston, and had accelerated westward, merging with the maddening Boston traffic. The images of the road swam before him and then receded, as if they existed at the end of a long tunnel.

By sheer strength of will, Cedric resisted the darkness that threatened to engulf him. Gradually, the scene brightened. He was still alive. Instead of pulling over, instinct told him his only chance was to get to a hospital as fast as possible. By lucky coincidence the Good Health Plan Clinic was not too far off. Hold on, he told himself.

Along with the pain came a drenching sweat that started on Cedric's forehead but soon spread to the rest of his body. Sweat stung his eyes, but he dared not loosen his grip on the steering wheel to wipe it away. He exited the highway onto the Fenway, a parklike complex in Boston, as the pain returned, squeezing his chest like a cinch of steel wire. Ahead cars were slowing for a traffic light. He couldn't stop. There was no time. Leaning forward, he depressed the horn and shot through the intersection. Cars went by, missing him by inches. He could see the faces of the startled and enraged drivers. He was now on Park Drive with the Back Bay Fens and the scruffy victory gardens on his left. The pain was constant now, strong and overpowering. He could hardly breathe.

The hospital was ahead on the right, on the previous site of a Sears building. Only a little further. Please. . . . A large white sign with a red arrow and red letters that said EMERGENCY loomed above.

Cedric managed to drive directly up to the emergency room platform, braking belatedly and crashing into the concrete abutment. He slumped forward, hitting the horn and gasping for breath.

The first person to reach his car was the security guard. He yanked open the door and after a glance at Cedric's frightening pallor yelled for help. Cedric barely choked out the words, "Chest pain." The head nurse, Hilary Barton, appeared and called for a gurney. By the time the nurses and the security man had Cedric out of the car, one of the emergency room residents had appeared and helped maneuver him onto the stretcher. His name was Emil Frank and he'd been a resident for only four months. A few years previously he would have been called an intern. He too noticed Cedric's cream-colored skin and profuse perspiration.

"Diaphoresis," he said with authority. "Probably a heart attack."

Hilary rolled her eyes. Of course it was a heart attack. She rushed the patient inside, ignoring Dr. Frank, who'd plugged his stethoscope into his ears and was trying to listen to Cedric's heart.

As soon as they reached the treatment room, Hilary ordered oxygen, IV fluids and electrocardiographic monitoring, attaching the three main EKG leads herself. As soon as Emil had the IV going, she suggested to him that he order 4 mg. of morphine to be given IV immediately.

As the pain receded a little, Cedric's mind cleared. Even though no one had told him, he knew he'd had a heart attack. He also knew he'd come very close to dying. Even now, staring at the oxygen mask, the IV, and the EKG machine as it spewed paper out onto the floor, Cedric had never felt so vulnerable in his life.

"We're going to move you to the coronary care unit," Hilary said. "Everything is going to be okay." She patted Cedric's hand. He tried to smile. "We've called your wife. She's on her way."

The coronary intensive care unit was similar to the emergency room as far as Cedric was concerned—and just as frightening. It was filled with esoteric, ultramodern electronic technology. He could hear his heartbeat being echoed by a mechanical beep, and when he turned his head he could see a phosphorescent blip trace across a round TV screen.

Although the machines were frightening, it was a source of some reassurance to know all that technology was there. Even more reassuring was the fact that his own doctor, who had been paged shortly after Cedric's arrival, had just come into the ICU.

Cedric had been a patient of Dr. Jason Howard's for five years. He had begun going when his employers, the Boston National Bank, insisted that senior executives have yearly physicals. When Dr. Howard suddenly sold his private practice several years previously and joined the staff of the Good Health Plan (GHP), Cedric had dutifully followed. The move required changing his health plan from Blue Cross to the prepaid variety, but it was Dr. Howard that had attracted him, not GHP, and Cedric had let Dr. Howard know it in no uncertain terms.

"How are you doing?" Jason asked, grasping Cedric's arm but paying more attention to the EKG screen.

"Not . . . great," Cedric rasped. It took several breaths to get out the two words.

"I want you to try to relax."

Cedric closed his eyes. *Relax! What a joke.*

"Do you have a lot of pain?"

Cedric nodded. Tears were running down his cheeks.

"Another dose of morphine," Jason ordered.

Within minutes of the second dose, the pain became more tolerable. Dr. Howard was talking with the resident, making sure all the appropriate blood samples had been drawn and asking for some kind of catheter. Cedric watched him, reassured just seeing Howard's handsome, hawklike profile and sensing the man's confidence and authority. Best of all, he could feel Dr. Howard's compassion. Dr. Howard cared.

"We have to do a little procedure," Jason was saying. "We want to insert a Swan-Ganz catheter so we can see what's going on inside. We'll use a local anesthesia so it won't hurt, okay?"

Cedric nodded. As far as he was concerned, Dr. Howard had carte blanche to do whatever he felt was necessary. Cedric appreciated Dr. Howard's approach. He never talked down to his patients—even when Cedric had had his physical three weeks ago and Howard had lectured him about his high-cholesterol diet, his two-pack-a-day cigarette habit, and his lack of exercise. *If only I'd listened,* Cedric thought. But despite Dr. Howard's doomsday approach to Cedric's lifestyle, the doctor had admitted that the tests were okay. His cholesterol was not too high, and his electrocardiogram had been fine. Reassured, Cedric put off attempts to stop smoking and start exercising.

Then, less than a week after his physical, Cedric

felt as if he were coming down with the flu. But that had been only the beginning. His digestive system began acting up, and he suffered terrible arthritis. Even his eyesight seemed to deteriorate. He remembered telling his wife it was as though he had aged thirty years. He had all the symptoms his father had endured during his final months in the nursing home. Sometimes when he caught an unexpected glimpse of his reflection, it was as if he were staring at the old man's ghost.

Despite the morphine, Cedric felt a sudden stab of white-hot, crushing pain. He felt himself receding into a tunnel as he had in the car. He could still see Dr. Howard, but the doctor was far away, and his voice was fading. Then the tunnel started to fill with water. Cedric choked and tried to swim to the surface. His arms frantically grappled the air.

Later, Cedric regained consciousness for a few moments of agony. As he struggled back to awareness, he felt intermittent pressure on his chest, and something in his throat. Someone was kneeling beside him, crushing his chest with his hands. Cedric started to cry out when there was an explosion in his chest and darkness descended like a lead blanket.

Death had always been Dr. Jason Howard's enemy. As a resident at Massachusetts General, he'd carried that belief to the extreme, never giving up on a cardiac arrest until a superior ordered him to stop.

Now he refused to believe that the fifty-six-year-old man whom he'd examined only three weeks earlier and had declared generally healthy was about to die. It was a personal affront.

Glancing up at the monitor, which still showed normal EKG activity, Jason touched Cedric's neck. He could feel no pulse. "Let me have a cardiac needle," he demanded. "And someone get a blood pressure." A large cardiac needle was thrust into his hand as he palpated Cedric's chest to locate the ridge on the sternum.

"No blood pressure," reported Philip Barnes, an anesthesiologist who had responded to the code call that automatically went out when Cedric arrested. He'd placed an endotracheal tube into Cedric's trachea and was ventilating him with oxygen by compressing the Ambu bag.

To Jason, the diagnosis was obvious: cardiac rupture. With the EKG still being recorded, yet no pumping action of the heart, a situation of electromechanical dissociation prevailed. It could mean only one thing. The portion of Cedric's heart that had been deprived of its blood supply had split open like a squashed grape. To prove this horrendous diagnosis, Jason plunged the cardiac needle into Cedric's chest, piercing the heart's pericardial covering. When he drew back on the plunger, the syringe filled with blood. There was no doubt. Cedric's heart had burst open inside his chest.

"Let's get him to surgery," Jason shouted, grabbing the end of the bed. Philip rolled his eyes at

Judith Reinhart, the coronary care head nurse. They both knew it was futile. At best they might get Cedric on the heart-lung machine, but what then?

Philip stopped ventilating the patient. But instead of helping to push the bed, he walked over to Jason and gently put an arm on his shoulder, restraining him. "It's got to be cardiac rupture. You know it. I know it. We've lost this one, Jason."

Jason made a motion to protest, but Philip tightened his hold. Jason glanced at Cedric's ivory-colored face. He knew Philip was right. As much as he hated to admit it, the patient was lost.

"You're right," he said, and reluctantly let Philip and Judith lead him from the unit, leaving the other nurses to prepare the body.

As they walked over to the central desk, Jason admitted that Cedric was the third patient to die just weeks after having a clean physical. The first had been another heart attack, the other a massive stroke. "Maybe I should think about changing professions," Jason said half seriously. "Even my inpatients have been doing poorly."

"Just bad luck," Philip said, giving Jason a playful poke in the shoulder. "We all have our bad times. It'll get better."

"Yeah, sure," Jason said.

Philip left to return to surgery.

Jason found an empty chair and sat down heavily. He knew he'd have to get ready to face Cedric's wife, who would be arriving at the hospital at any moment. He felt drained. "You'd think by now I'd have gotten a little more accustomed to death," he said aloud.

"The fact that you don't is what makes you a good doctor," said Judith, attending to the paperwork associated with a death.

Jason accepted the compliment, but he knew his attitude toward death went far beyond the profession. Just two years ago death had destroyed all that Jason held dear. He could still remember the sound of the phone at quarter past midnight on a dark November night. He'd fallen asleep in the den trying to catch up on his journals. He thought it would be his wife, Danielle, calling from Children's Hospital, saying she'd be delayed. She was a pediatrician and had been called back to the hospital that evening to attend to a preemie in respiratory distress. But it had been the turnpike police. They called to say that a semi coming from Albany with a load of aluminum siding had jumped the central divider and rammed into his wife's car head-on. She had never had a chance.

Jason could still remember the trooper's voice, as if it had been yesterday. First there'd been shock and disbelief, followed by anger. Then his own terrible guilt. If only he'd gone with Danielle as he sometimes had, and read at Countway Medical Library. Or if only he'd insisted she sleep at the hospital.

A few months later he'd sold the house that was haunted by Danielle's presence and his private practice and the office he'd shared with her. That was when he had joined the Good Health Plan. He'd done everything Patrick Quillan, a psychiatrist friend, had suggested he do. But the pain was still there, and the anger, too.

"Excuse me, Dr. Howard?"

Jason looked up into the broad face of Kay Ramn, the unit secretary.

"Mrs. Harring is in the waiting room," Kay said. "I told her you'd be out to talk with her."

"Oh, God," Jason said, rubbing his eyes. Speaking to the relatives after a patient died was difficult for any doctor, but since Danielle's death, Jason felt the families' pain as if it were his own.

Across from the coronary care unit was a small sitting room with outdated magazines, vinyl chairs and plastic plants. Mrs. Harring was staring out the window that faced north toward Fenway Park and the Charles River. She was a slight woman with hair that had been allowed to go naturally gray. When Jason entered, she turned and looked at him with red-rimmed, terrified eyes.

"I'm Dr. Howard," Jason said, motioning for her to sit. She did, but on the very edge of the chair.

"So it is bad . . ." she began. Her voice trailed off.

"I'm afraid it is very bad," Jason said. "Mr. Harring has passed away. We did all we could. At least he didn't suffer." Jason hated himself for voicing those expected lies. He knew Cedric had suffered. He'd seen the mortal fear in his face. Death was always a struggle, rarely the peaceful ebbing of life portrayed in film.

The color drained from Mrs. Harring's face, and for a moment Jason thought she would faint. Finally, she said, "I can't believe it."

Jason nodded. "I know." And know he did.

"It's not right," she said. She looked at Jason defiantly, her face reddening. "I mean, you just gave him a clean bill of health. You gave him all those tests and they were normal! Why didn't you find something? *You might have prevented this.*"

Jason recognized the anger, the familiar precursor to grief. He felt great compassion for her. "I didn't exactly give him a clean bill of health," he said gently. "His lab studies were satisfactory, but I warned him as I always did about his smoking and diet. And I reminded him that his father had died of a heart attack. All these factors put him in a high-risk category despite his lab values."

"But his father was seventy-four when he died. Cedric is only fifty-six! What's the point of a physical if my husband dies just three weeks later?"

"I'm sorry," Jason said softly. "Our predictive abilities are limited. We know that. We can only do the best we can."

Mrs. Harring sighed, letting her breath out. Her narrow shoulders sagged forward. Jason could see the anger fading. In its place came the crushing sadness. When she spoke, her voice was shaking. "I know you do the best you can. I'm sorry."

Jason leaned forward and put his hand on her shoulder. She felt delicate under her thin silk dress. "I know how hard this is for you."

"Can I see him?" she asked through her tears.

"Of course." Jason got to his feet and offered her a hand.

"Did you know Cedric had made an appointment to see you?" Mrs. Harring said as they walked into the corridor. She wiped her eyes with a tissue she'd taken from her purse.

"No, I didn't," Jason admitted.

"Next week. It was the first available appointment. He wasn't feeling well."

Jason felt the uncomfortable stirring of defensive concern. Although he was certain no malpractice had been committed, that was no guarantee against a suit.

"Did he complain of chest pain when he called?" Jason asked. He stopped Mrs. Harring in front of the CCU door.

"No, no. Just a lot of unrelated symptoms. Mostly exhaustion."

Jason breathed a sigh of relief.

"His joints ached," Mrs. Harring continued. "And his eyes were bothering him. He was having trouble driving at night."

Trouble driving at night? Although such a symptom did not relate to a heart attack, it rang some kind of a bell in Jason's mind.

"And his skin got very dry. And he had lost a great deal of hair—"

"Hair naturally replaces itself," Jason said mechanically. It was obvious that this litany of nonspecific complaints had nothing to do with the man's massive heart attack. He pushed open the heavy door to the unit and motioned Mrs. Harring to follow him. He guided her into the appropriate cubicle.

Cedric had been covered with a clean white sheet. Mrs. Harring put her thin, bony hand on her husband's head.

"Would you like to see his face?" Jason asked.

Mrs. Harring nodded, tears reappearing and streaming down her face. Jason folded back the sheet and stepped back.

"Oh, God!" she cried. "He looks like his father did before he died!" She turned away and murmured, "I didn't realize how death aged a person."

It doesn't usually, Jason thought. Now that he wasn't concentrating on Cedric's heart, he noticed the changes in his face. His hair had thinned. And his eyes appeared to have receded deep into their orbits, giving the dead man's face a hollow, gaunt look, a far cry from the appearance Jason remembered when he'd done Cedric's physical three weeks earlier. Jason replaced the sheet and led Mrs. Harring back to the small sitting room. He sat her back down and took a seat across from her.

"I know it's not a good time to bring this up," he said, "but we would like permission to examine your husband's body. Maybe we can learn something that will help someone in the future."

"I suppose if it could help others . . ." Mrs. Harring bit her lip. It was hard for her to think, much less make a decision.

"It will. And we really appreciate your generosity. If you'd just wait here, I'll have someone bring out the forms."

"All right," Mrs. Harring said, with resignation.

"I'm sorry," Jason told her again. "Please call me if there is anything I can do."

Jason found Judith and told her that Mrs. Harring had agreed to an autopsy.

"We called the medical examiner's office and spoke to a Dr. Danforth. She said they want the case," Judith told him.

"Well, make sure they send us all the results." Jason hesitated. "Did you notice anything odd about Mr. Harring? I mean, did he appear unusually old for a man of fifty-six?"

"I didn't notice," Judith said, hurrying away. In a unit with eleven patients, she was already involved in another crisis.

Jason knew that Cedric's emergency was putting him behind schedule, but Cedric's unexpected death continued to disturb him. Making up his mind, he called Dr. Danforth, who had a deep resonant voice, and convinced her to let the postmortem be done in house, saying death was due to a long family history of heart disease and that he wanted to compare the heart pathology with the stress EKGs that had been done. The medical examiner graciously released the case.

* * *

Before leaving the unit, Jason used the opportunity to check another of his patients who was not doing well.

Sixty-one-year-old Brian Lennox was another heart attack victim. He had been admitted three days previously, and although he'd done well initially, his course had taken a sudden turn for the worse. That morning when Jason had made rounds he had planned to move Lennox from CCU, but the man was in the early throes of congestive heart failure. It was an acute disappointment for Jason, since Brian Lennox had to be added to the list of Jason's inpatients who had recently gone sour. Instead of transferring the patient, Jason had instituted aggressive treatment for the heart failure.

Any hope of a rapid return by Mr. Lennox to his previous state was dashed when Jason saw him. He was sitting up, breathing rapidly and shallowly in an oxygen mask. His face had an evil grayness that Jason had learned to fear. A nurse attending him straightened up from adjusting the IV.

"How are things going?" Jason asked, forcing a smile. But he didn't have to ask. Lennox lifted a limp hand. He couldn't talk. All his attention was directed toward his breathing efforts.

The nurse pulled Jason from the cubicle into the center of the room. Her name tag said Miss Levay, RN. "Nothing seems to be working," she said, concernedly. "The pulmonary wedge pressure has gone up despite everything. He's had the diuretic, the hydralazine and the nitroprusside. I don't know what to do."

Jason glanced over Miss Levay's shoulder into the room. Mr. Lennox was breathing like a miniature locomotive. Jason didn't have any ideas save for a transplant, and of course, that was out of the question. The man was a heavy smoker and undoubtedly had emphysema as well as heart trouble. But Mr. Lennox should have responded to the medication. The only thing Jason could imagine was the area of the heart involved with the heart attack was extending.

"Let's get a cardiology consult stat," Jason said. "Maybe they'll be able to see if the coronary vessels are more involved. It's the only thing I can think of. Maybe he's a candidate for bypass."

"Well at least it's something," said Miss Levay. Without hesitation, she went to the central desk to call.

Jason returned to the cubicle to dispense some compassion to Brian Lennox. He wished he had more to give but the diuretic was supposed to reduce fluid while the hydralazine and nitroprusside were supposed to reduce pre-load and after-load on the heart. All of this was geared to lower the effort the heart had to expend to pump the blood. This would allow the heart to heal after the insult of the heart attack. But it wasn't working. Lennox was slipping downhill despite all the efforts and all the technology. His eyes now had a sunken, glazed appearance.

Jason put his hand on Brian's forehead and pushed the hair back from his perspiring brow. To Jason's surprise, some of the hair came out in his hand. Momentarily confused, Jason stared at it, then he carefully pulled on a few other strands. They came out as well with almost no resistance. Checking the pillow behind Brian's head, Jason noticed more hair. Not an enormous amount but more than he would suspect. It made him wonder if any of the medications he'd ordered had hair loss as a potential side effect. He made a mental note to look that up in the evening. Obviously hair loss was not a major concern at the time. But it reminded him of Mrs. Harring's comment. Curious!

After leaving word that he should be called after the cardiology consult on Brian Lennox and after one more masochistic glance at the sheet-wrapped corpse of Cedric Harring, Jason left the coronary care unit and took the elevator down to the second floor, which connected the hospital with the outpatient building. The GHP Medical Center was the impressive central facility of the large prepaid health plan. It incorporated a four-hundred-bed hospital with an ambulatory surgery center, separate outpatient department, a small research wing, and a floor of administrative offices. The main building, originally designed as a Sears office building, had an art deco flair. It had been gutted and totally renovated to incorporate the hospital and the administrative offices. The outpatient and research building was new, but it had been built to match the old structure, with the same careful details. It was built on pillars over a parking lot. Jason's office was on the third floor, along with the rest of the department of internal medicine.

There were sixteen internists at the GHP Center. Most were specialists, though a few like Jason maintained a generalized practice. Jason had always felt that the whole panoply of human illness interested him, not just specific organs or systems.

The doctors' offices were spread around the perimeter, with a central desk surrounded by a waiting area with comfortable seating. Examining rooms were clustered between the offices. At one end were small treatment rooms. There was a pool of support personnel who were supposed to rotate positions, but in actual fact the nurses and secretaries tended to work for one or another of the doctors. Such a situation promoted efficiency since there could be some adaptation to each doctor's eccentricities. A nurse by the name of Sally Baunan and a secretary by the name of Claudia Mockelberg had aligned themselves with Jason. He got along well with both women, but particularly Claudia, who took an almost motherly interest in Jason's well-being. She had lost her only son in Vietnam and contended that Jason looked just like him despite the age difference.

Both women saw Jason coming and followed him to his office. Sally had an armload of charts of waiting patients. She was the compulsive one, and

Jason's absence had disturbed her carefully planned routine. She was eager to "get the show on the road," but Claudia restrained her and sent her out of the room.

"Was it as bad as you look?" Claudia asked.

"Is it that obvious?" Jason said as he washed his hands at the sink in the corner of the room.

She nodded. "You look like you've been run over by an emotional train."

"Cedric Harring died," he said. "Do you remember him?"

"Vaguely," Claudia admitted. "After you got called to the emergency room, I pulled his chart. It's on your desk."

Jason glanced down and saw it. Claudia's efficiency was sometimes unnerving.

"Why don't you sit down for a few moments," Claudia suggested. More than anyone else at GHP, Claudia knew Jason's reaction to death. She was one of only two people at the Center in whom Jason had confided about his wife's fatal accident.

"We must be really behind schedule," Jason said. "Sally will get her nose bent out of shape."

"Oh, screw Sally." Claudia came around Jason's desk and pushed him gently into the seat. "Sally can hold her water for a few minutes."

Jason smiled in spite of himself. Leaning forward, he fingered Cedric Harring's chart. "Do you remember last month the two others who died just after their physicals?"

"Briggs and Connoly," Claudia said without hesitation.

"How about pulling their charts? I don't like this trend."

"Only if you promise me you're not going to let yourself"—Claudia paused, struggling for a word—"get into a dither over this. People die. Unfortunately it happens. It's the nature of the business. You understand? Why don't you just have a cup of coffee."

"The charts," Jason repeated.

"Okay, okay," Claudia said, going out.

Jason opened Cedric Harring's chart, glancing through the history and physical. Except for his unhealthy living habits, there was nothing remarkable. Turning to the EKG and the stress EKG, Jason scanned the tracing, looking for some sign of the impending disaster. Even armed as he was with hindsight, he could find nothing.

Claudia came back and opened the door without knocking. Jason could hear Sally whine, "Claudia . . ." but Claudia shut the door on her and came over to Jason's desk. She plopped down Briggs's and Connoly's charts in front of him.

"The natives are getting restless," she said, then left.

Jason opened the two charts. Briggs had died of a massive heart attack probably similar to Harring's. Autopsy had shown extensive occlusion of all of the coronary vessels despite the EKG done during his physical four weeks prior to his death being as normal-looking as Harring's. Also like Harring's, his stress EKG had been normal. Jason shook his head in dismay. Even more than the normal EKG, the stress EKG was supposed to pick up such potentially fatal conditions. It certainly suggested that the executive physical was an exercise in futility. Not only was the examination failing to pick up these serious problems, but it was giving the patients a false sense of security. With the results being normal, there wasn't motivation for the patients to change their unhealthy lifestyles. Briggs, like Harring, had been in his late fifties, was a heavy smoker, and never exercised.

The second patient, Rupert Connoly, had died of a massive stroke. Again, it had been a short time after an executive-style physical, which in his case had also revealed no alarming abnormalities. In addition to a generally unhealthy lifestyle, Connoly had been a heavy drinker, though not an alcoholic. Jason was about to close the chart when he noticed something he had missed before. In the autopsy report the pathologist had recorded significant cataract development. Thinking that he'd not remembered the man's age correctly, Jason flipped to the information page. Connoly was only fifty-eight. Now cataracts were not entirely unknown at fifty-eight, but it was nonetheless rare. Turning to the physical, Jason checked to see if he'd noted cataracts. Embarrassingly he'd failed to include them, noting he described the "eyes, ears, nose, and throat" as being within normal limits. Jason wondered if he were getting sloppy in his "old" age. But then he noticed he described the retinas as appearing normal as well. In order to have visualized the retinas, Jason would have had to have sighted through a cataract. Not being an ophthalmologist, he knew his limitations in this regard. He wondered if certain kinds of cataracts impede the passage of light more than others. He added that question to his mental list of things to investigate.

Jason stacked the charts. Three apparently healthy men had all died a month after their physicals. *Jesus,* he thought. People were often scared of going to hospitals. If this got out, they might stop getting checkups.

Grabbing all three charts in his arms, Jason emerged from his office. He saw Sally stand up in the central desk area and look at him expectantly. Jason silently mouthed "two minutes" as he walked the length of the waiting area. He passed several patients whom he treated with nods and smiles. He slipped into the hall leading to Roger Wanamaker's office. Roger was an internist who specialized in cardiology and whose opinion Jason held in high esteem. He found the man leaving one of the examination rooms. He was an obese man with a face like an old hound dog with wattles and lots of extra skin.

"How about a sidewalk consult?" Jason asked.

"It'll cost ya," Roger teased. "Whatcha got?"

Jason followed the man into his disheveled office. "Unfortunately, some pretty embarrassing evidence." Jason opened the charts of his three late patients to the EKG sections and placed them in front of Roger. "I'm ashamed to even discuss this, but I've had three middle-aged men die right after their fancy executive physicals showed them in pretty good health. One was today. Cardiac rupture after a massive MI. I did the physical exam three weeks ago. This is the one. Even knowing what I do now, I can't find even a bit of trouble or any of the tracings. What do you think?"

There was a moment of silence while Roger studied the EKGs. "Welcome to the club," he finally said.

"Club?"

"These EKGs are fine," Roger said. "All of us have had the same experience. I've had four such cases over the last few months. Just about everybody who's willing to bring it up has had at least one or two."

"How come it's not come up?"

"You tell me," Roger said, with a wry smile. "You haven't exactly been advertising your experience, have you? It's dirty laundry. We'd all rather not call attention to it. But you're acting chief of service. Why don't you call a meeting?"

Jason nodded glumly. Under the aegis of the GHP administration, which made all of the major organizational decisions, chief of service was not a desirable position. It was rotated on a yearly basis among all the internists, and had fallen onto Jason's shoulders two months previously.

"I guess I should," Jason said, collecting his charts from Roger's desk. "If nothing else, the other doctors should know they're not alone if they've had the same experience."

"Sounds good," Roger agreed. He heaved his considerable bulk to his feet. "But don't expect everybody to be quite as open as you are."

Jason headed back to the central desk, motioning to Sally to ready the next patient. Sally took off like a sprinter. He then turned to Claudia.

"Claudia, I need a favor. I want you to make a list of all the annual physicals I've done over the last year, pull their charts, and check on their state of health. I want to be sure none of the others have had serious medical problems. Apparently some of the other doctors have been having similar episodes. I think it's something we should look into."

"It's going to be a big list," Claudia warned.

Jason was aware of that. In its desire to promote what it called preventive medicine, GHP had been strongly advocating such physicals and had streamlined the process to take care of the maximum number of people. Jason knew that he did, on the average, between five and ten a week.

For the next several hours, Jason devoted himself to his patients, who treated him to an endless stream of problems and complaints. Sally was relentless, filling examining rooms the moment the previous patient vacated. By skipping lunch, Jason was actually able to catch up.

In the middle of the afternoon, as Jason was returning from one of the treatment rooms where he had done a sigmoidoscopy on a patient with recurrent ulcerative colitis, Claudia caught his attention and motioned for him to come over to the central desk. She was sporting a cocky smile as Jason approached. He knew something was brewing.

"You have an honored visitor," Claudia said with pursed lips, imitating a Lily Tomlin character.

"Who?" Jason asked, reflexly scanning the adjacent waiting room area.

"He's in your office," Claudia said.

Jason shifted his eyes toward his office. The door was closed. It wasn't like Claudia to put someone in there. He looked back at his secretary. "Claudia?" he questioned, extending her name out as if it were more than three syllables. "How come you allowed someone in my office?"

"He insisted," said Claudia, "and who am I to refuse?"

Obviously whoever it was had offended her. Jason knew her that well. And whoever it was certainly had some kind of stature at GHP. But Jason was tiring of the game. "Are you going to tell me who it is or am I supposed to be surprised?"

"Dr. Alvin Hayes," Claudia said. She batted her eyes and made a sneer. Agnes, the secretary who worked for Roger, snickered.

Jason waved at them in disgust and headed for his

office. A visit by Dr. Alvin Hayes was a unique occurrence. He was the GHP token and star researcher, hired by the Plan to promote its image. It had been a move reminiscent of the Humana Corporation's hiring Dr. William DeVries, the surgeon of artificial-heart fame. GHP, as a health-maintenance organization (HMO), did not support research per se, yet it had hired Hayes at a prodigious salary in order to expand and augment its image, especially in the Boston academic community. After all, Dr. Alvin Hayes was a world-class molecular biologist who had been on the cover of *Time* magazine after having developed a method of making human growth hormone from recombinant DNA technology. The growth hormone he had made was exactly like the human variety. Earlier attempts had resulted in a hormone that was similar but not exactly the same. It had been considered an important breakthrough.

Jason reached his office and opened the door. He could not fathom why Hayes would be paying him a visit. Hayes had all but ignored Jason from the day he had been hired over a year previously, despite the fact they'd been in the same Harvard Medical School class. After graduation they had gone their separate ways, but when Alvin Hayes had been hired by GHP, Jason had sought the man out and personally welcomed him. Hayes had been distant, obviously impressed by his own celebrity status and openly contemptuous of Jason's decision to stay in clinical medicine. Except for a few chance meetings, they ignored each other. In fact, Hayes ignored everyone at the GHP, becoming more and more what people referred to as the mad scientist. He'd even gone to the extreme of letting his personal appearance suffer by wearing baggy, unpressed clothes and allowing his unkempt hair to grow long like a throwback to the turbulent sixties. Although people gossiped, and he had few friends, everyone respected him. Hayes worked long hours and produced an unbelievable number of papers and scientific articles.

Alvin Hayes was sprawled in one of the chairs facing Jason's antique desk. About Jason's height, with pudgy, boyish features, Hayes's unkempt hair hung about his face, which appeared more sallow than ever. He'd always had that peculiar academic pallor that characterizes scientists who spend all their time in their laboratories. But Jason's clinical eye noted an increased yellowishness as well as a laxness that made Hayes look ill and overly exhausted. Jason wondered if this was a professional visit.

"Sorry to bother you," Hayes said, struggling to his feet. "I know you must be busy."

"Not at all," Jason lied, skirting his desk and sitting down. He removed the stethoscope draped around his neck. "What can we do for you?" Hayes appeared nervous and fatigued, as if he hadn't slept for several days.

"I have to talk to you," he said, lowering his voice and leaning forward in a conspiratorial fashion.

Jason flinched back. Hayes's breath was fetid and

his eyes had a glassy, unfocused look that gave him a slightly crazed appearance. His white laboratory coat was wrinkled and stained. Both sleeves were pushed up above his elbows. His watch fitted so loosely that Jason wondered how he kept from losing it.

"What's on your mind?"

Hayes leaned farther forward, knuckles resting on Jason's blotter. He whispered, "Not here. I want to talk with you tonight. Outside of GHP."

There was a moment of strained silence. Hayes's behavior was obviously abnormal, and Jason wondered if he should try to get the man to talk to his friend Patrick Quillan, thinking a psychiatrist might have more to offer him. If Hayes wanted to talk away from the hospital, it couldn't be about his health.

"It's important," Hayes added, striking Jason's desk impatiently.

"All right," Jason said quickly, afraid Hayes might throw a tantrum if he hesitated any longer. "How about dinner?" He wanted to meet the man in a public place.

"All right. Where?"

"Doesn't matter." Jason shrugged. "How about the North End for some Italian food?"

"Fine. When and where?"

Jason ran down the list of restaurants he knew in the North End section of Boston, a warren of crooked streets that made you feel you'd been mystically transplanted to southern Italy. "How about Carbonara?" he suggested. "It's on Rachel Revere Square, across from Paul Revere House."

"I know it," Hayes said. "What time?"

"Eight?"

"That's fine." Hayes turned and walked somewhat unsteadily toward the door. "And don't invite anyone else. I want to talk with you alone." Without waiting for a reply, he left, pulling the door shut behind him.

Jason shook his head in amazement and went back to his patients.

Within a few minutes, he was again absorbed in his work, and the bizarre episode with Hayes slipped into his unconscious. The afternoon drifted on without unwelcome surprises. At least Jason's outpatients seemed to be doing well and responding to the various regimens he'd ordered. That gave a needed boost to his confidence that the Harring affair had undermined. With only two more patients to be seen, Jason crossed the waiting room after having done a minor surgical procedure in one of the treatment rooms. Just before he disappeared into his office to dictate the procedure, he caught sight of Shirley Montgomery leaning on the central desk and chatting with the secretaries. Within the clinical environment, Shirley stood out like Cinderella at the ball. In contrast to the other women, who were dressed in white skirts and blouses or white pants suits, Shirley wore a conservative silk dress that tried but failed to hide her attractive figure. Although few people could guess when seeing her, Shirley was the chief executive officer of the entire Good Health Plan organization. She was as attractive as any model, and she had a PhD in hospital administration from Columbia and a master's degree from the Harvard Business School.

With her physical and mental attributes, Shirley could have been intimidating, but she wasn't. She was outgoing and sensitive and as a result she got along with everyone: maintenance people, secretaries, nurses, and even the surgeons. Shirley Montgomery could take personal credit for providing a good portion of the glue that held GHP together and made it work so smoothly.

When she spotted Jason, she excused herself from the secretaries. She moved toward him with the ease and grace of a dancer. Her thick brown hair was swept back from her forehead and layered along the side into a heavy mane. Her makeup was applied so expertly that she didn't seem to be wearing any. Her large blue eyes shone with intelligence.

"Excuse me, Dr. Howard," she said formally. At the very corners of her mouth there was the faint hint of a smile. Unknown to the staff, Shirley and Jason had been seeing each other on a social basis for several months. It had started during one of the semiannual staff meetings when they had met each other over cocktails. When Jason learned that her husband had recently died of cancer, he felt an immediate bond.

During the dinner that followed, she told Jason that one morning three years ago her husband had awakened with a severe headache. Within months he was dead from a brain tumor that had been unresponsive to any treatment. At the time they had both been working at the Humana Hospital Corporation. Afterward, like Jason, she had felt compelled to move and had come to Boston. When she told Jason the story, it had affected him so deeply that he'd broken his own wall of silence. That same evening he shared his own anguish concerning his wife's accident and death.

Fueled by this extraordinary commonality of emotional experience, Jason and Shirley began a relationship that hovered somewhere between friendship and romance. Each knew the other was too emotionally raw to move too quickly.

Jason was perplexed. She had never sought him out in such a fashion. As usual, he had only the vaguest notion of what was going on inside her expansive mind. In so many ways she was the most complicated woman he'd ever met. "Can I be of assistance?" he asked, watching for some hint of her intent.

"I know you must be busy," she was saying now, "but I was wondering if you were free tonight." She lowered her voice, turning her back on Claudia's unwavering stare. "I'm having an impromptu dinner party tonight with several Harvard Business School acquaintances. I'd like you to join us. How about it?"

Jason immediately regretted having made plans to eat with Alvin Hayes. If only he'd agreed to see the man for drinks.

"I know it's short notice," Shirley added, sensing Jason's hesitation.

"That's not the problem. The trouble is that I promised to have dinner with Alvin Hayes."

"Our Dr. Hayes?" Shirley said with obvious surprise.

"None other. I know it sounds peculiar, but he seemed almost distraught. And though he's hardly been friendly, I felt sorry for the man. Dinner was my suggestion."

"Damn!" Shirley said. "You'd have enjoyed this group. Well, next time . . ."

"I'll take a rain check," Jason said. She was about to leave when he remembered his conversation with Roger Wanamaker. "I probably should tell you I'm going to call a staff meeting. A number of patients have died of coronary disease which our physicals have missed. As acting chief of service I thought I should look into it. Dropping dead within a month of receiving a clean bill of health from us doesn't make for good PR."

"Dear God," Shirley said. "Don't go spreading rumors like that!"

"Well, it's a bit unnerving when someone you've examined with all your resources and declared essentially healthy comes back to the hospital with a catastrophic condition and dies. Avoiding such an event is the whole purpose of the executive physical. I think we should try to increase the sensitivity of our stress testing."

"An admirable goal," Shirley agreed. "All I ask is that you keep it low key. Our executive physicals play a major role in our campaign to lure some of the larger corporate clients in the area. Let's keep this an in-house issue."

"Absolutely," said Jason. "Sorry about tonight."

"Me too," Shirley said, lowering her voice. "I didn't think Dr. Hayes socialized much. What's up with him?"

"It's a mystery to me," Jason admitted, "but I'll let you know."

"Please," Shirley said. "I'm one of the main reasons GHP hired the man. I feel responsible. Talk to you soon." She moved off, smiling to nearby patients.

Jason watched her for a moment, then caught Claudia's stare. She guiltily looked down at her work. Jason wondered if the secret was out. With a shrug he went back to his last two patients.

2.

Late fall in Boston was an exhilarating season for Jason despite the bleak winter it heralded. Dressed in his Indiana Jones–style fedora and his "lived-in" Burberry trench coat, he was adequately protected from the chilly October night.

Gusts of wind blew the yellowed remains of the elm leaves around Jason's feet as he trudged up Mt. Vernon Street and passed through the columned passageway under the State House. Crossing the Government Center promenade, he skirted the Faneuil Hall Marketplace with its street performers and entered the North End, Boston's Little Italy. People were everywhere: men standing on street corners and talking with animated gestures; women leaning out the windows gossiping with their friends on the opposite side of the street. The air was filled with the smell of ground coffee and almond-flavored baked goods. Like Italy itself, the neighborhood was a delight to the senses.

Two blocks down Hanover Street, Jason turned right and quickly found himself in sight of Paul Revere's modest wood clapboard house. The cobblestoned square was defined by a heavy black nautical chain looped between metal stanchions. Directly across from Paul Revere's house was Carbonara, one of Jason's favorite restaurants. There were two other restaurants in the square but neither was as good as the Carbonara. He mounted the front steps and was greeted by the maître d', who led him to his table by the front window, affording him a view of the quaint square. Like many Boston locations the scene had an unreal quality, as though it were the set for some theme park.

Jason ordered a bottle of Gavi white wine and munched on a dish of antipasto while waiting for Hayes to appear. Within ten minutes, a cab pulled up and Hayes got out. For a few moments after the cab had left, he just stood on the sidewalk and peered back up North Street from the direction he had come. Jason watched, wondering what the man was waiting for. Eventually, he turned and entered the restaurant.

As the maître d' escorted him to the table, Jason noted how out of place Hayes seemed in the elegant decor and among the fashionably dressed diners. In place of his stained lab coat, Hayes was wearing a baggy tweed jacket with a torn elbow patch. He seemed to be having trouble walking, and Jason wondered if the man had been drinking.

Without acknowledging Jason's presence, Hayes threw himself into the empty seat and stared out the window, again looking up North Street. A couple had appeared, strolling arm in arm. Hayes watched them until they disappeared from view down Prince Street. His eyes still appeared glassy, and Jason noted that a web of new, red capillaries had spread out over his nose like a sea fan. His skin was pale as ivory, not too dissimilar to Harring's when Jason had seen him in the CCU. It seemed certain that Hayes was not well.

Fumbling in one of the bulging pockets of his tweed jacket, Hayes brought out a crumpled pack of unfiltered Camels. He lit one with trembling hands and said, his eyes glittering with some strong emotion, "Someone is following me."

Jason wasn't sure how to react. "Are you sure?"

"No doubt," Hayes said, taking a long drag on his cigarette. A smoldering ash fell onto the white tablecloth. "A dark guy, smooth—a sharp dresser, a foreigner," he added with venom.

"Does that make you concerned?" Jason asked, trying to play psychiatrist. Apparently, on top of everything else, Hayes was acutely paranoid.

"Christ, yes!" Hayes shouted. A few heads turned and Hayes lowered his voice. "Wouldn't you be upset if someone wanted to kill you?"

"Kill you?" Jason echoed, now sure Hayes had gone mad.

"Absolutely positive. And my son, too."

"I didn't know you had a son," Jason said. In fact, he hadn't even been aware Hayes was married. It was rumored in the hospital that Hayes frequented the disco scene on the rare occasions he wanted distraction.

Hayes mashed out his cigarette in the ashtray, cursed under his breath, and lit another, blowing the smoke away in short, nervous puffs. Jason realized that Hayes was at the breaking point and he'd have to tread carefully. The man was about to decompensate.

"I'm sorry if I sound dumb," Jason said, "but I would like to help. I presume that's why you wanted to talk to me. And frankly, Alvin, you don't look too well."

Hayes leaned the back of his right wrist on his forehead, his elbow on the table. His lit cigarette was dangerously close to his disheveled hair. Jason was tempted to move either the hair or the cigarette; he didn't want the man lighting himself like a pyre. But fearful of Hayes's distraught state, he did neither.

"Would you gentlemen like to order?" asked a waiter, silently materializing at the table.

"For Christ's sake!" Hayes snarled, his head popping up. "Can't you see we're talking?"

"Excuse me, sir," the waiter said, bowing and moving off.

After taking a deep breath, Hayes returned his attention to Jason. "So I don't look well?"

"No. Your color isn't good, and you seem exhausted as well as upset."

"Ah, the clairvoyant clinician," Hayes said sarcastically. Then he added, "I'm sorry—I don't mean to be nasty. You're right. I'm not feeling well. In fact, I'm feeling terrible."

"What's the problem?"

"Just about everything. Arthritis, GI upset, blurred vision. Even dry skin. My ankles itch so much they're driving me insane. My body is literally falling apart."

"Perhaps it would have been better to meet in my office," Jason said. "Maybe we should check you out."

"Maybe later—but that's not why I wanted to see you. It may be too late for me, anyway, but if I could save my son . . ." He broke off, pointing out the window. *"There he is!"*

Twisting in his seat, Jason barely caught sight of a figure disappearing up North Street. Turning back to Hayes, Jason asked, "How could you tell it was him?"

"He's been following me from the moment I left GHP. I think he plans on killing me."

With no way to tell fact from delusion, Jason studied his colleague. The man was acting weird, to put it mildly, but the old cliché "even paranoids have enemies" echoed in his brain. Maybe someone was in fact following Hayes. Fishing the chilled bottle of Gavi from the ice bucket, Jason poured Hayes a glass and filled his own. "Maybe you'd better tell me what this is all about."

Tossing back the wine as if it were a shot of aquavit, Hayes wiped his mouth with the back of his hand. "It's such a bizarre story. . . . How about a little more of the wine?"

Jason refilled the glass as Hayes continued. "I don't suppose you know too much of what my research interests are. . . ."

"I have some idea."

"Growth and development," Hayes said. "How genes turn on and off. Like puberty; what turns on the appropriate genes. Solving the problem would be a major achievement. Not only could we potentially influence growth and development, but we'd probably be able to 'turn off' cancers, or, after heart attacks, 'turn on' cellular division to create new cardiac muscle. Anyway, in simplified terms, the turning on and off of growth and development genes has been my major interest. But like so often in research, serendipity played a role. About four months ago, in the process of my research I stumbled onto an unexpected discovery, ironic but astounding. I'm talking about a major scientific breakthrough. Believe me: it is Nobel material."

Jason was willing to suspend disbelief, although he wondered if Hayes was exhibiting symptoms of a delusion of grandeur to go along with his paranoia.

"What was your discovery?"

"Just a moment," Hayes said. He put his cigarette in the ashtray and pressed his right hand against his chest.

"Are you all right?" Jason asked. Hayes appeared to have become a shade grayer, and a line of perspiration had formed at his hairline.

"I'm okay," Hayes assured him. He let his hand drop to the table. "I didn't report this discovery because I realized it was the first step toward an even bigger breakthrough. I'm talking about something akin to antibiotics or the helical structure of DNA. I've been so excited I've been working around the clock. But then I found out my original discovery was no longer a secret. That it was being used. When I suspected this, I . . ." Hayes stopped in midsentence. He stared at Jason with an expression that started out as confusion but rapidly changed to fear.

"Alvin, what's the matter?" Jason asked. Hayes didn't reply. His right hand again pressed against his chest. A moan escaped from his lips, then both hands shot out and gripped the tablecloth, clawing it toward him. The wine glasses fell over. He started to get to his feet but he never made it. With a violent choking cough, he spewed a stream of blood across the table, drenching the cloth and spraying Jason, who jumped backward, knocking over his chair. The blood didn't stop. It came in successive waves, splattering everything as nearby diners began to scream.

As a physician, Jason knew what was happening. The blood was bright red and was literally being pumped out of Hayes's mouth. That meant it was coming directly from his heart. In the seconds that followed, Hayes remained upright in his chair, confusion and pain replacing the fear in his eyes. Jason skirted the table and grabbed him by the shoulders. Unfortunately there was no way to staunch the flow of blood. Hayes was either going to exsanguinate or drown. There was nothing Jason could do but hold the man as his life flowed out of him.

When Hayes's body went flaccid, Jason let it slump to the floor. Although the human body contains about six quarts of blood, the amount on the table and floor appeared to be considerably more. Jason turned to a neighboring table that had been vacated and took a napkin to wipe his hands.

For the first time since the initial catastrophe, Jason became aware of his surroundings. The other patrons of the restaurant had all leaped from their tables and were crowded at the other end of the room. Unfortunately, several people had gotten sick.

The maître d' himself, with a green complexion, was swaying on his feet. "I've called for an ambulance," he managed to say through a hand clamped over his mouth.

Jason looked down at Hayes. Without an operating room right there, with a heart and lung machine primed and ready to go, there was no chance of saving him. An ambulance at this point was futile. But at least it could take the body away. Glancing again at the still body, Jason decided the man must have had a lung cancer. A tumor could have eroded through his aorta, causing the bleeding. Ironically, Hayes's cigarette was still lit in the ashtray that was now full of frothy blood. A bit of smoke languidly rose to the ceiling.

In the distance Jason heard the undulating sound of an approaching ambulance. But before it arrived, a police cruiser with a flashing blue light pulled up outside, and two uniformed policemen came bounding into the dining room. They both pulled up short when confronted by the bloody scene. The younger one, Peter Carbo, a blond-haired boy who looked about nineteen, immediately turned green. His partner, Jeff Mario, quickly sent him to interview the patrons. Jeff Mario was Jason's age, give or take a couple of years. "What the hell happened?" he asked, astounded at the amount of blood.

"I'm a physician," Jason offered. "The man is dead. He bled out. There was nothing that could have been done."

After squatting over Hayes, Jeff Mario gingerly felt for a pulse. Satisfied, he stood up and directed his attention to Jason. "You a friend?"

"More a colleague," said Jason. "We both work for Good Health Plan."

"He a physician also?" Jeff Mario asked, motioning toward Hayes with his thumb.

Jason nodded.

"Was he sick?"

"I'm not certain," Jason said. "If I had to guess, I'd say cancer. But I don't know."

Jeff Mario took out a pad and a pencil. He opened the pad. "What's the man's name?"

"Alvin Hayes."

"Does Mr. Hayes have a family?"

"I guess," Jason said. "To tell you the truth, I don't know too much about his private life. He mentioned a son, so I presume he has a family."

"Do you know his home address?"

"I'm afraid not."

Officer Mario regarded Jason for a moment, then reached down and carefully searched Hayes's pockets, coming up with a billfold. He went through Hayes's cards.

"The guy doesn't have a driver's license," Jeff Mario said. He looked at Jason for confirmation.

"I wouldn't know." Jason could feel himself begin to tremble. The horror of the episode was starting to affect him.

The sound of the ambulance, which had gotten progressively louder, trailed off outside the window. There was now a red flashing light in addition to the blue. Within a minute two uniformed emergency techs came into the room, one carrying a metal case that looked like a tackle box. They went directly over to Hayes.

"This man's a doctor," Jeff Mario said, pointing at Jason with his pencil. "He says it's all over. He says the guy bled out from cancer."

"I'm not sure it was cancer," Jason said. His voice was higher than he intended. He was visibly trembling now, so he clasped his hands together.

The EMTs examined Hayes briefly, then stood up.

The one who'd been carrying the case told the other to go down and get the stretcher.

"Okay, here's his address," said Jeff Mario, who had gone back to searching Hayes's wallet. He held up a card. "He lives over near Boston City Hospital." He copied the address down on his note pad. The younger policeman was taking down names and addresses, including Jason's.

When they were ready to leave, Jason asked if he could go along with the body. He felt bad sending Hayes to the morgue all alone. The cops said it was fine with them. As they emerged onto the square, Jason could see that a considerable crowd had formed. News like this traveled around the North End like wildfire, but the crowd was silent, awed by the presence of death.

Jason's eye caught one nattily dressed man who seemed to melt backward into the crowd. He looked like a businessman—more Latin American or Spanish than Italian—particularly his clothing—and for a moment Jason wondered at himself for even noticing.

Then one of the emergency techs said, "Want to ride with your friend?" Jason nodded and climbed into the back of the ambulance. Jason sat on a low seat across from Hayes, down near his feet. One of the EMTs sat on a similar seat closer to Hayes's head. With a lurch, the ambulance moved. Through the back window Jason saw the restaurant and the crowd recede. As they turned onto Hanover Street, he had to hold on. The siren had not been turned on, but the flashing light was still functioning. Jason could see it reflected in the glass of the store windows.

The trip was short; about five minutes. The EMT tried to make small talk, but Jason made it apparent he was preoccupied. Staring at the covered body of Hayes, Jason attempted to come to terms with the experience. He couldn't help but think that death was stalking him. It made him feel curiously responsible for Hayes, as if the man would still be alive if he'd not had the misfortune of meeting with Jason. Jason knew such thoughts were ridiculous on a rational level. But feelings didn't always rely on rationality.

After a sharp turn to the left, the ambulance backed up, then stopped. When the rear door was opened, Jason recognized where they were. They'd arrived at the courtyard of the Massachusetts General Hospital. It was a familiar place for Jason. He'd done his internal medicine residency there years ago. Jason climbed out. The two EMTs unloaded Hayes efficiently and the wheels dropped down under the stretcher. Silently, they pushed the body into the emergency room, where a triage nurse directed them to an empty trauma room.

Despite his being a physician, Jason did not know the protocol for handling a situation like Hayes's death. He was a bit surprised they'd even come to an emergency room, since Hayes was beyond care. But thinking about it, he realized Hayes had to be formally pronounced dead. He'd remembered doing it when he'd been a house officer.

The trauma room was set up in the usual fashion, with all sorts of equipment ready for instant use. In a corner was a scrub sink. Jason washed Hayes's blood off his hands. A small mirror over the sink revealed a significant amount of dried blood that had splattered his face as well. After rinsing his face, he dried himself with paper towels. There was blood on his jacket and shirtfront as well as his pants, but there was little he could do about that. As he was finishing washing, a house officer breezed into the room with a clipboard. He unceremoniously yanked back the sheet covering Hayes, then pulled his stethoscope from around his neck. Hayes's face looked eerily pale in the raw fluorescent light.

"You related?" asked the resident casually as he listened to Hayes's chest.

When the resident took the stethoscope from his ears, Jason spoke. "No, I'm a colleague. We worked together at Good Health."

"You an MD?" the resident asked, sounding a degree more deferential.

Jason nodded.

"What happened to your friend?" He shined a penlight into Hayes's eyes.

"He exsanguinated at the dinner table," Jason said, being deliberately blunt, mildly offended at the callous attitude of the resident.

"No kidding. Far out! Well, he sure is dead." He pulled the sheet back over Hayes's head.

It took all of Jason's self-control not to tell the resident what he thought of his insensitivity, but he knew it would be a waste of time. Instead, he wandered out into the hallway and watched the bustle of the emergency room, remembering his own days as a resident. It seemed a long time ago, but nothing had really changed.

Thirty minutes later, Hayes's body was wheeled back out to the ambulance. Jason followed and watched as it was reloaded.

"Do you mind if I still tag along?" he asked, uncertain as to his motives, realizing he was probably acting out of shock.

"We're just going to the morgue," the driver said, "but be my guest."

As they pulled out of the courtyard, Jason was suddenly surprised to see what looked like the same sharply dressed businessman he'd spotted outside the restaurant. Then he shrugged. That would be too much of a coincidence. Odd, though, the man's face had the same Hispanic cast.

Jason had never been to the city morgue. As they wheeled Hayes's body through scarred and battered swinging doors and entered the storage room, he wished he had not come on this occasion. The atmosphere was as unpleasant as his imagination had suggested it would be. The storage room was large and lined on both sides with square, refrigerator-like doors that had once been white. The walls and floor were surfaced with old, stained, and cracked tiles. There were a number of gurneys, some occupied by corpses covered with sheets, a few of which were bloody. The room reeked with an antiseptic, fishy smell that made Jason reluctant to breathe. A heavyset, florid man wearing a rubber apron and gloves came over to Hayes and helped transfer the corpse to one of the morgue's ancient and stained gurneys. Then they all disappeared to attend to the necessary paperwork.

For a few moments Jason stood in the body room and thought about the sudden end to Hayes's distinguished life. Then, pursued by a vivid image of his trip to the hospital after Danielle's death, he walked after the emergency technicians.

At the time the Boston City Morgue had been built a half century ago, it had been considered a state-of-the-art facility. As Jason mounted the wide steps leading up to the offices, he noticed some architectural detail work with ancient Egyptian motifs. But the building had suffered over the years. Now it was dark, dirty, and inadequate. What horrors it had seen was beyond Jason's imagination.

In a shabby office he found the two EMTs and the florid morgue worker. They had finished the paperwork and were laughing about something, completely oblivious to the oppressive atmosphere of death.

Jason interrupted their conversation to ask if any

of the medical examiners were there at the moment.

"Yup," said the attendant. "Dr. Danforth's finishing up an emergency case in the autopsy room."

"Is there someplace I can wait for her?" Jason asked. He was in no condition to visit the autopsy room.

"There's a library upstairs," the attendant said. "Right next to Dr. Danforth's office."

The library was a dark, musty place with large bound volumes of autopsy reports that dated back to the eighteenth century. In the center of the room was a large oak table with six captain's chairs. More important, there was a telephone. After some thought, Jason decided to call Shirley. He knew she was in the middle of entertaining, but he thought she would want to know.

"Jason!" she exclaimed. "Are you coming over?"

"Unfortunately, no. There's been some trouble."

"Trouble?"

"This is going to be a shock," Jason warned. "I hope you're sitting down."

"Stop teasing me," Shirley said. The concern in her voice rose a notch.

"Alvin Hayes is dead."

There was a pause. Inappropriate-sounding laughter could be heard in the background.

"What happened?"

"I'm not entirely sure," Jason said, wanting to shield her from the horrible details. "Some kind of internal medical catastrophe."

"Like a heart attack?"

"Something like that," Jason said evasively.

"My God! The poor man."

"Do you know anything about his family? They've asked me, but I don't know anything."

"I don't know much either. He's divorced. He has children, but I believe the wife has custody. She lives somewhere near Manhattan and that's about all I know. The man was very private about his personal life."

"I'm sorry to bother you about this now."

"Don't be silly. Where are you?"

"At the morgue."

"How did you get there?"

"I rode in the ambulance with Hayes's body."

"I'll come and pick you up."

"No need," Jason said. "I'll get a cab after I talk to the medical examiner."

"How are you feeling?" Shirley asked. "It must have been an awful experience."

"Well," Jason admitted, "I've been better."

"That settles it. I'm coming to pick you up."

"What about your guests?" Jason protested halfheartedly. He felt guilty ruining her party, but not guilty enough to refuse her offer. He knew he wasn't ready to be alone with tonight's memory.

"They can take care of themselves," Shirley said. "Where are you exactly?"

Jason gave her directions, then hung up. He let his head sink into his hands and closed his eyes.

"Excuse me," said a deep voice softened by a slight brogue. "Are you Dr. Jason Howard?"

"That's correct," Jason said, sitting up with a start.

A heavyset figure advanced into the room. The man had a broad face with lidded eyes, wide nose, and square teeth. His hair was dark with glints of red. "I'm Detective Michael Curran, Homicide." He stuck out a broad, callused hand.

Jason shook it, flustered by the sudden appearance of the plainclothes detective. He realized he was being evaluated as the detective's eyes went from his face to his feet and back again.

"Officer Mario reported that you were with the victim," Detective Curran said, taking a chair.

"Are you investigating Hayes's death?"

"Just routine," Curran said. "Rather a dramatic scene, according to Officer Mario's description. I don't want my detective sergeant on my back if there's any questions later on."

"Oh, I see," Jason said. In truth, Detective Curran's appearance made him remember Hayes's insistence that someone was trying to kill him. Though the man's death seemed a natural disaster rather than murder, Jason realized Hayes's fear in part had motivated Jason to come to the morgue to check the cause of death.

"Anyway," Detective Curran said, "I got to ask the usual questions. In your opinion, was Dr. Hayes's death expected? I mean, was he ill?"

"Not that I know of," Jason said, "though when I saw him this afternoon and then again this evening, I did have the feeling he wasn't well."

Detective Curran's heavy eyelids lifted slightly. "What do you mean?"

"He looked terrible. And when I mentioned the fact to him, he admitted he wasn't feeling well."

"What were the symptoms?" asked the detective. He'd taken out a small pad.

"Fatigue, stomach upset, joint discomfort. I thought he might have had a fever, but I couldn't be sure."

"What did you think about these symptoms?"

"They worried me," Jason admitted. "I told him that it might be better if we met in my office so I could have run a few tests. But he insisted we meet away from the hospital."

"And why was that?"

"I'm not sure." Then Jason went on to describe what was probably Hayes's paranoia and his statements about having made a breakthrough.

After writing all this down, Curran looked up. He seemed more alert. "What do you mean, 'paranoia'?"

"He said that someone was following him and wanted him and his son dead."

"Did he say who?"

"No," Jason said. "To be honest, I thought that he was delusional. He was acting strangely. I thought he was about to decompensate."

"Decompensate?" Curran asked.

"Nervous breakdown," Jason said.

"I see," Curran said, returning to his note pad. Jason watched as he wrote. He had the curious habit of licking the end of his pencil at odd intervals.

At that moment another figure appeared in the doorway. She walked around the table to Jason's right. Both Jason and the detective got to their feet. The newcomer was a diminutive woman barely five feet tall. She introduced herself as Dr. Margaret Danforth. In contrast to her size, her voice resounded in the small room.

"Sit down," she commanded, smiling at Curran, whom she obviously knew.

Jason guessed the woman to be in her upper thirties. She had small, delicate features with highly arched eyebrows that gave her an innocent appeal. Her hair was short and very curly. She wore a dark, demure dress with a lace collar. Jason had trouble associating her appearance with her position as one of the medical examiners of the city of Boston.

"What's the problem?" she asked, getting right to business. There were dark circles under her eyes, and Jason guessed she'd been working since early that morning.

Detective Curran tipped his chair back and teetered. "Sudden death of a physician in a North End restaurant. Apparently he vomited a large amount of blood . . ."

"Coughed up would be a better term," interrupted Jason.

"How so?" Detective Curran asked, coming forward with a thump. He licked the end of his pencil to make a correction.

"Vomiting would mean it came from his digestive

system," Jason said. "This blood obviously came from his lungs. It was bright red and frothy."

"Frothy! I like that word," Curran said. He bent over his pad, making a correction.

"I presume it was arterial blood," Dr. Danforth said.

"I believe so," Jason said.

"Which means . . . ?" Curran questioned.

"Probably a rupture of the aorta," Danforth answered. She had her hands folded in her lap as if she were at a tea party. "The aorta is the main vessel that leaves the heart," she added for Curran's benefit. "It carries oxygenated blood out to the body."

"Thank you," Curran said.

"Sounds like either lung cancer or aneurysm," Danforth added. "An aneurysm is an abnormal outpocketing of the blood vessel."

"Thank you again," Curran said. "It's so handy when people know I'm ignorant."

Jason had a momentary flash of Peter Falk playing Detective Columbo. He was quite sure that Curran was anything but ignorant.

"Would you agree, doctor?" Danforth asked, looking directly at Jason.

"I'd vote for lung cancer," Jason said. "Hayes was a prodigious smoker."

"That does raise the probability."

"Any possibility of foul play?" Curran asked, looking at the medical examiner from under his heavy lids.

Dr. Danforth gave a short laugh. "If the diagnosis

is what I think it is, the only foul play involved would have been perpetrated by his Maker—or the tobacco industry."

"That's what I thought," Curran said, flipping his notebook closed and pocketing his pencil.

"Are you going to do an autopsy now?" Jason asked.

"Heavens no," Dr. Danforth said. "If there were some pressing reason, we could. But there isn't. We'll get to it first thing in the morning. We should have some answers by ten-thirty or so, if you'd like to call about then."

Curran put his hands on the table as if he were about to stand. Instead, he said, "Dr. Howard has alleged that the victim thought someone was trying to kill him. Am I right, doctor?"

Jason nodded.

"So . . ." Curran said. "Could you keep that in mind when you do the autopsy?"

"Absolutely," Dr. Danforth said. "We keep an open mind in all cases we do. That's our job. Now, if you'll excuse me, I'd like to get home. I haven't even had a chance to eat dinner."

Jason felt a mild wave of nausea. He wondered how Margaret Danforth could feel hungry after spending her day cutting up corpses. Curran actually said as much to Jason as they descended to the first floor. He offered Jason a lift, but Jason told him he was expecting a friend. No sooner had he said it than the street door opened and Shirley walked in.

"Some friend," Curran whispered with a wink as he left.

Once again Shirley stood out like a mirage. For entertaining she'd dressed in a red, fitted, silk shirt-dress, cinched with a wide black leather belt. Her appearance bespoke so strongly of life and vitality that her presence in the dirty morgue was a collision of opposites. Jason had the unnatural urge to get her out of there as soon as possible, lest some evil force touch her. But she was resistant to his urging. She'd thrown her arms around him and pressed his head against hers in a genuine show of sympathy. Jason melted. His response surprised him. He found himself fighting back tears like an adolescent. It was embarrassing.

She pulled back and looked him in the eyes. He managed a crooked smile. "What a day," he said.

"What a day!" she agreed. "Any reason you have to stay here?"

Jason shook his head.

"Come on, I'm taking you home," she said, hurrying him outside to where her BMW was parked in a no-parking zone. They got in and the car roared to life.

"Are you okay?" Shirley asked as they headed toward Massachusetts Avenue.

"I'm much better now." Jason looked at Shirley's profile as the city lights illuminated it in flashes. "I'm just overwhelmed by all the deaths. As if I should be doing something better."

"You're too hard on yourself. You can't take responsibility for everyone. Besides, Hayes wasn't your patient."

"I know."

They drove for a while in silence. Then Shirley said, "It is a tragedy about Hayes. He was pretty close to a genius, and he couldn't have been more than forty-five."

"He was my age," Jason said. "He was in my class in medical school."

"I didn't know that," Shirley said. "He looked a lot older."

"Especially lately," Jason said. They passed Symphony Hall. Some affair was just getting out, and men in black tie were emerging on the front steps.

"What did the medical examiner have to say?" Shirley asked.

"Probably cancer. But they aren't going to do the autopsy until morning."

"Autopsy? Who gave the authorization?"

"No need if the medical examiner thinks there is some question about the death."

"But what kind of question? You said the man had a heart attack."

"I didn't say it was a heart attack. I said it was something like that. At any rate, it's apparently protocol for them to do a postmortem on any unexpected death. A detective actually questioned me."

"Seems like a waste of taxpayers' money," Shirley said as they turned left on Beacon Street.

"Where are we going?" Jason asked suddenly.

"I'm taking you home with me. My guests will still be there. It will be good for you."

"No way," Jason said. "I'm in no shape to be social."

"Are you sure? I don't want you brooding. These people will understand."

"Please," Jason said. "I'm not strong enough to argue. I just need to sleep. Besides, look at me, I'm a wreck."

"Okay, if you put it that way," Shirley said. She turned left on the next block, then left again on Commonwealth Avenue, heading back to Beacon Hill. After a period of silence, she said, "I'm afraid Hayes's death is going to be a big blow to GHP. We were counting on him to produce some exciting results. The fallout is going to be especially tough for me, since I was responsible for his being hired."

"Then take some of your own advice," Jason said. "You can't hold yourself responsible for his medical condition."

"I know. But try telling that to the board."

"In that case I guess I should tell you. There's more bad news," Jason said. "Apparently Hayes believed he'd made a real scientific breakthrough. Something extraordinary. Do you know anything about it?"

"Not a thing," Shirley said with alarm. "Did he tell you what it was?"

"Unfortunately no," Jason said. "And I wasn't

sure whether to believe him or not. He was acting rather bizarre, to say the least, claiming someone wanted him dead."

"Do you think he was having a nervous breakdown?"

"It crossed my mind."

"The poor man. If he did make some sort of discovery, then GHP is going to have a double loss."

"But if he had made some dramatic discovery, wouldn't you be able to find out what it was?"

"Obviously you didn't know Dr. Hayes," Shirley said. "He was an extraordinarily private man, personally and professionally. Half of what he knew he carried around in his head."

They skirted the Boston Garden, then navigated the roundabout route to get into Beacon Hill, a residential enclave of brick-fronted townhouses in the center of Boston, whose one-way streets made driving a nightmare.

After crossing Charles Street, Shirley drove up Mt. Vernon Street and turned into the cobblestoned Louisburg Square. When he'd decided to give up suburban living and try the city, Jason had been lucky enough to find a one-bedroom apartment overlooking the square. It was in a large townhouse whose owner had a unit in the building, but was rarely there. It was a perfect location for Jason, since the apartment came with a true urban prize: a parking place.

Jason got out of the car and leaned in the open

window. "Thanks for picking me up. It meant a lot." He reached in and gave Shirley's shoulder a squeeze.

Shirley suddenly reached out and grabbed Jason by the tie, pulling his head down to her. She gave him a hard kiss, gunned the motor, and was off.

Jason stood at the curb in a pool of light from the gas lamp and watched her disappear down Pinckney Street. Turning to his door, he fumbled for his keys. He was pleased she had come into his life, and for the first time considered the possibility of a real relationship.

3.

It had not been a good night. Every time Jason had closed his eyes, he'd seen Hayes's quizzical expression just before the catastrophe and re-experienced the awful feeling of helplessness as he watched Hayes's lifeblood pump out of his mouth.

The scene haunted him as he drove to work, and he remembered something he'd forgotten to tell either Curran or Shirley. Hayes had said his discovery was no longer a secret and it was being used. Whatever that meant. Jason planned to call the detective when he reached GHP, but the moment he entered he was paged to come directly to the coronary care unit.

Brian Lennox was much worse. After a brief examination, Jason realized there was little he could do. Even the cardiac consult he'd requested the day before was not optimistic, though Harry Sarnoff had scheduled an emergency coronary study for that morning. The only hope was if immediate surgery might have something to offer.

Outside Brian's cubicle the nurse asked, "If he arrests, do you want to code him? Even his kidneys seem to be failing."

Jason hated such decisions, but said firmly that he wanted the man resuscitated at least until they had the results from the coronary study.

The remainder of Jason's rounds were equally as depressing. His diabetes cases, all of whom had multisystem involvement, were doing very poorly. Two of them were in kidney failure and the third was threatening. The depressing part was that they had not entered the hospital for that reason. The kidney failure had developed while Jason was treating them for other problems.

Jason's two leukemia patients were also not responding to treatment as he'd expected. Both had developed significant heart conditions even though they had been admitted for respiratory symptoms. And his two AIDS sufferers had made very distinct turns for the worse. The only patients doing well were two young girls with hepatitis. The last patient was a thirty-five-year-old man in for an evaluation of his heart valves. He'd had rheumatic fever as a child. Thankfully he was unchanged.

Arriving at his office, Jason had to be firm with Claudia. News of Hayes's death had already permeated the entire GHP complex, and Claudia was beside herself with curiosity. Jason told her that he wasn't going to talk about it. She insisted. He ordered her out of his office. Later he apologized and gave her an abridged version of the event. By ten-thirty he got a call from Henry Sarnoff with depressing news. Brian Lennox's coronary arteries were much worse but without focal blockage. In other words, they were uniformly filling up with atherosclerosis at a rapid rate, and there was no chance for surgery. Sarnoff said he'd never seen such rapid progression and asked Jason's permission to write it up. Jason said it was fine with him.

After Sarnoff's call, Jason kept himself locked in his office for a few minutes. When he felt emotionally prepared, he called the coronary care unit and asked for the nurse taking care of Brian Lennox. When she came on the line, he discussed with her the results of the coronary artery study. Then he told her that Brian Lennox should be a no-code. Without hope, the man's suffering had to be curtailed. She agreed. After he'd hung up, he stared at the phone. It was moments like that that made him wonder why he'd gone into medicine in the first place.

When the lunch break came, Jason decided to check out Hayes's autopsy results in person. In the daylight, the morgue was not such an eerie place—just another aging, run-down, not-too-clean building. Even the Egyptian architectural details were more comical than imposing. Yet Jason avoided the body storage room and went directly to find Margaret Danforth's narrow office next to the library. She was hunched over her desk eating what looked like a Big Mac. She waved him in, smiling. "Welcome."

"Sorry to bother you," Jason said, sitting down. Once again he marveled how small and feminine Margaret seemed in light of her job.

"No bother," she said. "I did the post on Dr. Hayes this morning." She leaned back in her chair, which squeaked softly. "I was a little surprised. It wasn't cancer."

"What was it?"

"Aneurysm. Aortic aneurysm that broke into the tracheobronchial tree. The man never had syphilis, did he?"

Jason shook his head. "Not that I know of. I'd kinda doubt it."

"Well, it looked strange," Margaret said. "Do you mind that I continue eating? I have another autopsy in a few minutes."

"Not at all," Jason said, wondering how she could. His own stomach did a little flip-flop. The whole building had a slightly fishy odor. "What looked strange?"

Margaret chewed, then swallowed. "The aorta looked kind of cheesy, friable. So did the trachea, for that matter. I'd never seen anything quite like it, except in this one guy I'd posted who was one hundred and fourteen. Can you believe it? It was written up in *The Globe*. He was forty-four when the First World War started. Amazing."

"When will you have a microscopic report?"

Margaret made a gesture of embarrassment. "Two weeks," she said. "We're not funded for adequate support personnel. Slides take quite a while."

"If you could give me some samples, I could have our path department process them."

"We have to process them ourselves. I'm sure you understand."

"I don't mean for you not to do it," Jason said. "I just meant we could too. It would save some time."

"I don't see why not." Standing up, Margaret took another large bite out of her hamburger and motioned for Jason to follow her. They used the stairwell and went up a floor to the autopsy room.

It was a long rectangular room with four stainless steel tables oriented perpendicular to the long axis. The smell of formaldehyde and other unspeakable fluids was overpowering. Two tables were occupied, and the two others were in the process of being cleaned. Margaret, perfectly at home in the environment, was still chewing her last bite of lunch as she led Jason over to the sink. After scanning through a profusion of plastic-capped specimen bottles, she separated a number from the rest. Then, taking each in turn, she fished out the contents, placed them on a cutting board, and sliced off a piece of each with a blade that looked very much like a standard kitchen carving knife. Then she got new specimen bottles, labeled them, poured in formaldehyde, and dropped in the respective samples. When she was done, she packed them in a brown paper bag and handed it to Jason. It had all been done with remarkable efficiency.

Back at GHP, Jason headed to pathology, where he found Dr. Jackson Madsen at his microscope. Dr.

Madsen was a tall, gaunt man who at sixty was still proudly running marathons. As soon as he saw Jason, he commiserated with him about Jason's experience with Hayes.

"Not many secrets around here," Jason said a little sourly.

"Of course not," Jackson said. "Socially, the medical center is like a small town. It thrives on gossip." Eyeing the brown paper bag, he added, "You have something for me?"

"In a manner of speaking." Jason went on to explain what the specimens were, and added that since it was going to take two weeks for the slides to be processed at the city lab, he wondered if Jackson would mind running them at the GHP lab.

"I'd be happy to," Jackson said, taking the bag. "By the way, are you interested in hearing the results of the Harring case now?"

Jason swallowed. "Of course."

"Cardiac rupture. First case I've seen in years. Split open the left ventricle. It appeared as if most of the heart had been involved in the infarct, and when I sectioned the heart, I had the impression that all of the coronary vessels were involved. That man had the worst coronary heart disease I've seen in years."

So much for our wonderful predictive tests, Jason thought. He felt defensive enough to explain to Jackson that he'd gone back and reviewed Harring's record and still couldn't find any evidence of the impending problem on an EKG taken less than a month before Harring's death.

"Maybe you'd better check your machines," Jackson said. "I'm telling you, this man's heart was in bad shape. The microscopic sections should be ready tomorrow if you're interested."

Leaving the pathology department, Jason considered Jackson's comment. The idea of a defective EKG machine hadn't occurred to him. But by the time he got to his office, he discarded the notion. There would be too many ways to tell if the EKG machine wasn't functioning properly. Besides, two different machines were used for the resting EKG and the stress EKG. But in thinking about it, he remembered something. Like Jason himself, on joining the GHP staff, Hayes would have been given a complete physical. Everyone was.

After Claudia had given Jason his phone messages, he asked her to see if Dr. Alvin Hayes had a patient chart, and if he did, to get it. Meanwhile, he avoided Sally and headed up to radiology. With the help of one of the department secretaries, he located Alvin Hayes's folder. As he'd expected, it contained a routine chest X ray taken six months previously. He looked at it briefly. Then, armed with the film, he sought out one of the four staff radiologists. Milton Perlman, MD, was emerging from the fluoroscopy room when Jason buttonholed him, described Hayes's death and the results of the autopsy, and handed Milton the chest film. Milton took the film back to his office, placed it on the viewing box, and flipped on the light. He scanned the film for a full minute before turning to Jason.

"There ain't no aneurysm here," he said. He was from West Virginia and liked to talk as if he'd left the farm the day before. "Aorta looks normal, no calcification."

"Is that possible?" Jason asked.

"Must be." Milton checked the name and unit number on the film. "I guess there's always a chance we could have mixed up the names, but I doubt it. If the man died of an aneurysm, then he developed it in the last month."

"I never heard of that happening."

"What can I say?" Milton extended his hands, palms up.

Jason returned to his office, mulling over the problem. An aneurysm could balloon quickly, especially if the victim had a combination of vessel disease and high blood pressure, but when he checked Hayes's physical exam, his blood pressure and heart sounds were, as he suspected, normal. With no signs of vascular disease, Jason realized that there was little he could do at that point besides wait for the microscopic sections. Maybe Hayes had contracted some strange infectious disease that had attacked his blood vessels, including his aorta. For the first time, Jason wondered if they were seeing the beginnings of a new and terrible disease.

Changing his suit jacket for a white coat, Jason left his office, practically bumping into Sally.

"You're behind schedule!" she scolded.

"So what else is new?" Jason said, heading for exam room A.

By a combination of hard work and luck, Jason caught up to his schedule. The luck involved not having any new patients that needed extensive work-ups or old patients with new problems. By three there was even a break. Someone had canceled.

The whole afternoon, Jason could not get the Hayes affair out of his mind. And with a little extra time on his hands, he headed up to the sixth floor. That was where Dr. Alvin Hayes's lab was located. Jason thought perhaps Hayes's assistant would have some idea if the big breakthrough Hayes had mentioned had any basis in fact.

As soon as he stepped from the elevator, Jason felt as if he were in another world. As part of Hayes's incentive to come to GHP, the GHP board had built him a brand new lab which occupied a good portion of the sixth floor.

The area near the elevator was furnished with comfortable leather seating, deep pile carpets, and even a large glass-fronted bookcase filled with current references in molecular biology. Beyond this reception room was a clean room where visitors were expected to don long white coats and protective coverings over their shoes. Jason tried the door. It was open, so he entered.

Jason put on the coat and booties and tried the inner door. As he expected, it was locked. Next to the door was a buzzer. He pushed it and waited. Above the lintel a small red light blinked on over a closed-circuit TV camera. Then the door buzzed open and Jason entered.

The lab was divided into two main sections. The first section was constructed of white Formica and white tile and included a large central room with several offices on one side. With overhead fluorescent lighting, the effect was dazzling. The room was filled with sophisticated equipment, most of which Jason did not recognize. A locked steel door separated the first section from the second. A sign next to the door read: ANIMAL ROOM AND BACTERIAL INCUBATORS: NO ENTRY!

Sitting at one of the extensive lab benches in the first section was a very blond woman Jason had seen on several occasions in the GHP cafeteria. She had sharp features, a slightly aquiline nose, and her hair was tightly pulled back into a French knot. Jason saw that her eyes were red, as if she had been crying.

"Excuse me, I'm Dr. Jason Howard," he said, extending his hand. She took it. Her skin was cool.

"Helene Brennquivist," she said with a slight Scandinavian accent.

"Do you have a moment?"

Helene didn't answer. Instead, she closed her notebook and pushed away a stack of petri dishes.

"I'd like to ask a few questions," Jason continued. He saw that she had an uncanny ability to maintain an absolutely neutral facial expression.

"This is, or was, Dr. Hayes's lab?" Jason asked, with a short wave of his hand to the surroundings.

She nodded.

"And I presume you worked with Dr. Hayes?"

Another nod, less perceptible than the first. Jason

had the feeling he'd already evoked a defensiveness in the woman.

"I'm assuming that you've heard the bad news about Dr. Hayes," Jason said. This time she blinked, and Jason thought he saw the glint of tears.

"I was with Dr. Hayes when he died," Jason explained, watching Helene carefully. Except for the watery eyes, she seemed strangely devoid of emotion, and Jason wondered if it was a form of grief. "Just before Hayes died, he told me that he'd made a major scientific breakthrough . . ."

Jason let his comment hang in the air, hoping for some appropriate response. There was none. Helene merely stared back at him.

"Well, was there?" Jason said, leaning forward.

"I didn't know you were finished speaking," Helene said. "It wasn't a question, you know."

"True," Jason admitted. "I was merely hoping you'd respond. I do hope you know what Dr. Hayes meant."

"I'm afraid I don't. Other people in the administration have already been up here asking me the same question. Unfortunately, I have no idea what Dr. Hayes could have been referring to."

Jason imagined that Shirley had been to see Helene first thing that morning.

"Are you the only person besides Dr. Hayes who works in this lab?"

"That's right," Helene said. "We had a secretary, but Dr. Hayes dismissed her three months ago. He thought she talked too much."

"What was he afraid she'd talk about?"

"Anything and everything. Dr. Hayes was an intensely private person. Especially about his work."

"So I'm learning," Jason said. His initial impression that Hayes had become paranoid seemed to be substantiated. Yet Jason persisted: "What exactly do you do, Miss Brennquivist?"

"I'm a molecular biologist. Like Dr. Hayes, but nowhere near his ability. I use recombinant DNA techniques to alter E. coli bacteria to produce various proteins that Dr. Hayes was interested in."

Jason nodded as if he understood. He'd heard the term "recombinant DNA," but had only the vaguest notion what it really meant. Since he'd been in medical school there had been a virtual explosion of knowledge in the field. But there was one thing he did remember, and that was a fear that recombinant DNA studies might produce bacteria capable of causing new and unknown diseases. With Hayes's sudden death in mind, he asked, "Had you come up with any new and potentially dangerous strains?"

"No," Helene said without hesitation.

"How can you be so sure?"

"For two reasons. First of all, I did all the recombinant bacterial work, not Dr. Hayes. Secondly, we use a strain of E. coli bacteria that cannot grow outside of the laboratory."

"Oh," Jason said, nodding encouragingly.

"Dr. Hayes was interested in growth and development. He spent most of his time isolating the growth factors from the hypothalamic-pituitary axis responsible for puberty and sexual development. Growth factors are proteins. I'm sure you know that."

"Of course," Jason said. *What a curious woman*, he thought. At first, conversation had been like pulling teeth. Now that she was on scientific ground, she was extremely vocal.

"Dr. Hayes would give me a protein and I'd set out to produce it by recombinant DNA techniques. That's what I'm doing here." She turned to the stacks of petri dishes, and, lifting one, removed the cover. She extended it toward Jason. On the surface were whitish clumps of bacterial colonies.

Helene replaced the dish on its appropriate stack. "Dr. Hayes was fascinated by the on/off switching of genes, the balance between repression and expression, and the role of repressor proteins and where they bind to the DNA. He's used the growth hormone gene as the prototype. Would you like to see his latest map of chromosome 17?"

"Sure," Jason said, forcing a smile.

A buzzer resounded in the lab, momentarily drowning out the low hum of the electronic equipment. A screen in front of Helene flashed to life, showing four people and a dog in the foyer. Jason recognized two of them immediately—Shirley Montgomery and Detective Michael Curran. The other two were strangers.

"Oh, dear," Helene said, as she reached for the buzzer.

Jason stood as the new arrivals filed into the

room. Shirley registered a momentary flash of surprise when she saw Jason, but calmly introduced Detective Curran to Helene. As he began to question her, Shirley took Jason by the arm and steered him into the nearest office, which Jason realized must have been Hayes's. Covering the walls were progressive close-up photos of human genitalia going through the anatomical evolution of puberty. They were all nicely framed in stainless steel squares.

"Interesting decor," Jason commented wryly.

Shirley acted as if she didn't even see the photos. Her usually calm face wore an expression of concern and irritation. "This affair is getting out of hand."

"What do you mean?" Jason asked.

"Apparently last night the police got an anonymous tip that Dr. Alvin Hayes dealt drugs. They searched his apartment and found a significant amount of heroin, cocaine, and cash. Now they have a warrant to search his lab."

"My God!" Jason suddenly understood the dog's presence.

"And as if that's not enough, they found out he's been living with a woman by the name of Carol Donner."

"That name sounds familiar," Jason said.

"Well, it shouldn't be," Shirley said sternly. "Carol Donner is an exotic dancer at the Club Cabaret in the Combat Zone."

"Well, I'll be damned." Jason chuckled.

"Jason!" Shirley snapped. "This is not a laughing matter."

"I'm not laughing," he protested. "I'm just astounded."

"If you think *you're* astounded, what's the board of directors going to say? And to think I insisted on hiring Hayes. The man's death alone was bad enough. This is fast becoming a public relations nightmare."

"What are you going to do?" Jason asked.

"I haven't the slightest idea," Shirley admitted. "At the moment my intuition tells me the less we do, the better."

"What are your thoughts about Hayes's supposed breakthrough?"

"I think the man was fantasizing," Shirley said. "I mean, he was involved with drugs and an exotic dancer, for God's sake!"

Exasperated, she returned to the main part of the lab, where Detective Curran was still talking intently with Helene. The other two men and the dog were methodically searching the lab. Jason watched for a few moments, then excused himself to finish office hours. He still had a handful of outpatients to see as well as hospital rounds to do.

On the way home, even though he was more convinced than ever that Hayes had been on the verge of a nervous breakdown, rather than a breakthrough, Jason stopped at the library and took out a slim volume titled *Recombinant DNA: An Introduction for the Nonscientist.*

Rush hour traffic was the usual dog-eat-dog Boston rally, and when Jason stepped on the emergency brake in his parking place in front of his townhouse, he felt the usual relief that he'd survived unscathed. He carried his briefcase up to his apartment, and put it on the desk in the small study that looked out onto the square. The now leafless elms were like skeletons against the night sky. Daylight Saving was already over, and it was dark outside even though it was only six forty-five. Changing into his jogging clothes, Jason ran down Mt. Vernon Street, crossed over Storrow Drive on the Arthur Fiedler Bridge, and ran along the Charles. He ran to the Boston University Bridge before turning. In contrast to the summer, there were few joggers. On the way back he stopped at De Luca's Market and picked up some fresh, local bluefish, makings for a salad, and a cold bottle of California Chardonnay.

Jason liked to cook, and after taking his shower, he prepared the fish by broiling it with a small amount of garlic and virgin olive oil. He tossed the salad, then rescued the wine from the freezer where he'd put it to give it an icy kick. He poured himself a glass. When all was ready he carried it into the study on a tray. Thus prepared, he opened the small book on recombinant DNA and settled in for the night.

The first part of the book served as a review. Jason was well aware that deoxyribonucleic acid, better known as DNA, was a molecule, shaped like a twisted, double-stranded string. It was made up of repeating subunits called bases that had the property of pairing with each other in very specific ways. Particular areas of the DNA were called genes, and each gene was associated with the production of a specific protein.

Jason felt encouraged as he took a sip of his wine. The book was well written and made the subject matter seem clear. He liked the little tidbits like the fact that each human cell had four billion base pairs. The next part of the book dealt with bacteria, and the fact that bacteria reproduce easily and rapidly. Within days, trillions of identical cells could be made from a single initial cell. This was important, because in genetic engineering bacteria served as the recipient of small fragments of DNA. This "foreign" DNA was incorporated into the bacterium's own DNA, and then, as the cell divided, it manufactured the original fragments. The bacterium with the newly incorporated DNA was called a recombinant strain and the new DNA molecule was called recombinant DNA. So far so good.

Jason ate some of his fish and salad and washed it down with wine. The next chapter got a little more complicated. It talked about how the genes in the DNA molecule went about producing their respective proteins. The first part entailed making a copy of the segment of DNA with a molecule called messenger RNA. The messenger RNA then directed the production of the protein in a process called transcription. Jason drank a little more wine. The last part of the chapter got particularly interesting, since it explained the elaborate mechanisms that turned genes on and off.

Getting up from his desk, Jason walked across his

living room into the kitchen. Opening the freezer, he poured himself another glass of wine. Back in his study he stared out the window, seeing the lights across the square in St. Margaret's Convent. It always amused him that there was a convent on the most desirable residential square in Boston: Give up the material world, become a nun, and move to Louisburg! Jason smiled, then looked back down at the recombinant DNA book. Sitting down again, he reread the section on the timing of gene expression. It was complicated and fascinating. Apparently, a host of proteins had been discovered that served as repressors of gene function. These proteins attached to the DNA or caused the DNA to coil, to cover up the involved genes.

Jason closed the book. He'd had enough for one night. Besides, the section on the control of gene function was what he'd been unconsciously looking for. Reading that section brought back Hayes's comment that his main interest was "how genes turned on and how they turned off." Helene had said the same thing but in different words.

Taking his wine, Jason wandered into his living room. Absently fondling the cut-glass sconces over the fireplace, he allowed his mind to consider the possibilities. What could Hayes have meant when he said he'd made a major scientific breakthrough? For the moment Jason dismissed the idea of Hayes having delusions of grandeur. After all, he was a world-class researcher, and he was working prodigious hours. So there was a chance he'd been telling the truth. If he'd made a discovery, it would be in the area of turning genes on and off, and probably have to do with growth and development. The image of the photos of the genitals clouded Jason's mind for a moment.

Jason was brought out of his reverie by the phone. It was the head nurse in the coronary care unit. "Brian Lennox just died. He had a terminal episode of V-tack that progressed to asystole."

"I'll be right over," Jason said. He hung up and thought of the nurse's scientific jargon, recognizing that it was an emotional defense. Once again the shadow of death hung over him like a noxious cloud.

4.

The radio alarm blasted Jason out of bed. He'd turned up the volume for fear of oversleeping. He'd spent a good portion of the night consoling Brian Lennox's wife. Retrieving his newspaper from the front steps, he shaved and showered while his Mr. Coffee performed its usual morning miracle. By the time he was dressed, the apartment was filled with the aromatic smell of the freshly brewed coffee. With mug in hand, he retreated to the den, slipping the *Boston Globe* out of its protective clear plastic sheath.

Planning to turn directly to the sports section, he stopped at a front-page headline— DOCTOR, DRUGS AND DANCER. It was not a flattering article about Dr. Alvin Hayes. It played up Hayes's shocking death and unfairly associated it with the drugs found in his apartment, even likening his affair with the dancer to the case involving the Tufts Medical School professor who had been convicted of murdering a prostitute. Along with the article there were two photos: the *Time* cover shoot of Hayes and another of a woman entering the Club Cabaret, captioned, "Carol Donner entering her place of business." Jason tried to see what Carol Donner looked like, but it was impossible. She had one hand up, shielding her face. In the background was a sign that said, TOPLESS COLLEGE GIRLS. *Sure,* thought Jason with a smile.

He read the rest of the article, feeling sorry for Shirley. The police reported that a significant amount of heroin and cocaine was found at the South End apartment that Hayes had shared with Carol Donner.

Jason went to the hospital to find his inpatients generally in poor shape. Matthew Cowen, who had had a cardiac catheterization the day before, displayed odd symptoms alarmingly like the late Cedric Harring: arthritis, constipation, and dry skin. None of these would normally cause Jason much concern. But in view of recent events, they made him feel uneasy. They again brought up the specter of some new unknown infectious disease that he could not control. He had the feeling Matthew's course was about to change for the worse.

After ordering a dermatology consult for Cowen, Jason gloomily went down to his office, where Claudia greeted him with the information that she had pulled the executive physicals through the letter P. She had called the patients and discovered that only two complained of health problems.

Jason reached for the charts and opened them.

The first one was Holly Jennings, the other Paul Klingler. Both had had their physicals within a month. "Call them back," Jason said, "and ask both to come in as soon as they can without alarming them."

"It's going to be hard not to upset them. What should I say?"

"Tell them we want to repeat some test. Use your imagination."

Later in the day he decided to see if he could charm some more information on Hayes out of his lab technician, but the moment he saw Helene she made it clear she was not about to be charmed.

"Did the police find anything?" he asked, already knowing the answer was no. Shirley had called him and told him after the police had departed, saying, "Thank God for small favors."

Helene shook her head.

"I know you're busy," Jason said, "but do you think you could spare a minute? I'd like to ask a few more questions."

She finally stopped working and turned toward him.

"Thank you," he said, and smiled. Her expression didn't change. It wasn't unpleasant, just neutral.

"I hate to belabor the subject," Jason said, "but I keep thinking of what Dr. Hayes said about a significant breakthrough. Are you sure you have no idea what it could be? It would be tragic if a real medical discovery were lost."

"I told you what I know," Helene said. "I could show you the latest map he did of chromosome 17. Would that help?"

"Let's give it a try."

Helene led the way into Hayes's office. She ignored the photos that covered the walls, but Jason couldn't. He wondered what kind of man could work in such an environment. Helene produced a large sheet of paper covered with minute printing, giving the sequence of base pairs of the DNA molecule comprising a portion of chromosome 17. There was a staggering number of base pairs: hundreds and hundreds of thousands.

"Dr. Hayes's area is here." She pointed to a large section where the pairs were done in red. "These are the genes associated with growth hormone. It's very complex."

"You're right there," Jason said. He knew he'd have to do a lot more reading to make any sense of it all.

"Is there any chance this mapping could have led to a major scientific breakthrough?"

Helene thought for a moment, then shook her head. "The technique has been known for some time."

"What about cancer?" Jason asked, giving the idea a shot. "Could Dr. Hayes have discovered something about cancer?"

"We didn't work with cancer at all," Helene said. "But if he was interested in cell division and maturation, it's possible he could have discovered something about cancer. Especially with his interest in the switching on and off of genes."

"I suppose it's possible," Helene said without enthusiasm.

Jason was sure that Helene was not being as helpful as she could be. As Hayes's assistant, she should have had a better idea of what Hayes was doing. But there was no way he could force the issue.

"What about his lab books?"

Helene returned to her spot at the lab bench. Opening the second drawer at the table, she pulled out a ledger. "This is all I have," she said, and handed it to Jason.

The book was three-quarters filled. Jason could see it was only a data book without experimental protocols, and without those, the data was meaningless.

"Aren't there other lab books?"

"There were some," Helene admitted, "but Dr. Hayes kept them with him, especially over the last three months. Mostly he kept everything in his head. He had a fabulous memory, especially for figures. . . ." For a brief moment Jason saw a light in Helene's eyes and thought she might open up, but it didn't last.

She trailed off into silence. She took the data book from Jason and replaced it in its drawer.

"Let me ask one other question," Jason said, struggling over the wording. "As far as you could tell, did Dr. Hayes act normally over the last few weeks? He seemed anxious and overtired when I saw him." Jason deliberately understated Hayes's condition.

"He seemed normal to me," said Helene flatly.

Oh, brother, Jason thought. Now he was sure Helene wasn't being open with him. Unfortunately, there was nothing he could do about it. Thanking her and excusing himself, he retreated from Hayes's lab. He descended in the elevator, avoided being seen by Sally, crossed to the main building, and rode up to pathology.

He found Jackson Madsen in the chemistry lab, where there was a problem with one of the automated machines. Two company reps were there, and Jackson was happy to return to his office with Jason to show him the slides of Harring's heart.

"Wait until you see this," he said as he positioned a slide under his microscope. He peered through the eyepiece, moving the slide deftly with his thumb and index finger. Then he stepped back and let Jason take a look.

"See that vessel?" he asked. Jason nodded. "Notice the lumen is all but obliterated. It's some of the worst atherosclerosis I've seen. That pink stuff looks like amyloid. It's amazing, especially if you say his EKG was okay. And let me show you something else." Jackson substituted another slide. "Take a look now."

Jason peered into the microscope. "What am I supposed to see?"

"Notice how swollen the nuclei are," Jackson said. "And the pink stuff. That's amyloid for certain."

"What does that mean?"

"It's as if the guy's heart was under siege. Notice the inflammatory cells."

Unaccustomed to looking at microscopic sections, Jason hadn't noticed them at first, but now they jumped out at him. "What do you make of it?" he asked.

"I'm not sure. How old did you say this guy was?"

"Fifty-six." Jason straightened up. "Is there any chance, in your estimation, that we are seeing some new infectious disease?"

Jackson thought for a moment, then shook his head. "I don't think there's enough inflammation for that. It looks more metabolic, but that's all I can say. Oh, one more thing," he added, putting in another slide. While he focused he said: "This is part of the red nucleus in the brain. Tell me what you see." He leaned back for Jason. Jason peered into the scope. He saw a neuron. Within the neuron was a prominent nucleus as well as a darkly stained granular area. He described it to Jackson.

"That's lipofuscin," said Jackson. He removed the slide.

Jason straightened up. "What does it all mean?"

"Wish I knew," said Jackson. "All nonspecific, but certainly a suggestion that your Mr. Harring was a sick cookie. These slides could have belonged to my grandfather."

"That's the second time I've heard something like

that," said Jason slowly. "Can't you give me anything more specific?"

"I'm sorry," said Jackson. "I wish I could be more cooperative. I'll be running some tests to be sure these deposits in the heart and elsewhere are amyloid. I'll let you know."

"Thanks," said Jason. "What about the slides on Hayes?"

"Not ready yet," said Jackson.

Jason returned to the second floor and walked over to the outpatient area. As a doctor he'd always had questions about the efficacy of certain tests, procedures and drugs. But he had never had reason to question his general competence. In fact, in most situations he'd always thought of himself as well above average. Now, he wasn't so sure. Such misgivings were disturbing, especially because he'd been using work as his major sense of self since Danielle's death.

"Where have you been?" demanded Sally, catching up to Jason as he tried to slip into his office. Within minutes Sally had Jason buried beneath a host of minor problems that thankfully absorbed his attention. By the time he could catch his breath, it was just after twelve. He saw his last patient, who wanted advice and shots for a trip to India, and then he was free.

Claudia tried to get him to join her and some other secretaries for lunch, but Jason declined. He retreated to his office and brooded. The worst part for Jason was the frustration. He felt something was terribly wrong, but he didn't know what it was or what to do about it. A loneliness descended over him.

"Damn," said Jason, slapping the top of his desk with his open palm, hard enough to send unattached papers flying. He had to avoid slipping into a depression. He had to do something. Changing from his white coat to his jacket, he grabbed his beeper and descended to his car. He drove around the Fenway, passing the Gardner Museum and then the Museum of Fine Arts on his right. Then, heading south on Storrow Drive, he got off at Arlington. His destination was Boston Police Headquarters.

At police headquarters a policeman directed Jason to the fifth floor. As soon as he got off the elevator, he saw the detective coming down the hall, balancing a full mug of coffee. Curran was jacketless, with the top button of his shirt open and his tie loosened. Under his left arm dangled a worn leather holster. When he saw Jason he seemed perplexed until Jason reminded him that they'd met at the morgue and at GHP.

"Ah, yes," Curran said, with his slight brogue. "Alvin Hayes business."

He invited Jason into his office, which was starkly utilitarian with a metal desk and metal file cabinet. On the wall was a calendar with the Celtics' basketball schedule.

"How about some coffee?" Curran suggested, putting his mug down.

"No, thank you," Jason said.

"You're smart," Curran said. "I know everybody complains about institutional coffee, but this stuff is lethal." He pulled a metal chair away from the wall and motioned to it for Jason to sit.

"So what can I do for you, doctor?"

"I'm not sure. This Hayes business disturbs me. Remember I told you that Dr. Hayes said he'd made a major discovery? Well, now I think there's a good chance he did. After all, the man was a world-famous researcher, and he was working in a field with a lot of potential."

"Wait a minute. Didn't you also tell me you thought Hayes was having a nervous breakdown?"

"At the time I thought he was displaying inappropriate behavior," Jason said. "I thought he was paranoid and delusional. Now I'm not sure. What if he did make a major discovery which he hadn't revealed because he was still perfecting it? Suppose someone found out and for some reason wanted it suppressed?"

"And had him killed?" Curran interrupted patronizingly. "Doctor, you're forgetting one major fact: Hayes died of natural causes. There was no foul play, no gunshot wounds to the head, no knife in the back. And on top of that, he was dealing. We found heroin, coke, and cash in his Southie pad. No wonder he acted paranoid. The drug scene is a serious world."

"Wasn't that anonymous tip a bit strange?" Jason asked, suddenly curious.

"It happens all the time. Somebody's pissed about something so they call us to get even."

Jason stared at the detective. He thought the drug connection was out of character, but didn't know why. Then he remembered that Hayes had been living with an exotic dancer. Maybe it wasn't so out of character after all.

As if reading Jason's thoughts, Curran said, "Listen, doctor, I appreciate you taking the time to come down, but facts are facts. I don't know if this guy made a discovery or not, but let me tell you something. If he was dealing drugs, he was taking them too. That's the pattern. I had the Vice department run his name through their computers. They came up with zip, but that just means he hadn't been caught yet. He's lucky he got to die of natural causes. In any case, I can't justify spending Homicide time on the death."

"I still think there's more to it."

Curran shook his head.

"Dr. Hayes was trying to tell me something," Jason persisted. "I think he wanted help."

"Sure," Curran said. "He probably wanted to pull you into his drug ring. Listen, doctor, take my advice. Forget this affair." He stood up, indicating the interview was over.

Descending to the street, Jason removed the parking ticket from his windshield wiper. Sliding in behind the wheel, he thought about his conversation with Detective Curran. The man had been cordial, but he obviously gave little credence to Jason's thoughts and intuition. As Jason started his car, he remembered something else Hayes had said about his discovery. He'd said it was "ironic." Now that was a weird way to characterize a major scientific breakthrough, especially if someone were contriving the story.

Back at the GHP, Jason returned to his patients, going from room to room listening, touching, sympathizing, and advising. That was what he loved about medicine. People opened themselves to him, literally and figuratively. He felt privileged and needed. Some of his confidence ebbed back.

It was close to four when he approached exam room C and took the chart. He remembered the name. It was Paul Klingler, the man whose physical exam he had done. Before entering the room, Jason quickly reviewed his workup. The man appeared to be healthy, with low normal cholesterol and triglycerides and normal EKG. Jason entered the room.

Klingler was slender, with sandy blond hair and the quiet confidence of an old moneyed Yankee. "What was wrong with my tests?" he asked, concerned.

"Nothing, really."

"But your secretary told me you wanted to repeat some. That I had to come today."

"Sorry about that. There was no need for alarm. When she heard you weren't feeling well, she thought we should take a look."

"I'm just getting over the flu," Paul said. "Kids brought it home from school. I'm much better. The only problem is that it has kept me from exercise for over a week."

The flu didn't scare Jason. Healthy people didn't die of it. But he still examined Paul Klingler carefully and repeated the various cardiac tests. Finally he told Klingler that he'd call if the blood work revealed any abnormalities.

Two patients later, Jason confronted Holly Jennings, a fifty-four-year-old executive from one of the largest Boston advertising firms. She was not happy and certainly not shy about expressing her feelings. And although there was a sign specifically forbidding it, she'd been smoking in the exam room while she had been waiting.

"What the hell is going on?" she demanded as Jason entered the room. Her physical a month ago had given her a clean bill of health, though Jason had warned her to stop smoking and take off the twenty to thirty extra pounds she had put on in the last five years.

"I'd heard you weren't feeling well," Jason said mildly. He noticed she looked tired, and saw the dark circles under her eyes.

"Is that what this is all about?" she snapped. "The secretary told me you wanted to repeat some tests. What was wrong with them?"

"Nothing. We just wanted to do some follow-up. Tell me about your health."

"Jesus Christ! You drag me down here, scaring the

hell out of me, making me miss two important presentations, just to have a conversation. Couldn't this have been done on the phone?"

"Well, since you're here, why don't you tell me how you've been feeling."

"Tired."

"Anything else?"

"Just generally lousy. I haven't been able to sleep. My appetite's been poor. Nothing specific . . . well, that's not true. My eyes have been bothering me. I've had to wear sunglasses a lot, even in the office."

"Anything else?" Jason asked, feeling an uncomfortable prickle of fear.

Holly shrugged. "For some goddamn reason my hair's been thinning."

As carefully as possible, Jason examined the woman. Her pulse and blood pressure were up, although that could have been due to stress. Her skin was dry, particularly on her extremities. When he repeated her EKG, he thought there might have been some very mild ST changes suggesting reduced oxygen to her heart. When he suggested they do another stress test, she declined.

"Can I come back for that?"

"I'd rather do it now," Jason said. "In fact, would you consider staying in the hospital for a couple of days?"

"Are you kidding? I don't have time. Besides, I don't feel that bad. Why do you even suggest it?"

"Just to get everything done. I'd like you to see a cardiologist and an ophthalmologist as well."

"Next week. Monday or Tuesday. But I've got some big deadlines."

Reluctantly, Jason let Holly go after drawing some blood. There was no way he could force her to stay, and he had nothing specific enough to convince her she was in trouble. It was just a feeling: a bad feeling.

Following his usual routine after returning home, Jason jogged, stopped into De Luca's Market where he got a Perdue chicken, put his meal in the oven, showered and retreated to his den with an ice-cold beer. Making himself comfortable, he continued his reading on DNA. He began to understand how Hayes could isolate specific genes. That was what Helene Brennquivist had probably been doing that morning. Once an appropriate bacterial colony was found, it was cultivated to produce trillions of bacteria. Then, using enzymes, the bacteria DNA was separated, fragmented, and the desired gene was isolated and purified. Later, it could be spliced back into different bacteria into regions of the DNA that could be "switched on" by the researcher. In that form, the recombinant strain of bacteria acted like miniature factories to produce the protein the gene was coded for. It had been this method that Hayes had used to produce his human growth hormone. He had started with a piece of human DNA, the gene that made growth hormone, cloned it by the help of bacteria, then spliced it into bacteria DNA in an area controlled by a gene responsible for digesting lactose. By adding lactose to the culture, Hayes's recombinant strain of bacteria had been "turned on" to produce human growth hormone.

Jason drained his beer and went into the kitchen and popped another. He was overwhelmed by what he'd learned. No wonder scientists like Hayes were strange. They knew they had the power to manipulate life. This comprehension thrilled Jason and disturbed him at the same time. The DNA technology had awesome potential to do good and harm. The direction, he thought, was a toss-up.

Armed with this information, Jason was even more inclined to believe that Hayes, though under general stress, had been telling the truth—at least about the scientific breakthrough. Jason was not so sure about Hayes's statement that someone wanted him dead. He wished he'd spent more time with the man over the last months. He wished he knew more about him.

Opening the oven, Jason checked his chicken. It was browning nicely and looked delicious. He put water on to boil for rice, then went back to the den. Lifting his legs onto the desktop and tilting back his chair, he started the next chapter on the laboratory techniques of genetic engineering. The first part dealt with the methods by which DNA molecules were fragmented with enzymes called restriction endonucleases. Jason had to read the section several times. It was difficult material.

The shrill whine of the smoke detector startled

Jason. Leaping up from the desk where he'd fallen fast asleep, he dashed into the kitchen. The water for the rice had boiled away, and the Teflon lining was smoking, filling the kitchen with acrid vapors. Jason shoved it under running water, where it spattered and hissed. Turning on the exhaust fan and opening one of the living room windows slowly emptied the kitchen of smoke, and finally the smoke detector fell silent. Jason was glad the landlord was out of town as usual.

When his dinner was finally prepared, without rice, Jason carried it to his desk in the den, pushing papers and books aside. As he started eating he found himself looking at the front of the *Boston Globe* with the article "Doctor, Drugs and Dancer" staring him in the face. Picking the paper up in his left hand, he looked at Carol Donner again. The idea that Hayes would have been living with the woman confounded him. Jason wondered if Hayes had fallen prey to the age-old male fantasy of rescuing the prostitute who, despite her work, had a heart of gold. Thinking of Hayes as a colleague with similar background including the same medical school, Jason found the idea of him falling for such a cliché farfetched. But as Curran had said, facts were facts. Obviously Hayes had been living with the girl. Jason tossed the paper aside.

After reading what he could find about dry skin, which wasn't much, Jason carried his soiled dishes to the kitchen and rinsed them. The image of Carol

Donner with her hand in front of her face kept popping up in his mind. He looked at his watch. It was ten-thirty. "Why not," he said aloud. After all, if Hayes had been living with the woman, maybe she knew something that could give Jason a clue about Hayes's breakthrough. At any rate, he had nothing to lose. Donning a sweater and a tweed jacket, Jason left the apartment.

From Beacon Hill it was only a fifteen-minute walk to the Combat Zone. But fifteen minutes took Jason an enormous social distance. Beacon Hill was the epitome of comfortable wealth and propriety, with its cobblestone streets and gas lamps. The Combat Zone was the sordid opposite. To get there, Jason skirted the edge of the Boston Common, reaching Washington Street with its row of bottomless bars by way of Boylston Street. There were roaming packs of street people mixing uneasily with groups of boisterous students and leather-jacketed blue-collar workers from Dorchester. The Club Cabaret was in the middle of the block, nestled between an X-rated cinema and an adult bookstore with a variety of supposed sexual aids on display in its window. The TOPLESS COLLEGE GIRLS sign glowed with fluorescent paint.

Jason walked up to the door and went inside. He found himself in the bar, a long, dark room illuminated in the center to spotlight a wooden runway. The bar itself was U-shaped and surrounded the runway. Behind there were small booths, and rock music thudded into the room from large speakers flanking the stairs that led to the runway from the floor above.

The air was foul with cigarette smoke and that peculiar chemical odor which smells like cheap room-deodorant. The place was almost filled with men hunched over drinks at the bar. It was difficult to see into the booths, but as Jason passed, he glimpsed numerous women in low-cut spaghetti-strap dresses. He found a stool at the bar. A waitress wearing a white shirt and tight black shorts took his order almost instantly.

As she brought his beer and a glass, a seminude dancer came down the stairs and pranced along the runway. Jason gazed up at her, catching her eye for a brief instant. She looked bored. Her face was heavily made up, and her bleached hair had the consistency of straw. Jason guessed her age to be over thirty, certainly no coed.

Glancing around the room, he noticed equivalent expressions of boredom on the faces of the men as their eyes reflexively followed the progress of the dancer up and down the runway. Jason sipped his beer from the bottle. There was no way he'd allow his lips to touch a glass in that place.

When the rock-and-roll piece ended, the dancer acted as if she'd been momentarily stranded. Self-consciously, she shifted her weight from one four-inch heel to the other, waiting for the next number. Jason noticed a tattooed heart on her right thigh.

Heralded by the heavy beat of drums, the next number began, and the blonde immediately recommenced her gyrations. As she did so, she slipped off her brief top. Now all she had on was a G-string and her shoes. Still, the men at the bar appeared carved in stone. The only movements were those necessary to bring their drinks or cigarettes to their lips. At least until the dancer began moving along the runway. Then a few customers would hold out dollar bills.

Jason watched for a while, then scanned the room again. About twenty feet away was a booth occupied by a man in a dark suit with a cigar, studying a ledger through dark glasses. Jason had no idea how the man could see anything at all, but decided he was management. Several body-builder types with eighteen-inch necks, wearing white T-shirts, stood on either side of the booth, their beefy arms crossed and their heads constantly turning to survey the room.

As the music ended, the blond stripper picked up her things and ran up the stairs. There was scattered applause. When the music began again, a new dancer descended the stairs and whirled about the runway. Dressed in a flashy, voluminous gypsy costume, she could have been the first dancer's sister—her older sister.

Very quickly, Jason got the hang of the program. A girl would appear in some wild costume and dance, taking off more of her clothes as the number progressed. Forty-five minutes passed and Jason wondered if Carol Donner was scheduled to appear that night. He asked one of the waitresses.

"She should be next. Want another round, mister?"

Jason shook his head. He was content to nurse his first beer for the entire visit. Looking around, he noticed that several of the strippers had come back down to the floor. They would stop and talk to the man in the dark glasses and then wander around the room, chatting up the customers. Jason tried to imagine Hayes, the famous molecular biologist, there at the bar. Try as he might, he couldn't.

There was a pause in the music and the runway lights dimmed. A PA system crackled to life for the first time and announced the next performer: the famous Carol Donner. The bored patrons propped up on the bar suddenly seemed to wake up. There were a few catcalls.

The music changed to a softer rock and a figure appeared on the runway. As the lights came up, Jason was stunned. To his amazement, Carol Donner was a beautiful young woman. Her skin had a healthy glow and her eyes sparkled. She was dressed in a body suit, headband, and leg warmers as though she were in an aerobics class. Her feet were bare. She moved down the runway with effortless grace, and Jason noticed that her smile held genuine enjoyment.

As her number progressed, she removed her leg

warmers, a silk sash around her waist, and then the body suit. The sodden audience actually cheered as she danced topless back up the stairs. As soon as she disappeared, the customers sank back into their torpor. Jason kept waiting for Carol to appear on the floor like the other girls, but after twenty minutes he decided she might not. He pushed off his stool and walked back to the man in the sunglasses. One of the body-builders noticed his approach and unfolded his arms. "Excuse me," Jason said to the man with the ledger. "Would it be possible to talk with Carol Donner?"

The man removed his cigar. "Who the hell are you?" Jason was reluctant to give his real name, and while he hesitated, the man in the dark glasses motioned to one of the body-builders. Jason felt large hands take hold of his arm and urge him toward the door. "I only want . . ." But he didn't get to say any more. He was grabbed by his jacket and hastily escorted the length of the bar and through the dark curtain, his feet barely touching the floor. With a good deal of humiliation, he found himself propelled out into the street.

5.

After the radio alarm had awakened him, Jason had to stand under the shower for several minutes to feel capable of facing the day. The night before, after he'd returned from the unpleasant visit to the Club Cabaret, he'd been called back to the hospital. One of his AIDS patients, a man named Harvey Rachman, had arrested. When Jason had arrived, the staff had been giving CPR for fifteen minutes. They'd kept it up for two hours before conceding defeat. The head nurse's comment that at least the man didn't have to suffer anymore was not much consolation to a stricken Jason. For Jason it seemed that death was winning the competition.

The only positive side of inpatient rounds later that morning was the discharge of one of his hepatitis cases. Jason was sorry to see the girl go. Now he had only a single patient who was doing well.

In the CCU, Matthew Cowen was no better. In addition to his other complaints, he was now having trouble seeing. The symptom bothered Jason. Harring and Lennox had also complained of impaired vision in the weeks before their deaths, and again the possibility of some new multisystem illness crossed Jason's mind. He ordered an ophthalmology consult. After finishing rounds, Jason headed to pathology to see if the slides from Hayes's autopsy were done. Maybe they would help explain why so many seemingly healthy people were suffering cardiovascular catastrophe.

He had to wait while Jackson called a report on a frozen section down to the OR. It was a breast biopsy and it was positive.

"That always makes me feel terrible," Jackson said, hanging up the phone. Then, in a more cheerful voice, he added, "I bet you want to see the Hayes slides." He searched around on his desk until he found the right folder. Opening it up, he took out a slide and focused it for Jason. "Wait until you see this.

"That's Alvin Hayes's aorta," Jackson explained as Jason looked in. The cellular death and disorganization were evident even to his unpracticed eye. "It's no wonder it blew," Jackson continued. "I've never seen such deterioration in anyone under seventy except with established aortic disease. And let me show you something else." He replaced the slide with another. "That's Hayes's heart. Look at the coronary vessel. It's like Cedric Harring's. All the coronary vessels are almost closed. If Hayes's aorta hadn't blown, he'd have died of a heart attack. The man was a walking time bomb. And not only that, he had inflammation in the thyroid, again like Harring.

In fact, there were so many parallels that I went back and looked at Harring's aorta. And guess what? Harring's aorta was on the verge of blowing too."

"What exactly are you saying?" Jason asked.

Jackson spread his hands. "I don't know. There are strong similarities between these two cases. The widespread inflammation—but I don't think it's infectious. It has more the look of autoimmunity, as if their immune system had started attacking their own organs."

"You mean like lupus?"

"Yeah, something like that. Anyway, Alvin Hayes was in terrible shape. Just about every organ was in a state of deterioration. He was falling apart at the seams."

"He said he wasn't feeling too well," Jason said.

"Ha!" Jackson exclaimed. "That's the understatement of the year."

Jason left pathology, trying to make sense of Jackson's statement. Again he considered the possibility of an unknown infectious disease despite Jackson's opinion. After all, what kind of an autoimmune disease could work so quickly? Jason answered his own question: none.

Before starting the office patients, Jason decided to stop by Hayes's lab. Not that he expected Helene to be helpful, but he thought she might be interested in the fact that Hayes had been so ill the last few weeks of his life. To his surprise, he saw Helene had been crying.

"What's the matter?"

Helene shook her head. "Nothing."

"Aren't you working?"

"I finished," Helene said.

All at once Jason realized that without Hayes there to give her instructions, she was lost. Apparently she'd not been apprised of the big picture, a fact that made Jason pessimistic that she would have knowledge of Hayes's breakthrough, if there'd been one. The man's penchant for secrecy was to be society's loss.

"Do you mind if I talk with you for a few minutes?" Jason asked.

"No," Helene said in her usual laconic manner. She motioned him into Hayes's office. Jason followed, assaulted once again by the graphic genital photos.

"I've just come from pathology," Jason began, once they were seated. "Dr. Hayes apparently was a very sick man. Are you sure he didn't complain of feeling ill?"

"He did," Helene admitted, reversing her previous stand. "He kept saying he felt weak."

Jason stared across at her. She seemed softer, more open, and he realized that in contrast to the previous times he'd seen her, her hair was loose, falling to her shoulders instead of severely pulled back.

"Last time you said his behavior was unchanged," he said.

"It was. But he said he felt terrible."

Frustrated by this semantic distinction, Jason again was convinced that she was covering up something. He wondered why, but he felt he'd get nowhere by confronting her.

"Miss Brennquivist," Jason said, speaking patiently, "I want to ask once again. Are you absolutely certain you have no idea what Dr. Hayes could have been referring to when he told me he'd made a major scientific breakthrough?"

She shook her head. "I really don't know. The truth was that things had not been going well in the lab. About three months ago, the rats receiving growth hormone–releasing factors had mysteriously begun to die."

"Where did the releasing factors come from?"

"Dr. Hayes extracted them himself from rat brains. Mostly the hypothalamus. Then I produced them by recombinant DNA techniques."

"So the experiments were a failure?"

"Completely," Helene said. "But, like any great researcher, Dr. Hayes was not daunted. Instead he worked harder. He tried different proteins, but unfortunately with the same fatal results."

"Do you think Dr. Hayes was lying when he told me he'd made a breakthrough?"

"Dr. Hayes never lied," Helene said indignantly.

"Well, how do you explain it?" Jason asked. "At first I thought Hayes was having a nervous breakdown. Now I'm not so sure. What do you think?"

"Dr. Hayes was not having a nervous breakdown,"

Helene said, rising to make it clear the conversation was over. Jason had hit a raw nerve. She was not about to listen to her late boss be calumniated.

Frustrated, Jason went down to his office, where Sally already had two patients waiting for physicals. Between them Jason escaped Sally long enough to check the laboratory values on Holly Jennings. The only significant change from her earlier tests was an elevated gamma globulin, again making Jason consider a non-AIDS-related epidemic involving the autoimmune system. Instead of turning the immune system off, as with AIDS, this problem seemed to turn it on in a destructive fashion.

Midmorning Jason got a call from Margaret Danforth, who stated without preamble, "Thought you should know that Dr. Hayes's urine showed moderate levels of cocaine."

So Curran was right, Jason realized, hanging up. Hayes was using drugs. But whether that was related to his claim of discovery, his fear of being attacked, or even his actual death, Jason couldn't tell.

He was forced to put aside his speculation as the heavy patient load pushed him further and further behind. The pressure was heightened by a call from Shirley, who had apparently learned of his visit to Helene.

"Jason," she said with an edge to her voice, "please don't stir the pot. Just let the Hayes affair calm down."

"I think Helene knows more than she's telling us," Jason said.

"Whose side are you on?" Shirley asked.

"Okay, okay," he said, rudely cutting her off as he was confronted by Madaline Krammer, an old patient who had been squeezed in as an emergency. Up until now her heart condition had been stable. Suddenly she was presenting swollen ankles and chest rales. Despite strong medication, her congestive heart disease had increased in severity to the point that Jason insisted on hospitalization.

"Not this weekend," Madaline protested. "My son is coming from California with his new baby. I've never seen my granddaughter. Please!" Madaline was a cheerful woman in her mid-sixties with silver-gray hair. Jason had always been fond of her, since she rarely complained and was extraordinarily grateful for his ministrations.

"Madaline, I'm sorry. I wouldn't do this unless I thought it was necessary. But the only way we can adjust your medications is with constant monitoring."

Grumbling but resigned, Madaline agreed. Jason told her he'd see her later, and left her in the capable hands of Claudia. By four P.M., Jason had just about caught up to his appointment schedule. Emerging from his office, Jason ran into Roger Wanamaker, whose impressive bulk completely blocked the narrow hallway.

"My turn," Roger said. "Got a minute for a chat?"

"Sure," said Jason, who never said no to a colleague. He led the way back to his office. Roger ceremoniously dropped a chart on his desk.

"Just so you don't feel lonely," he said. "That's the chart of a fifty-three-year-old executive from Data General who was just brought into the emergency room deader than a doorknob. I'd given him one of our full-scale executive physicals less than three weeks ago."

Jason opened the chart and glanced through the physical, including the EKG and laboratory values. The cholesterol was high but not terrible. "Another heart attack?" he asked, flipping to the report of the chest X ray. It was normal.

"Nope," Roger said. "Massive stroke. The guy had a seizure right in the middle of a board meeting. His wife is madder'n hell. Made me feel terrible. She said he'd been feeling crummy ever since he'd seen us."

"What were his symptoms?"

"Nothing specific," Roger said. "Mostly insomnia and tension, the kind of stuff executives complain about all the time."

"What the hell is going on?" Jason asked rhetorically.

"Beats me," Roger said. "But I'm getting a bad feeling—like we're on the edge of some kind of epidemic or something."

"I've talked with Madsen in pathology. I asked him about an unknown infectious disease. He said no. He said it was metabolic, maybe autoimmune."

"I think we'd better do something. What about the meeting you suggested?"

"I haven't called it yet," Jason admitted. "I'm having Claudia pull all my physicals over the last year and checking to see how the patients are doing. Maybe you should do the same."

"Good idea."

"What about the autopsy on this case?" Jason asked, handing the chart back to Roger.

"The medical examiner has it."

"Let me know what they find."

When Roger left, Jason made a note to call a meeting of the other internists early the following week. Even if he didn't want to know how widespread the problem was, he knew he couldn't sit back and watch while patients with seemingly healthy check-ups ended up in the morgue.

En route to his final patient, Jason found himself again thinking of Carol Donner. Suddenly getting an idea, he made a detour to the central desk and found Claudia. He asked her to go down to personnel and see if she could get Alvin Hayes's home address. Jason was confident that if anybody could do it, Claudia could.

Once again heading for his last outpatient, Jason wondered why he'd not thought of getting Hayes's address sooner. If Carol Donner had been living with the man, it would be vastly easier to talk with her at her apartment than at the Club Cabaret, where they obviously felt rather protective. Maybe she'd have some ideas about Hayes's breakthrough, or if nothing else, his health. By the time Jason had finished with his last patient, Claudia had the address. It was in the South End.

After all the outpatients had been seen, and Jason had dictated the necessary correspondence, he headed up the main elevator to begin his inpatient rounds. He saw Madaline Krammer first.

She was already looking better. An increased diuretic had reduced her swollen feet and hands considerably, but when he went over her again he was disturbed to find that her pupils seemed widely dilated and unreactive to light. He made a note on her chart before continuing his rounds.

Before he went in to see Matthew Cowen, Jason pulled his chart to see what the ophthalmology consult had said about his eyes. Shocked, Jason read, "Mild cataract formation in both eyes. Check again in six months." Jason couldn't believe what he was seeing. Cataracts at thirty-five? He remembered the autopsy had noted cataracts in Connoly's eyes. He also remembered just seeing Madaline Krammer's dilated pupils. What the hell were they dealing with? He was further confused when he went down the hall to see Matthew.

"Are you giving me any weird drugs?" he demanded as soon as he glimpsed Jason.

"No. Why do you ask?"

"Because my hair is coming out." To make his point, he tugged on a few strands, which indeed came right out. He scattered them on the pillow.

Jason picked one up, rolling it slowly between his

thumb and index finger. It looked normal save for a grayness at the root. Then he examined Matthew's scalp. It too was normal, with no inflammation or soreness.

"How long has this been going on?" he asked, remembering Brian Lennox with startling vividness, as well as Mrs. Harring's comment that her husband's hair had started to fall out.

"It's gotten much worse today," Matthew said. "I don't mean to sound paranoid, but everything seems to be happening to me."

"It's just coincidence," Jason said, trying to buoy his own confidence as much as Matthew's. "I'll have the dermatologist take another look. Maybe it's associated with your dry skin. Has that improved?"

"It's worse, if anything. I shouldn't have come into the hospital."

Jason tended to agree, especially since so many of his patients were doing poorly. By the time he finished rounds, he was exhausted. He almost forgot that some well-meaning friends had insisted he attend a dinner party that night so they could fix him up with a cute thirty-four-year-old lawyer named Penny Lambert. With an hour to kill, Jason decided it wasn't worth going home. Instead, he pulled out the Boston map he kept in his car and located Springfield Street, where Hayes's apartment was located. It was off Washington Street. Thinking it would be a good time to catch Carol Donner, he decided to drive directly there. But that was easier said than done. Heading south, he found himself caught in bumper-to-bumper traffic on Massachusetts Avenue. With persistence, he reached Washington Street and turned left, then left again at Springfield. He located Hayes's building, then found a parking spot.

The neighborhood was a mixture of renovated and unrenovated buildings. Hayes's was in the latter category. Graffiti was spray-painted on the front steps. Jason entered the foyer and noted that several of the mailboxes were broken and that the inner door was unlocked. In fact, the lock had been broken sometime in the distant past and never replaced. Hayes's apartment was on the third floor. Jason started up the poorly lit steps. The smell was musty and damp.

The building was large, with single apartments on each floor. On three Jason tripped over several *Boston Globe*s still in their plastic covers. There was no bell so Jason knocked. Hearing no response, he knocked again, harder. The door squeaked open about an inch. Looking down, Jason saw that the lock had recently been forced and that part of the doorjamb was missing. Using his index finger, Jason gingerly pushed the door open. It squeaked again as if in pain. "Hello," he called. There was no answer. He stepped into the apartment. "Hello." There was no noise except a running toilet. He closed the door behind him and started across a dark hall toward a partially opened door.

Jason took one look and almost fled. The place had

been trashed. The living room, once decorated with attractive antiques and reproductions, was a wreck. All the drawers in the desk and sideboard had been pulled out and dumped. The sofa cushions had been slashed, and the contents of a large bookcase were strewn about the floor.

Picking his way carefully through the mess, Jason peered into a small bedroom, which was in the same condition as the living room, then went down the hall to what he assumed was the master bedroom. It too was a wreck. Every drawer had been dumped, and the clothes in the walk-in closet had been ripped from hangers and thrown on the floor. Picking some up, he noted they were all men's clothes.

Suddenly the front door squeaked, sending a shiver down Jason's spine. He let the clothes fall to the floor. He started to call out again, hoping that it was Carol Donner, but for a moment he was too scared to speak. He froze, his ears straining for sound. Maybe a draft had pushed the door. . . . Then he heard a thud, like the sound of a shoe knocking against a book or an overturned drawer. Someone was definitely in the apartment, and Jason had the feeling whoever it was knew he was there. Perspiration appeared on his forehead and ran down the side of his nose. Detective Curran's warning that the drug world was dangerous flashed through his mind. He wondered if there was a way to sneak out. Then he realized he was at the end of a long hallway.

All at once a large figure filled the doorway. Even

in the darkness Jason could tell that it was carrying a gun.

Panic filled Jason as his heart raced. But still he did not move.A second,smaller figure joined the first and together they stepped into the room. Then they advanced toward Jason, inexorably, step by step. It seemed like an eternity. Jason wanted to cry out or run.

6.

The next instant Jason thought he'd died. There was a flash. But then he realized it was not the gun, but a light bulb over his head. He was still alive. Two uniformed policemen stood before him. Jason could have hugged them in his relief.

"Am I glad to see you guys," Jason said.

"Turn around," the larger cop ordered, ignoring Jason's comment.

"I can explain . . ." Jason began, but he was told to shut up and put his hands on the wall, his feet spread apart.

The second cop searched him, removing his wallet. When they were satisfied Jason was unarmed, they pulled his arms off the wall and handcuffed him. Then they marched him back through the apartment, down the stairs, and into the street. Some passersby stopped to watch as Jason was forced into the back seat of an unmarked car.

The cops remained silent during the ride to the stationhouse, and Jason decided there was no point trying to explain until they got there. Now that he had calmed down, he began to think of what he should do. He guessed he'd be able to make a phone call, and he wondered if he should call Shirley or the lawyer he'd used when he'd sold his house and practice.

But when they arrived, the cops just marched Jason to a small, bare room and left him there. The door clicked when they went out and Jason realized he was locked in. He'd never been in jail before and it did not feel good.

As the minutes slipped by, Jason realized the gravity of the situation. He remembered Shirley's request that he not stir the pot. God knows the effect his arrest would have on the clinic if it became public.

Finally the door to the room opened and Detective Michael Curran came in, followed by the smaller policeman. Jason was glad to see Curran, but he was immediately aware the detective did not reciprocate the emotion. The lines on his face seemed deeper than ever.

"Uncuff him," Curran said without smiling. Jason stood up while the uniformed policeman released his hands. He watched Curran's face, trying to fathom his thoughts, but he remained impenetrable.

"I want to talk with him alone," he said to the policeman, who nodded and left.

"Here's your goddamn wallet," Curran said, slapping it into Jason's palm. "You don't take advice too well, do you? What do I have to do to convince you this drug business is serious stuff?"

"I was only trying to talk with Carol Donner . . ."

"Wonderful. So you butt in and screw things up for us."

"Like what?" Jason asked, beginning to feel his temper rise.

"Vice has been staking out Hayes's apartment since we learned it had been searched. We hoped to pull in someone a bit more interesting than you."

"I'm sorry."

Curran shook his head in frustration. "Well, it could have been worse. You could have gotten yourself hurt. Please, doctor—would you get back to your doctoring?"

"Am I free to go?" Jason asked with disbelief.

"Yeah," Curran said, turning to the door. "I'm not going to book you. No sense wasting our time."

Jason left the police station and took a cab back to Springfield Street, where he retrieved his car. He glanced up at Hayes's building and shivered. It had been an unnerving experience.

With enough adrenaline in his system now to run a four-minute mile, Jason was glad he had plans for the evening. His friends the Alics had invited a lively group of people, and the food and wine were really good. The girl they wanted him to meet, Penny Lambert, struck him as a bit of a yuppie, conservatively dressed in a blue suit with a voluminous silk bow tie. Luckily, she was cheerful and talkative and willingly filled the gap left by Jason's inability to stop thinking about Hayes's apartment and his need to speak to Carol Donner.

When coffee and brandy were cleared away, Jason had an idea. Maybe if he offered to take Penny home, he could persuade her to stop at Carol's club. Obviously, Carol was no longer living at Hayes's apartment, and Jason figured he might have a better chance talking to her if he were accompanied by another woman. Penny happily accepted his offer of a lift, and when they were in the car, he asked her if she were feeling adventurous.

"What do you mean?" she asked cautiously.

"I thought you might like to see another side of Boston."

"Like a disco?"

"Something like that," Jason said. In a mildly perverse way, Jason thought the experience might be good for Penny. She was nice enough, but a bit too predictable.

She relaxed, smiling and chatting until they pulled up in front of the Club Cabaret. "Are you sure this is a good idea?" she asked.

"Come on," Jason urged. He'd given her a little background en route, explaining that he wanted to see the girl Dr. Hayes had been involved with. Penny had remembered the story from the newspapers and it had not buoyed her confidence, but with a bit more cajoling he persuaded her to let him park and go in.

Friday was obviously a big night. Gripping Penny's hand, Jason worked his way down the room, hoping to avoid the man with the dark glasses and his two he-man bodyguards. With the help of a five-dollar bill he got one of the waitresses to give them a booth against the side wall, several steps up from the floor. They could see the runway while remaining partially concealed from the dancers by the dark silhouettes of men standing two deep at the bar.

They'd entered between numbers. They had just ordered drinks when the speakers roared to life. Jason's eyes had adjusted to the darkness, and he could just make out Penny's face. What he could see best were the whites of her eyes. She wasn't doing much blinking.

A stripper appeared in a swirl of diaphanous crepe. There were a few catcalls. Penny remained silent. As he paid the waitress for their drinks, Jason asked if Carol Donner was dancing that night. The waitress said her first set was at eleven. Jason was relieved—at least she hadn't been trashed along with Hayes's apartment.

When the waitress left he saw the dancer was down to her G-string and that Penny's lips were tightly pursed.

"This is disgusting," she spat.

"It's not the Boston Symphony," Jason agreed.

"She even has cellulite."

Jason looked more carefully when the dancer went back up the stairs. Sure enough, the backs of her thighs were heavily dimpled. Jason smiled. It was curious what a woman noticed.

"Are these men really enjoying themselves?" Penny asked with distaste.

"Good question. I don't know. Most of them look bored."

But not one was bored when Carol came out. Like the night before, the crowd came alive when she began her routine.

"What do you think?" Jason asked.

"She's a good dancer, but I can't believe your friend was involved with her."

"That's exactly what I thought," Jason said. But now he wasn't so sure. Carol Donner projected a very different personality than he had expected.

After Carol finished, and again did not appear among the patrons, Jason had had enough. Penny was eager to leave, and Jason noticed she had little to say on the way home. He guessed the Club Cabaret hadn't made a great impression. When he left her at her door, he didn't even bother to say he'd call. He knew the Alics would be disappointed, but he figured they should have known better than to fix him up with a bow tie.

Back in his own apartment, Jason undressed and picked up the DNA book from the den. He got into bed and started reading. Remembering his exhaustion that afternoon, he thought he'd drop off to sleep quickly. But that wasn't the case. He read about bacteriophages, the viral particles that infected bacteria, and how they were used in genetic engineering. Then he read a chapter on plasmids, which he'd never even heard of before he'd started reading about DNA. He marveled that plasmids were small circular DNA molecules that existed in bacteria and reproduced faithfully when the bacteria reproduced. They, too, served an enormously important function as vehicles for introducing segments of DNA into bacteria.

Still wide awake, Jason looked at the time. It was after two A.M., and sleep was out of the question. Getting up, he went into his living room and stared out at Louisburg Square. A car pulled up. It was the tenant who occupied the garden apartment in Jason's building. He, too, was a doctor and although they were friendly, Jason knew little about the man other than he dated a lot of beautiful women. Jason wondered where he found them all. True to form, the man emerged from his car with an attractive blonde and amid soft laughter disappeared out of sight below. Jason heard the front door to the building close. Silence returned. He could not get Carol Donner out of his mind, wishing he could speak with her. Looking at the clock on the mantel, Jason had an idea. Quickly, he returned to the bedroom, redressed, and went out to his car.

With some misgivings about the possible consequences, Jason drove back to the Combat Zone. In contrast to the rest of the city, it was still very much awake. He drove past the Club Cabaret once, then circled and backed into a side street and parked. He switched off the motor. There were some unsavory types lingering in doorways and on the side street who made Jason feel uncomfortable. He made sure all his doors were locked.

Within a quarter hour of his arrival, a large group of people emerged from the club and went their separate ways. About ten minutes later, a group of dancers appeared. They chatted together in front of the club, then split up. Carol was not among them. Just when Jason had begun to worry that he'd missed her, Carol came out with one of the bodybuilders. He wore a leather jacket over his T-shirt, but it was not zipped up. They turned right, heading up Washington Street toward Filene's.

Jason started his car, unsure of what to do. Luckily there was plenty of traffic, both cars and pedestrian. To keep Carol in sight, he nudged out into the street, staying to the side. A policeman saw him and waved him on. Carol and her friend turned left on Boylston Street, walked into an open parking lot, and got into a large black Cadillac.

Well, at least he'll be easy to keep in sight, Jason thought. But, never having followed anyone, he discovered it wasn't as easy as he'd imagined, especially if he didn't want to be observed. The Cadillac skirted the edge of the Common, went north on Charles Street, then made a left on Beacon, passing the Hampshire House. Several blocks later, the car pulled over to the left side of the street and double-parked. This was an area of town called Back Bay, composed of large, turn-of-the-century brownstones, most of which had been converted into rental units or condos. Jason passed the Cadillac as Carol alighted. Slowing, he watched in the rearview mirror as she ran up the steps of a building with a large bay window. Jason turned left on Exeter, then left on Marlborough. After waiting about five minutes, he rounded the block. Arriving back on Beacon Street, he looked for the black Cadillac. It was gone.

Jason parked in front of a fire hydrant half a block from Carol's building. At three A.M. Back Bay was peaceful—no pedestrians and only an occasional passing car. Turning into the walk leading to Carol's building, Jason surveyed the six-story façade and saw no lights in any of the windows. Entering the building's outer foyer, he scanned the names opposite the buzzers. There were fourteen. To his disappointment there was no Donner listed.

Stepping back outside, Jason debated what he should do. Remembering there was an alley running between Beacon and Marlborough, he walked around the block, counting the buildings until he located Carol's. There was a light in the window on the fourth floor. He guessed that had to be Carol's since it was unlikely anyone else would be up.

Intending to go back to the entrance and press the appropriate buzzer, Jason turned and headed back up the alley. He saw the lone figure immediately, but he kept walking, hoping the man would merely pass by. As the distance between them closed, Jason's steps slowed, then stopped. To his dismay he realized it was the body-builder. His leather motorcycle jacket was unzipped, showing a white T-shirt stretched tight across powerful muscles. It was the same individual who had thrown him out of the Club Cabaret the night before.

The man kept coming at Jason, his fingers flexing in apparent anticipation. Jason guessed him to be in his mid-twenties, with a full face that suggested he took steroids. It obviously spelled trouble. And Jason's hope that the man might not recognize him was banished as the goon growled, "What the fuck you doing, creep?"

That was all Jason needed. He spun on his heels and started for the other end of the alley. Unfortunately, his leather-soled loafers were no competition for the body-builder's Nikes. "You goddamn pervert!" he shouted, pulling Jason to a stop.

Jason ducked a roundhouse left hook and grabbed the goon's thigh, hoping to trip him. Unfortunately, it was like grabbing a piano leg. Instead, Jason was jerked upright. The unevenness of the match was already apparent to Jason, who decided he'd prefer some kind of dialogue. "Why don't you find someone your own size!" he yelled in exasperation.

"Because I don't like perverts," the body-builder said, practically lifting Jason off his feet.

Twisting to one side, then the other, Jason wriggled out of his jacket and shot off down the alley, knocking over a garbage can as he fled.

"I'll teach you not to come sniffing around Carol!"

the goon shouted, kicking aside the garbage can as he started off after Jason. But Jason's years of jogging paid off. Although the body-builder was quick despite his size, Jason could hear the man's breathing becoming increasingly labored. Jason was almost at the end of the alley when he skidded on loose pebbles, momentarily losing his balance. He scrambled back to his feet just as a heavy hand grabbed his shoulder and spun him around.

7.

"Hold it! Police!" A voice shattered the stillness of the Boston night. Jason froze and so did the body-builder. The doors of an unmarked police car parked next to the mouth of the alley suddenly opened and three plainclothesmen leaped out. Once again Jason was ordered, "Up against the wall. Feet apart!" He obeyed, but the body-builder thought about it for a moment. Finally he growled to Jason, "You're a lucky son of a bitch." He then complied.

"Shut up!" a policeman yelled. Jason and his pursuer were quickly searched, then turned around and told to put their hands behind their heads. One cop took out a flashlight and checked their identification.

"Bruno DeMarco?" questioned the man holding the light on the body-builder. Bruno nodded. The light switched to Jason.

"Dr. Jason Howard?"

"That's correct."

"What's going on here?" the policeman asked.

"This little creep was trying to bother my

girlfriend," Bruno informed him in an outraged voice. "He followed her."

The policeman looked back and forth between Jason and Bruno, then walked over to the car, opened the door, and took something from the back seat. When he returned, he handed Bruno his wallet and told him to go home and get some sleep. At first Bruno acted as though he hadn't understood, but then he took his wallet.

"I'll remember you, asshole!" he shouted at Jason as he disappeared toward Beacon Street.

"You," the policeman said, pointing to Jason. "In the car!"

Jason was stunned. He couldn't believe they let the bouncer go and not him. He was about to complain when the policeman grasped his arm and forced him into the back seat.

"You are becoming one big pain in the ass," Detective Curran said. He was sitting stolidly, smoking. "I should have let that hunk work you over."

Jason was at a loss for words.

"I hope you have some idea," Curran continued, "of just how much you are screwing up this case. First we have Hayes's apartment covered. You blew that. Then we're watching Carol Donner and you blow that. We might as well bag the whole operation. We're certainly not going to learn anything from her at this point. Where the hell is your car? I presume you came in a car?"

"Just around the corner," Jason said meekly.

"I suggest you get in it and go home," Curran said slowly. "Then I suggest you get back to doctoring and leave this investigation to us. You're making our job impossible."

"I'm sorry," Jason began. "I didn't think . . ."

"Just leave!" Curran said with a wave of dismissal.

Jason climbed out of the police car, feeling pretty dumb. Of course they'd be watching Carol. If she had been living with Hayes, she was probably involved with drugs too. In fact, with her line of work, it was almost a given. Getting into his own car, Jason thought about his jacket, said the hell with it, and drove home.

It was three-thirty when he trudged up the stairs to his apartment and dutifully called his service. He hadn't taken his beeper with him when he left to follow Carol Donner, and he hoped there had been no calls. He was too tired to handle an emergency. There was nothing from the hospital, but Shirley had left a message asking him to call the moment he got in, no matter what time. The page operator told him it was urgent.

Perplexed, Jason dialed. Shirley answered on the first ring. *"Where on earth have you been?"*

"That's a story in itself."

"I want you to do me a favor. Come over right now."

"It's three-thirty," Jason pleaded.

"I wouldn't ask if it weren't important."

Jason put on another jacket, returned to his car, and drove out to Brookline, wondering what emergency couldn't have waited a little longer. The only certainty was that it involved Hayes.

Shirley lived on Lee Street, a road that curved around Brookline Reservoir and wound its way up into a residential area of fine old homes. Her house was a fieldstone building of comfortable proportions with a gambrel roof and twin gables. As Jason entered the cobblestone driveway, he saw that the house was ablaze with light. He pulled up across from the entrance, and by the time he was out of the car, Shirley had the door open.

"Thank you for coming," she said, giving him a hug. She was dressed in a white cashmere sweater and faded jeans and seemed, for the first time since Jason had met her, totally distraught.

She led him into a large living room and introduced him to two GHP executives who also seemed visibly upset. Jason shook hands first with Bob Walthrow, a small, balding man, and then Fred Ingelnook, a Robert Redford lookalike.

"How about a cocktail?" Shirley asked. "You look like you need it."

"Just soda," Jason said. "I'm dead on my feet. What's going on?"

"More trouble. I got a call from security. Hayes's lab was broken into tonight and practically demolished."

"Vandalism?"

"We're not sure."

"Hardly," Bob Walthrow said. "It was searched."

"Was anything taken?" Jason asked.

"We don't know yet," Shirley said. "But that's not the problem. We want to keep this out of the papers. Good Health can't take much more bad publicity. We have two large corporate clients on the fence about joining the Plan. They might be scared off if they hear that the police think Hayes's lab was searched for drugs."

"It's possible," Jason said. "The medical examiner told me Hayes had cocaine in his urine."

"Shit," Bob Walthrow said. "Let's hope the newspapers don't get ahold of this."

"We've got to limit the damage!" Shirley said.

"How do you propose to do that?" Jason asked, wondering why he'd been called.

"The governing board wants us to keep this latest incident quiet."

"That might be difficult," Jason said, taking a sip of his soda. "The papers will probably get it from the police blotter."

"That's exactly the point," Shirley said. "We've decided not to tell the police. But we wanted your opinion."

"Mine?" Jason asked, surprised.

"Well," Shirley said, "we want the opinion of the medical staff. You're a current chief. We thought you could quietly find out how the others felt."

"I suppose," said Jason, wondering how he'd go

about polling the other internists and still keep the episode undercover. "But if you want my personal opinion, I don't think it's a good idea at all. Besides, you won't be able to collect insurance unless you inform the police."

"That's a point," Fred Ingelnook said.

"True," Shirley said, "but it's still minor in relation to the public relations problem. For now we will not report it. But we'll check with insurance and hear from the department chiefs."

"Sounds good to me," Fred Ingelnook said.

"Fine," Bob Walthrow said.

The conversation wound down and Shirley sent the two executives home. She held Jason back when he tried to follow, suggesting he meet her at eight o'clock that morning. "I've asked Helene to come in early. Maybe we can make some sense out of what's going on."

Jason nodded, still wondering why Shirley couldn't have told him all this on the phone. But he was too tired to care, and after giving her a brief kiss on the cheek, he staggered back out to his car, hoping for two or three hours' sleep.

8.

It was just after eight that Saturday morning when Jason, bleary-eyed, entered Shirley's office. It was paneled in dark mahogany, with dark green carpet and brass fixtures, and looked more like it belonged to a banker than to the chief executive of a health care plan. Shirley was on the phone talking to an insurance adjuster, so Jason sat and waited. After she hung up she said, "You were right about the insurance. They have no intention of paying a claim unless the break-in is reported."

"Then report it."

"First let's see how bad the damage is and what's missing."

They crossed into the outpatient building and took the elevator up to the sixth floor. A security guard was waiting for them and unlocked the inner door. They dispensed with the booties and white coat.

Like Hayes's apartment, the lab was a mess. All the drawers and cabinets had been emptied onto the floor, but the high-tech equipment appeared untouched, so it was obvious to both of them that it had been a search and not a destructive visit. Jason glanced into Hayes's office. It was equally littered, with the contents of the desk and several file cabinets strewn about the floor.

Helene Brennquivist appeared in the doorway to the animal room, her face white and drawn. Her hair was again severely pulled back from her face, but without her usual shapeless lab coat, Jason could see she had an attractive figure.

"Can you tell if anything is missing?" Shirley asked.

"Well, I don't see my data books," Helene said. "And some of the E. coli bacterial cultures are gone. But the worst is what's happened to the animals."

"What about them?" Jason asked, noting that her usually emotionless face was trembling with fear.

"Maybe you should look. They've all been killed!"

Jason stepped around Helene and through the steel door into the animal area. He was immediately confronted with a pungent, zoolike stench. He turned on the light. It was a larger room, some fifty feet long and thirty feet wide. The animal cages were organized in rows and stacked one on top of the other, sometimes as many as six high.

Jason started down the nearest row, glancing into individual cages. Behind him the door closed with a decisive click. Helene had not been exaggerating: all the animals that Jason saw were dead, hideously curled in contorted positions, often with bloodied tongues as if they'd chewed them in their final agony.

Suddenly Jason stopped short. Staring into a group of large cages, he saw something that made his stomach turn: rats the likes of which he had never seen. They were huge, almost the size of pigs, and their bald, whiplike tails were as thick as Jason's wrists. Their exposed teeth were four inches long. Moving along, Jason came to rabbits the same size, and then white mice the size of small dogs.

This side of genetic engineering horrified Jason. Although he was afraid of what he might see, morbid curiosity drove him on. Slowly, he looked into other cages, seeing distortions of familiar creatures that made him sick. It was science gone mad: rabbits with several heads and mice with supernumerary extremities and extra sets of eyes. For Jason, genetic manipulation of primitive bacteria was one thing; distortion of mammals was quite another.

He retreated back to the central part of the lab, where Shirley and Helene had been checking the scintillation cultures.

"Have you seen the animals?" Jason asked Shirley with disgust.

"Unfortunately. When Curran was here. Don't remind me."

"Did the GHP authorize those experiments?" Jason demanded.

"No," Shirley said. "We never questioned Hayes. We never thought we had to."

"The power of celebrity," Jason said cynically.

"The animals were part of Dr. Hayes's growth hormone work," Helene said defensively.

"Whatever," Jason said. He was not interested in any ethical argument with Helene at the moment. "At any rate, they're all dead."

"All of them?" Shirley questioned. "How bizarre. What do you think happened?"

"Poison," Jason said grimly. "Though why anyone searching for drugs would bother to kill lab animals beats me."

"Do you have any explanation for all of this?" Shirley said angrily, turning to Helene.

The younger woman shook her head, her eyes darting nervously about the room.

Shirley continued to stare at Helene, who was now shifting uncomfortably from foot to foot. Jason watched, intrigued by Shirley's suddenly aggressive behavior.

"You'd better cooperate," she was saying, "or you're going to be in a lot of trouble. Dr. Howard is convinced you're keeping something from us. If that's true and we find out, I hope you realize what that can do to your career."

Helene's anxiety was finally apparent. "I just followed Dr. Hayes's orders," she said, her voice breaking.

"What orders?" Shirley asked, lowering her voice threateningly.

"We did some free-lance work here . . ."

"What kind?"

"Dr. Hayes moonlighted for a company called Gene, Inc. We developed a recombinant strain of E. coli to produce a hormone for them."

"Were you aware that moonlighting was specifically forbidden under Dr. Hayes's contract?"

"That's what he told me," Helene admitted.

Shirley glared at Helene for another minute. Finally she said, "I don't want you to speak of this to anyone. I want you to make a detailed list of every animal and item missing or damaged in this lab and bring it directly to me. Do you understand?"

Helene nodded.

Jason followed Shirley out of the lab. She had obviously succeeded where he had failed, in breaking through Helene's façade. But she hadn't asked the right questions.

"Why didn't you press her about Hayes's breakthrough?" he said as they arrived at the elevator. Shirley hit the down button repeatedly, obviously furious.

"I didn't think of it. Every time I think the Hayes problem is under control, something new comes up. I had specifically demanded the no-moonlighting clause in his contract."

"It doesn't much matter now," Jason said, boarding the elevator after Shirley. "The man is dead."

She sighed. "You're right. Maybe I'm overreacting. I just wish this whole affair was over."

"I still think Helene knows more than she's telling."

"I'll talk to her again."

"And after seeing those animals, you don't think you should call the police?"

"With the police come the newspapers," Shirley reminded him. "With the newspapers comes trouble. Aside from the animals, it doesn't appear that anything terribly valuable is damaged."

Jason held his tongue. Obviously, reporting the break-in was an administrative decision. He was more concerned about discovering Hayes's breakthrough, and he knew the police and newspapers wouldn't help in finding that. He wondered if the breakthrough could have involved the monstrous animals. The thought gave him a shiver.

Jason started rounds with Matthew Cowen. Unfortunately, there'd been a new development. Besides his other problems, Matthew was now acting bizarrely. Only a few minutes earlier the nurses had found him wandering in the halls, mumbling nonsense to himself. When Jason entered the room he was restrained in the bed, regarding Jason as a stranger. The man was acutely disoriented as to time, place, and person. As far as Jason was concerned, that could have meant only one thing. The man had thrown emboli, probably blood clots, from his injured heart valves into his brain. In other words he'd had a stroke or perhaps even multiple strokes.

Without delay, Jason placed a call for a neurology consult. He also called the cardiac surgeon who'd seen the case. Although he debated immediate anticoagulation, he decided to wait for the neurologist's opinion. In the interim, he started the patient on aspirin and Persantine to reduce platelet adhesiveness. Strokes were a disturbing development and a very bad sign.

Jason did the rest of his rounds quickly and was about to leave for home and for some much-needed sleep when he was paged by the emergency room for one of his patients. Cursing under his breath, he ran downstairs, hoping whatever the problem was, it could be easily solved. Unfortunately, that was not to be the case.

Arriving breathless in the main treatment room, he found a group of residents giving CPR to a comatose patient. A quick look at the monitor screen told him there was no cardiac activity at all.

Jason stepped over to Judith Reinhart, who told him the patient had been found unconscious by her husband when he tried to waken her in the morning.

"Did the EMTs see any cardiac or respiratory activity?"

"None," Judith said. "In fact, she feels cold to me."

Jason touched the woman's leg and agreed. Her face was turned away from him.

"What's the patient's name?" Jason asked, intuitively bracing himself for the blow.

"Holly Jennings."

Jason felt like he'd been hit in the stomach. "My God!" he murmured.

"Are you all right?" Judith asked.

Jason nodded, but he insisted that the ER team maintain the CPR long past any reasonable time. He'd suspected trouble when he'd seen Holly on Thursday, but not this. He just couldn't accept the fact that, like Cedric Harring, Holly would die less than a month after her fancy GHP physical told her she was okay, and two days after he'd seen her again.

Shaken, Jason picked up the phone and called Margaret Danforth.

"So once again there's no cardiac history?" Margaret asked him.

"That's correct."

"What are you people doing down there?" Margaret demanded.

Jason didn't answer. He wanted Margaret to release the case so they could do the autopsy at GHP, but Margaret hesitated.

"We'll do the case today," Jason said. "You'll have a report early next week."

"I'm sorry," Margaret said, making a decision. "There are questions in my mind, and I think I'm obligated by law to do the autopsy."

"I understand. But I suppose you wouldn't mind supplying us with specimens so we can process them here as well."

"I suppose," Margaret said without enthusiasm. "To tell the truth, I don't even know the legality. But I'll find out. I'd rather not wait two weeks for the microscopic."

Jason went home and fell into bed. He slept for four hours, interrupted by a call from the neurologist concerning Matthew. He wanted to anticoagulate and CAT-scan the patient. Jason implored him to do whatever he thought was best.

Jason tried to go back to sleep, but he couldn't. He felt shell-shocked and anxious. He got up. It was a gloomy, late fall day with a slight drizzle that made Boston look dreadful. Fighting a depression, he paced his apartment, searching for something to occupy his mind. Realizing he couldn't stay there, he put on casual clothes and went down to his car. Knowing he was probably asking for trouble, he drove over to Beacon Street and parked in front of Carol's apartment.

Ten minutes later, as if God had finally decided to give him a break, Carol emerged. Dressed in jeans and a turtleneck, with her thick brown hair gathered in a ponytail, she seemed the young college student the Club Cabaret advertised. Feeling the light drizzle, she opened a flower print umbrella and started up the street, passing within a few feet of Jason, who scrunched down in his car seat, unreasonably afraid she'd recognize him.

Giving her a good lead, Jason got out of his car to follow on foot. He lost sight of her on Dartmouth Street, but picked her up at Commonwealth Avenue. As he continued to follow her, he kept a sharp eye out for the likes of Bruno or Curran. At the corner of Dartmouth and Boylston, Jason stopped at a magazine stand and thumbed through a periodical. Carol passed him, waited for the light, then hurried across Boylston. Jason studied the people and the cars, looking for anything suspicious. But there was no indication that Carol was not alone.

She was now passing the Boston Public Library, and Jason guessed she was heading for the Copley Plaza Shopping Mall. After buying the magazine, which turned out to be *The New Yorker,* Jason continued after her. When she folded her umbrella and went into the Copley Plaza, Jason quickened his step. It was a large shopping and hotel complex, and he knew he could easily lose her.

For the next three-quarters of an hour, Jason busied himself by pretending to study window displays, reading his *New Yorker,* and eyeing the crowds. Carol happily hopped from Louis Vuitton to Ralph Lauren to Victoria's Secret. At one point Jason thought she was being tailed, but it turned out the man in question was simply trying to pick her up. She apparently rebuffed his advance when he finally approached her, because he quickly disappeared.

At a little after three-thirty, Carol took her bags and umbrella and retreated into Au Bon Pain. Jason followed, standing next to her as they waited to order and taking the opportunity to note her lovely oval face, smooth olive complexion, and dark liquid eyes. She was a handsome young woman. Jason guessed she was about twenty-four.

"Good day for coffee," he said, hoping to start a conversation.

"I prefer tea."

Jason smiled sheepishly. He wasn't good at pick-ups or small talk. "Tea's good, too," he said, afraid he was making a fool of himself.

Carol ordered soup, tea, and a plain croissant, then carried her tray to one of the large communal tables.

Jason ordered a cappuccino and then, hesitating as though he could find no place to sit, approached her table.

"Do you mind?" he asked, pulling back a chair.

Several of the people at the table looked up, including Carol. A man moved several of his packages. Jason sat down, giving everyone a limp smile.

"What a coincidence," Jason said to Carol. "We meet again."

Carol eyed him over her teacup. She didn't say anything, but she didn't have to. Her expression reflected her irritation.

At once Jason recognized that his whole act appeared to be a come-on and that he was about to be sent packing. "Excuse me," he said. "I don't mean to be a bother. My name is Dr. Jason Howard. I was a colleague of Dr. Alvin Hayes. You're Carol Donner, and I'd like very much to talk with you."

"You're with GHP?" Carol asked suspiciously.

"I'm the current chief of the medical staff." It was the first time Jason had ever used the title. At a regular academic hospital it had great significance, but at GHP the job was a bothersome sinecure.

"How can I be sure?" Carol asked.

"I can show you my license."

"Okay."

Jason reached behind for his wallet, but Carol grasped his arm.

"Never mind," she said. "I believe you. Alvin used to speak of you. Said you were the best clinician there."

"I'm flattered," Jason said. He was also surprised, considering the little contact he'd had with Hayes.

"Sorry to be so suspicious," Carol said, "but I get hassled a lot, especially the last few days. What would you like to talk about?"

"Dr. Hayes," Jason said. "First, I'd like to say that his death was a real loss to us. You have my sympathy."

Carol shrugged.

Jason wasn't sure what to make of her response. "I still have trouble believing Dr. Hayes was involved with drugs. Did you know about that?" he asked.

"I did. But the newspapers had it wrong. Alvin was a minimal user, usually marijuana but occasionally cocaine. Certainly not heroin."

"Not a dealer?"

"Absolutely not. Believe me, I would have known."

"But a lot of drugs and cash were found in his apartment."

"The only explanation I can think of is that the police put both the drugs and the money in the apartment. Alvin was always short of both. If he ever had extra cash, he sent it to his family."

"You mean his ex-wife?"

"Yes. She had custody of his children."

"Why would the police do such a thing?" Jason asked, thinking her comment echoed Hayes's paranoia.

"I don't know, really. But I can't think of any other way the drugs could have gotten there. I can assure you, he didn't have them when I left at nine o'clock that evening."

Jason leaned forward, lowering his voice. "The night Dr. Hayes died he told me he'd made a major discovery. Did he tell you anything about it?"

"He mentioned something. But that was three months ago."

For a moment Jason allowed himself to feel optimistic. Then Carol explained that she didn't know what the discovery was.

"He didn't confide in you?"

"Not lately. We'd kinda drifted apart."

"But you were living together—or did the newspapers get that wrong too?"

"We were living together," Carol admitted, "but in the end just as roommates. Our relationship had deteriorated. He really changed. It wasn't just that he felt physically ill; his whole personality was different. He seemed withdrawn, almost paranoid. He kept talking about seeing you and I tried to get him to do it."

"You really have no idea what the discovery was?" Jason persisted.

"Sorry," Carol said, spreading her hands in apology. "The only thing I remember was that he said the breakthrough was ironic. I remembered because it seemed an odd way to describe success."

"He said the same to me."

"At least he was consistent. His only other comment was that if all went well, I would appreciate it because I was beautiful. Those were his exact words."

"He didn't elaborate?"

"That was all he said."

Taking a sip of his cappuccino, Jason stared at Carol's face. How could an ironic discovery help her beauty? His mind tried to reconcile that statement with his guess that Hayes's discovery had something to do with a cancer cure. It didn't fit.

Finishing her tea, Carol stood up. "I'm glad to have met you," she said, thrusting out her hand.

Jason stood up, awkwardly catching his chair to keep it from falling over. He was nonplussed by her sudden departure.

"I don't mean to be rude," she said, "but I have an appointment. I hope you solve the mystery. Alvin worked very hard. It would be a tragedy if he'd discovered something important and it was lost."

"My feelings exactly," said Jason, frantic not to see her disappear. "Can we meet again? There's so much more I'd like to discuss."

"I suppose. But I'm quite busy. When did you have in mind?"

"How about tomorrow?" Jason suggested eagerly. "Sunday brunch."

"It would have to be late. I work at night and Saturday is the busiest."

Jason could well imagine. "Please," he said. "It could be important."

"All right. Let's say two P.M. Where?"

"How about the Hampshire House?"

"Okay," Carol said, gathering up her bags and umbrella. With a final smile she left the café.

Glancing at her watch, Carol quickened her step. The impromptu meeting with Jason hadn't figured in her tight schedule, and she didn't want to be late for the meeting with her PhD adviser. She'd spent the late evening and early afternoon polishing the third chapter of her dissertation and she was eager to hear her professor's response. Carol took the escalator down to the street level, thinking about her conversation with Dr. Howard.

It had been a surprise to meet the man after hearing about him for so long. Alvin had told her that Jason had lost his wife and had reacted to the tragedy by completely changing his environment and submerging himself in his work. Carol had found the story fascinating because her thesis involved the psychology of grief. Dr. Jason Howard sounded like a perfect case study.

The Weston Hotel doorman blew his whistle with a shriek that hurt Carol's ears, making her wince. As the taxi lumbered toward her, she admitted that her response to Dr. Jason Howard went a bit further than pure professional interest. She'd found the man unusually attractive, and realized that her knowledge of his vulnerabilities contributed to his appeal. Even his social awkwardness had an endearing quality.

"Harvard Square," Carol said as she got into the cab. She found herself looking forward to brunch the following morning.

Still seated in front of his cooling coffee, Jason admitted to being totally bowled over by Carol's unexpected intelligence and charm. He'd expected an unsophisticated small-town girl who'd somehow been lured away from high school by money or drugs. Instead she was a lovely, mature woman quite capable of holding her own in any conversation. What a tragedy that a person with her obvious assets had become mixed up in the sordid world she inhabited. . . .

The insistent and jarring sound of his beeper snapped Jason back to reality. He switched it off and looked at the LCD display. The word "urgent" blinked twice, followed by a telephone number Jason did not recognize. After seeing his medical identification, the Au Bon Pain manager allowed Jason to use the phone behind the cash register.

"Thank you for calling, Dr. Howard. This is Mrs. Farr. My husband, Gerald Farr, has developed terrible chest pains and he's having trouble breathing."

"Call an ambulance," Jason said. "Bring him to the GHP emergency. Is Mr. Farr a patient of mine?"

Jason thought the name sounded familiar but he couldn't place it.

"Yes," Mrs. Farr said. "You did a physical on him two weeks ago. He's the senior vice president of the Boston Banking Company."

Oh, no, Jason thought as he hung up the receiver. *It's happening again.* Deciding to leave his car on Beacon Street until he'd handled the emergency, he ran from the café, dashed over the pedestrian connection to the hotel side of the Copley Plaza complex, and leaped into a cab.

Jason arrived at the GHP emergency room before the Farrs. He told Judith what he expected and even called anesthesia, pleased to learn Philip Barnes was on call.

When he saw Gerald Farr, Jason knew immediately that his worst fears were realized. The man was in agonizing pain and was pale as skim milk, with crystalline beads of perspiration on his forehead.

The initial EKG showed that a large area of the man's heart had been damaged. It was not going to be an easy case. Morphine and oxygen helped to calm the patient, and lidocaine was given for prophylaxis against irregular heartbeats. But, despite everything, Farr wasn't responding. Studying another EKG, Jason had the feeling that the infarcted area of the heart was expanding.

In desperation, he tried everything. But it was all for naught. At five minutes to four, Gerald Farr's eyes rolled up inside his head and his heart stopped.

Unwilling as usual to give up, Jason commanded the resuscitative efforts. They got the heart to start several more times, but each time it would slip back into a deadly pattern and fail again.

Farr never regained consciousness. At six-fifteen, Jason finally declared the patient dead.

"Shit!" said Jason with disgust at himself and life in general. He was unaccustomed to swearing, and the effect of his doing so was not lost on Judith Reinhart. She leaned her forehead against Jason's shoulder and put her arm around his neck.

"Jason, you did the best you could," she said softly. "You did the best anybody could. But our powers are limited."

"The man's only fifty-eight," said Jason, choking back tears of frustration.

Judith cleared the room of the other nurses and residents. Coming back to Jason, she put her hand on his shoulder, "Look at me, Jason!" she said.

Reluctantly, Jason turned his face toward the nurse. A single tear had run down from the corner of his eye, along the crease of his nose. Softly but firmly she told Jason that he could not take these episodes so personally. "I know that two in one day is an awful burden," she added. "But it's not your fault."

Jason knew intellectually that she was right, but emotionally it was another story. Besides, Judith had no idea how badly his inpatients were doing, especially Matthew Cowen, and Jason was embarrassed to tell her. For the first time, he seriously contemplated giving up medicine. Unfortunately, he had no idea of what else he could do. He wasn't trained for anything else.

After promising Judith that he was okay, Jason went out to face Mrs. Farr, steeling himself against the expected anger. But Mrs. Farr, in the depths of her grief, had decided to take the burden of guilt on herself. She said her husband had been complaining of feeling ill for a week, but that she'd ignored his complaints because, frankly, he'd always been a bit of a hypochondriac. Jason tried to comfort the woman as Judith had tried to comfort him. He was about equally successful.

Confident that the medical examiner would take the case, Jason didn't burden Mrs. Farr with an autopsy request. By law, the ME didn't need authorization to do a postmortem in cases of questionable death. But to be sure, he called Margaret Danforth. The response was as expected: she indeed wanted the case, and while she had Jason on the phone, she spoke to him about Holly Jennings.

"I take back that snide comment I made this morning," Margaret said. "You people are just having bad luck. The Jennings woman was as bad off as Cedric Harring. All her vessels looked terrible, not just the heart."

"That's not a lot of consolation," Jason said. "I had just given her a physical showing everything was fine. I did a follow-up EKG on Thursday, but that showed only minimal changes."

"No kidding? Wait till you see the sections.

Grossly the coronary vessels looked ninety percent occluded, and it was disseminated, not focal. Surgery wouldn't have done a damn thing. Oh, by the way, I checked and it's okay for us to give you small specimens from Jennings's case. But I should have a formal request in writing."

"No problem," Jason said. "Same with Farr?"

"Sure thing."

Jason took a cab back to his car and drove home. Despite the fog and rain, when he got home, he went for a jog. Getting mud-spattered and soaked had a mild cathartic effect, and after a shower he felt some relief from his burdensome emotions and depressive feelings. Just when he was starting to think about food, Shirley called and asked him over for dinner. Jason's first response was to say no. But then he recognized he felt too depressed to be alone, so he accepted. After changing into more reasonable clothes, he went down to his car and headed west toward Brookline.

Eastern's flight #409, nonstop from Miami to Boston, banked sharply before lining up for the final approach. It touched down at seven thirty-seven as Juan Díaz closed his magazine and looked out at the fog-shrouded Boston skyline. It was his second trip to Boston and he wasn't all that pleased. He wondered why anyone would choose to live in such predictably bad weather. It had rained on his previous trip just a few days ago. Looking down on the tarmac, he saw the wind and rain in the puddles and thought nostalgically of Miami, where late fall had finally put an end to the searing summer heat.

Getting his bag from under the seat in front of him, Juan wondered how long he'd be in Boston. He remembered that on the previous trip he'd been there only two days, and he hadn't had to do a thing. He wondered if he'd have the same good fortune. After all, he got his five thousand no matter what.

The plane taxied toward the terminal. Juan looked around the compartment with a sense of pride. He wished his family back in Cuba could see him now. Would they be surprised! There he was, flying first class. After being sentenced to life in prison by the Castro government, he'd been released after only eight months and sent first to Mariel and then, to his astonishment, to the USA. That was to be his punishment for having been convicted of multiple murder and rape—being sent to the USA! It was so much easier to do his type of work in the United States. Juan felt that the one person in the world whose hand he'd most like to shake was a peanut farmer someplace in Georgia.

The plane gave a final lurch, then was still. Juan rose to his feet and stretched. Taking his carry-on bag, he headed for baggage. After retrieving his suitcase, he caught a cab to the Royal Sonesta Hotel, where he registered as Carlos Hernández from Los Angeles. He even had a credit card in that name, with a legitimate number. He knew the number was good, since he'd taken it off a receipt he'd found at the Bal Harbour shopping plaza in Miami.

Once he was comfortably relaxed in his room, with his second silk suit hanging in the closet, Juan sat at the desk and called a number he'd been given in Miami. When the phone was answered, he told the person he needed a gun, preferably a .22 caliber. With that business taken care of, he got out the name and address of the hit and looked up the location on the map supplied by the hotel. It wasn't far away.

The evening with Shirley was a great success. They dined on roast chicken, artichokes, and wild rice. Afterward they had Grand Marnier in front of the fire in the living room and talked. Jason learned that Shirley's father had been a doctor and that back in college she'd entertained the idea of following in his footsteps.

"But my father talked me out of it," Shirley said. "He said that medicine was changing."

"He was right about that."

"He told me that it would be taken over by big business and that someone who cared about the profession should go into management. So I switched to business courses, and I believe I made the right choice."

"I'm sure you did, too," Jason agreed, thinking about the explosion of paperwork and the malpractice dilemma. Medicine had indeed changed. The fact that he now worked for a salary for a corporation stood as testament to that change. When he'd been in medical school he'd always imagined he'd work for himself. That had been part of the appeal.

At the end of the evening, there was a bit of awkwardness. Jason said he'd best be going, but Shirley encouraged him to stay.

"You think that would be a good idea?" Jason asked.

She nodded.

Jason wasn't so sure, saying he'd have to get up early for rounds and wouldn't want to disturb her. Shirley insisted she was up at seven-thirty as a matter of course, Sundays included.

They stared at each other for a time, the firelight making Shirley's face glow.

"There's no obligation," Shirley said softly. "I know we both have to be slow about this. Let's just be together. We've both been under stress."

"Okay," Jason said, recognizing he did not have the strength to resist. Besides, he was flattered that Shirley was so insistent. He was becoming more open to the idea that not only could he care about another person but another person could care about him.

But Jason did not get to sleep the whole night through. At three-thirty he felt a hand on his shoulder, and he sat up, momentarily confused as to his whereabouts. In the half light, he could just make out Shirley's face.

"I'm sorry to have to bother you," she said gently, "but I'm afraid the phone is for you." She handed him the receiver from the nightstand.

Jason took the phone and thanked her. He hadn't even heard the phone ring. Propping himself on one elbow, he put the receiver to his ear. He was certain it would be bad news, and he was right. Matthew Cowen had been found dead in his bed, apparently having suffered a final, massive stroke.

"Has the family been notified?" Jason asked.

"Yes," said the nurse. "They live in Minneapolis. They said they'd come in the morning."

"Thanks," Jason said, absently giving the phone back to Shirley.

"Trouble?" Shirley asked. She set the receiver back in the cradle.

Jason nodded. Trouble had become his middle name. "A young patient died. Thirty-five or so. He had rheumatic heart disease. He was in for evaluation for surgery."

"How bad was his heart disease?" asked Shirley.

"It was bad," Jason said, seeing Matthew's face, remembering him as he'd been when he entered the hospital. "Three of his four valves were affected. They would have had to replace all of them."

"So there were no guarantees," Shirley said.

"No guarantees," Jason agreed. "Three valve replacements can be tricky. He's had congestive heart failure for a long time, undoubtedly affecting his heart, lungs, kidneys and liver. There would have been problems, but he had age on his side."

"Maybe it was for the best," Shirley suggested. "Maybe he's been spared from a lot of suffering. Sounds like he would have been in and out of the hospital for the rest of his life."

"Maybe so," Jason said without conviction. He knew what Shirley was doing: she was trying to make him feel better. Jason appreciated her effort. He patted the thigh through the thin cover of her robe. "Thanks for your support."

The night seemed awfully cold when Jason ran out to his car. It was still raining, in fact, harder than before. Turning up the heat, he rubbed his thighs to get his circulation going. At least there was no traffic. At four A.M., Sunday morning, the city was deserted. Shirley had tried to get him to stay, arguing that there was nothing for Jason to do if the man had died and the family was not available. As true as this was, Jason felt an obligation to his patient that he could not dismiss. Besides, he knew he'd not be able to get back to sleep. Not with yet another death on his conscience.

The GHP parking lot was mostly empty. Jason was able to park close to the hospital entrance rather than under the outpatient building where he usually parked. As he stepped out of his car, preoccupied with thoughts of Matthew Cowen, he didn't notice a darkened figure hunched over at the side of the hospital door. Rounding the front of his car, the figure lunged at Jason. Caught completely unaware, Jason screamed. But the figure turned out to be one of the drunken street people who frequented the

GHP emergency room, asking for spare change. With a shaking hand, Jason gave him a dollar, hoping he'd at least buy himself a little food.

Shirley had been right. There was nothing for Jason to do but write a final note in Matthew Cowen's chart. He went in and viewed his body. At least Matthew's face looked calm, and as Shirley suggested, he was now spared further suffering. Silently, Jason apologized to the dead man.

Paging the resident on call, Jason instructed him to ask the family for an autopsy. Jason explained he might not be immediately available. Then, feeling as ineffectual as ever, after these deaths, he left the hospital and returned to his apartment. He lay for some time, staring at the ceiling, unable to sleep. He wondered what kind of job he could get in the pharmaceutical industry.

9.

Cedric Harring, Brian Lennox, Holly Jennings, Gerald Farr, and now Matthew Cowen. Jason had never lost so many patients in such a short period of time. All night the parade of their faces had interrupted his dreams, and when he awakened about eleven he was as exhausted as though he'd never slept at all. He forced himself to do his regular Sunday six miles, then showered and dressed carefully in a pale yellow shirt with white collar and cuffs, dark brown pants, and a muted brown plaid jacket of linen and silk. He was glad he had the meeting with Carol to distract him.

The Hampshire House was on Beacon Street, overlooking the Boston Public Gardens. In contrast to Saturday's rain, the sky was filled with bright sunshine and scudding clouds. The American flag flying over the Hampshire entrance snapped in the late autumn breeze. Jason arrived early and asked for a table in the front room on the first floor. A fire crackled comfortably and a piano player kept up a stream of old favorites.

Jason regarded the people around him. They were all respectably dressed and were engaged in lively conversation, obviously unaware of whatever new medical horror was sweeping their city. . . . Then Jason warned himself not to let his imagination run wild. Half a dozen deaths didn't mean an epidemic. Besides, he wasn't even sure it was infectious. Still, he couldn't get the fatalities out of his mind.

Carol arrived at five minutes after two. Jason stood up, waving to get her attention. She was appealingly dressed in a white silk blouse with black wool pants. Her fresh, young innocent appearance away from the club always amazed Jason. Noticing him, she smiled broadly and made her way over to the table. She acted mildly out of breath.

"Sorry I'm late," she said, arranging her things, which included a suede jacket, a canvas bag full of papers, and a shoulder handbag. As she did so, she glanced frequently at the entrance.

"Are you expecting someone?" Jason asked.

"I certainly hope not. But I have this crazy boss who insists on being overprotective. Especially since Alvin died. He's keeping someone with me most of the time, supposedly for my protection. At night I don't mind, but during the day I don't like it. Mr. Muscle showed up this morning, but I sent him on his way. He may have followed me anyway."

Jason wondered if he should mention he'd met Bruno, but decided against it. It was only after they had been served without glimpsing Bruno's hulk that they both began to relax a bit.

"I probably should be more grateful to my boss," Carol said. "He's been so good to me. Right now I'm living in one of his apartments on Beacon Street. I don't even pay rent."

Jason didn't want to consider all the reasons for which Carol's boss might want her to have a nice apartment. Embarrassed, he turned his attention to his omelette.

"So . . ." Carol said, brandishing her fork. "What else did you want to ask me?" She took a sizable bite of her French toast.

"Have you remembered anything else about Alvin Hayes's discovery?"

"Nope," Carol said, swallowing. "Besides, even when he used to discuss his work with me, I found it incomprehensible. He always forgot that not everyone is a nuclear physicist." Carol laughed, her eyes sparkling attractively.

"I've been told that Alvin free-lanced for another bioengineering company," Jason said. "Did you know anything about that?"

"I guess you're referring to Gene, Inc." Carol paused, her smile fading. "That was supposed to be a big secret." She cocked her head to the side. "But now that he's gone, I guess it doesn't matter. He'd worked for them for about a year."

"Do you know what he did for them?"

"Not really. Something with growth hormone. But lately they'd gotten into a row. Something to do with finances. I don't know the details. . . ."

Jason realized that he'd been right after all.

Helene had been holding back. If Hayes had been feuding with Gene, Inc., she must have known.

"What do you know about Helene Brennquivist?"

"She's a nice lady." Carol put down her fork. "Well . . . that's not quite sincere. She's probably okay. But to tell you the truth, Helene is the reason Alvin and I stopped being lovers. Because they worked together so much, she started coming over to the apartment. Then I found out they were having an affair. That I couldn't handle. It irked me she'd been so secret about it, especially right under my nose in my own house."

Jason was amazed. He'd guessed that Helene was withholding information, but it had never dawned on him that she was sleeping with Hayes. Jason studied Carol's face. He could see that mentioning the affair had brought back unpleasant feelings. Jason wondered if Carol had been as angry with Hayes as she was with Helene.

"What about Hayes's family?" he asked, deliberately changing the subject.

"I don't know much about them. I spoke to his ex-wife on the phone once or twice, but never in person. They'd been divorced for five years or so."

"Did Hayes have a son?"

"Two. Two boys and a girl."

"Do you know where they lived?"

"A small town in New Jersey. Leonia or something like that. I remember the street though—Park Avenue. I remembered that because it sounded so pretentious."

"Did he ever say anything about one of his sons being sick?"

Carol shook her head. Motioning to a waitress, Carol indicated she wanted more coffee. They ate in silence for a while, enjoying the food and the atmosphere.

When Jason's beeper went off, it startled them both. Luckily, it was just his service saying Cowen's family had finally arrived from Minneapolis and hoped to meet him at the hospital around four.

Returning from the phone, Jason suggested they take advantage of the nice weather and walk in the garden. After they'd crossed Beacon Street, she surprised him by taking his arm. He surprised himself by enjoying it. Despite her somewhat dubious profession, Jason had to admit he enjoyed her company immensely. Aside from her wholesome good looks, her vitality was infectious.

They skirted the swan boat pond, passed under the mounted bronze statue of Washington, then crossed the bridge spanning the central neck of the waterway. The swan boats had been retired for the season. Finding an empty bench under a now naked willow tree, Jason turned the conversation back to Hayes.

"Did he do anything out of the ordinary over the last three months? Anything unexpected . . . out of character?"

Carol picked up a pebble and tossed it into the water. "That's a hard question," she said. "One of the things I liked about Alvin was his impulsiveness.

We would do a lot of things on the spur of the moment, like taking trips."

"Had he done much traveling recently?"

"Oh, yes," Carol said, searching for another stone. "Last May he went to Australia."

"Did you go?"

"No. He didn't take me. He said it was strictly business—and that he needed Helene to help him with various tests. At the time I believed him, chump that I was."

"Did you ever find out what his business was?"

"Something involving Australian mice. I remember him saying they had peculiar habits. But that's all I knew. He had lots of mice and rats in his lab."

"I know," Jason said, vividly picturing the revolting dead animals. Jason had asked if Hayes had been behaving oddly. A sudden trip to Australia might be considered bizarre, but without knowing his current studies it was hard to be sure. He'd have to take the issue up with Helene.

"Any other trips?"

"I got to go to Seattle."

"When was that?"

"In the middle of July. Apparently old Helene wasn't feeling up to par, and Alvin needed a driver."

"A driver?"

"That was another weird thing about Alvin," Carol said. "He couldn't drive. He said he'd never learned and never would."

Jason recalled the police commenting the night he

died that Hayes had no driver's license.

"What happened in Seattle?"

"Not a lot. We were only in the city a couple of days. We did visit the University of Washington. Then we headed up into the Cascades. Now, that's beautiful country, but if you think it rains a lot in Boston, wait until you visit the Pacific Northwest. Have you?"

"No," Jason said absently. He tried to imagine a discovery that would involve trips to Seattle and Australia.

"How long were you away?"

"Which time?"

"You went more than once?"

"Twice," Carol said. "The first trip was for five days. We visited the University of Washington and saw the sights. On the second trip, which was several weeks later, we only stayed two nights."

"Did you do the same things both times?"

Carol shook her head. "The second trip we bypassed Seattle and went directly into the Cascades."

"What on earth did you do?"

"I just hung out, relaxed. We went to a lodge. It was gorgeous."

"What about Alvin? What did he do?"

"About the same. But he was interested in the ecology and all that stuff. You know, always the scientist."

"So it was like a vacation?" Jason asked, thoroughly perplexed.

"I suppose." She tossed another stone.

"What did Alvin do at the University of Washington?" Jason asked.

"He saw an old friend. Can't think of his name. Someone he trained with at Columbia."

"A molecular geneticist like Alvin?"

"I believe so. But we weren't there very long. I visited the Psychology Department while they were talking."

"That must have been interesting." Jason smiled, thinking the Psychology Department would have enjoyed getting their academic hands on the likes of Carol Donner.

"Damn," she said, suddenly checking her watch. "I've got to run. I have another appointment."

Jason stood up, taking her hand. He was impressed by the delicacy with which Carol described her work. "An appointment" sounded so professional. They walked to the edge of the park.

Refusing a ride, Carol said good-bye and started up Beacon Street. Jason watched as her figure receded in the distance. She seemed so carefree and happy. *What a tragedy,* he thought. *Time, which seems boundless to her youthful mind, will soon catch up with her.* What kind of life was topless dancing and dates with men? He didn't like to think about it. Turning in the opposite direction, Jason walked to De Luca's Market and bought the makings for a simple supper: barbecued chicken and salad greens. All the while he went over his conversation with Carol. He had a lot more information, but it provided more questions than conclusions. Still, he was now sure of two things. One, Hayes had definitely made a discovery, and two, the key was Helene Brennquivist.

In less than twenty-four hours, Juan had the whole scenario planned out. Since this was not supposed to look like a traditional hit, it required more thought. The usual ploy was to nail the victim in a crowd, putting a low-caliber pistol to the head, and pow, it was all over. That kind of operation needed little planning, only the right circumstances. The whole performance relied on the peculiar mentality of crowds. After any shocking event, everyone was so intent on the victim that the perpetrator could melt away unnoticed, even pretending to be one of the curious onlookers. All he had to do was drop the gun.

But the instructions on this job were different. The hit was to be staged as a rape, Juan's specialty. He smiled to himself, amazed that he could get paid for something he used to do as a sport. The United States was a strange and wonderful place, where the law often gave the felon more consideration than the victim.

This time Juan realized he'd have to get his victim alone. That was what made it a challenge. It was also what made it fun, because without witnesses he could do what he liked with the woman, as long as when he left she was dead.

Juan decided to follow the victim and accost her in the foyer of her building. The threat of immediate bodily injury made in a soft, reasonable voice should be enough to persuade her to take him up to her apartment. Once inside, it would be all fun and games.

He followed the mark on a short shopping excursion in Harvard Square. She bought a magazine at a corner kiosk, then headed for a grocery store called Sages. Juan lingered across the street, examining the window of a bookstore, surprised the place was open on Sunday. The mark came out of the grocery store with a plastic shopping bag, cut diagonally across the street, and disappeared into a bakery café. Juan followed—coffee sounded good, even if it was the American kind. He preferred Cuban coffee: thick, sweet, and rich.

While he sipped the watery brew, he stared at his victim. He was astounded at his good luck. The woman was beautiful. He guessed mid-twenties. *What a deal,* he thought. He could already feel himself getting hard. He wouldn't have to fake this one.

Half an hour later, the mark finished, paid, and walked out of the café. Juan tossed a ten-dollar bill on the table. He felt generous. After all, he'd be five thousand richer when he got back to Miami.

To his delight, the woman continued up Brattle Street. Juan slowed his pace, content to just keep her in view. When she turned onto Concord, he speeded up, knowing she was almost home. When she reached Craigie Arms Apartment Complex, Juan was right behind her. A quick glance up and down

Concord Avenue suggested the timing was perfect. Now it depended on what was happening inside the building.

Juan paused long enough to be sure the inner door had been opened. With split-second timing he was in the foyer and had one foot over the threshold of the inner door. It was then that he spoke.

"Miss Brennquivist?"

Momentarily startled, Helene looked into Juan's darkly handsome Hispanic face.

"Ja," she said with her Scandinavian accent, thinking he must be a fellow tenant.

"I've been dying to meet you. My name is Carlos."

Helene paused fatally, her keys still in her hand. "Do you live here?" she asked.

"Sure do," Juan said with practiced ease. "Second floor. How about you?"

"Third," Helene said. She stepped through the door, Juan directly behind her.

"Nice to meet you," she added. She debated using the stairs or the elevator. Juan's presence made her feel uncomfortable.

"I was hoping we could talk," Juan said, coming alongside her. "How about inviting me up for a drink?"

"I don't think that . . ." Helene saw the gun and gasped.

"Please don't make me angry, miss," Juan said in a soothing voice. "I do things I regret when I'm angry." He hit the elevator button. The doors opened.

He motioned for Helene to enter and stepped in behind her. Everything was working perfectly.

As the elevator clanked and thumped upward, Juan smiled warmly. It was best to keep everything calm.

Helene was paralyzed by panic. Not knowing what to do, she did nothing. The man terrified her, yet he seemed reasonable, and he was very well dressed. He looked like a successful businessman. Maybe he was associated with Gene, Inc., and they wanted to search her apartment. She thought briefly about screaming or trying to run, but then she remembered the gun.

The elevator grated open on the third floor. Juan graciously motioned for her to proceed. With her keys in her shaking hand, she walked toward her door and opened it. Juan immediately put his foot over the threshold, just as he'd done downstairs. After they'd both entered, he closed the door and locked it, using all three latches. Helene stood dumbly in the small entrance hall, unable to move.

"Please," Juan said, politely motioning for her to enter the living room. To his surprise, a plump blonde was sitting on the sofa. Juan had been told Helene lived alone. *Never mind,* he thought. "What is that saying you people have?" he murmured. "When it rains, it pours. This party is going to be twice as good as I expected."

He brandished his weapon, motioning for Helene to sit opposite her roommate. The women exchanged anxious looks. Then Juan yanked the telephone line from the wall, leaving the three color-coded wires to dangle nakedly in the air. He went over to Helene's stereo and turned on the tuner. A classical station came on. Figuring out the digital controls, he switched to a hard-rock station and turned up the volume.

"What kind of party is it without some music?" he shouted as he took some thin rope out of his pocket.

10.

Jason got to the hospital early Monday morning and suffered through rounds. No one was doing well. After he got to his office, he began calling Helene at every spare moment. She never answered. At mid-morning he even ran up to the sixth floor lab only to find it dark and deserted. Returning to his office, Jason was irritated. He felt that Helene had been obstructive from the start, and now by not making herself available, she was compounding the problem.

Jason picked up the telephone, called personnel, and got Helene's home address and phone number. He called immediately. After the phone rang about ten times, he slammed the receiver down in frustration. He then called personnel and asked to speak to the director, Jean Clarkson. When she came on the line, Jason inquired about Helene Brennquivist: "Has she called in sick? I've been trying to reach her all morning."

"I'm surprised," Ms. Clarkson said. "We haven't heard from her, and she's always been dependable. I don't think she's missed a day in a year and a half."

"But if she were ill," Jason asked, "you would expect her to call?"

"Absolutely."

Jason hung up the phone. His irritation changed to concern. He had a bad feeling about Helene's absence.

His office door opened and Claudia stuck her head in. "Dr. Danforth's on line two. Do you want to talk with her?"

Jason nodded.

"Do you need someone's chart?"

"No, thanks," Jason said as he lifted the phone.

Dr. Danforth's resonant voice came over the line: "I'd say Good Health had better start screening their patients. I've never seen corpses in such bad shape. Gerald Farr is as bad as the rest. He didn't have an organ that appeared less than one hundred years old!"

Jason didn't answer.

"Hello?" Margaret said.

"I'm here," Jason said. Once again he was embarrassed to tell Margaret that a month ago he'd done a complete physical on Farr and found nothing wrong despite the man's unhealthy lifestyle.

"I'm surprised he didn't have a stroke several years ago," Margaret said. "All his vessels were atheromatous. The carotids were barely open."

"What about Roger Wanamaker's patient?" Jason asked.

"What was the name?"

"I don't know," he admitted. "The man died on Friday of a stroke. Roger said you were getting the case."

"Oh, yes. He also presented almost total degeneration. I thought health plans were supposed to provide largely preventive medicine. You people aren't going to make much money if you sign up such sick patients." Margaret laughed. "Kidding aside, it was another case of multisystem disease."

"Do you people do routine toxicology?" Jason asked suddenly.

"Sure. Especially nowadays. We test for cocaine, that sort of stuff."

"What about doing more toxicology on Gerald Farr? Would that be possible?"

"I think we still have blood and urine," Margaret said. "What do you want us to look for?"

"Just about everything. I'm fishing, but I have no idea what's going on here."

"I'll be happy to run a battery of tests," Margaret said, "but Gerald Farr wasn't poisoned, I can tell you that. He just ran out of time. It was as if he were thirty years older than his actual age. I know that doesn't sound very scientific, but it's the truth."

"I'd appreciate the toxicology tests just the same."

"Will do," Margaret said. "And we'll be sending some specimens for your people to process. I'm sorry it takes us so long to do our microscopics."

Jason hung up and went back to work, vacillating

between self-doubt and the discomfiting sense that something was going on that was beyond his comprehension. Every time he got a moment, he dialed Hayes's lab. There was still no answer. He called Jean Clarkson again, who said that she'd call if she heard from Miss Brennquivist and to please stop bothering her. Then she slammed down the phone. Nostalgically Jason remembered those days when he got more respect from the hospital staff.

After seeing the last morning patient, Jason sat at his desk nervously drumming his fingers. All at once a wave of certainty spread through him, telling him that Helene's absence was not only significant, it was serious. In fact, he was convinced that it was so serious that he should inform the police immediately.

Jason traded his white coat for his suit jacket, and went to his car. He decided he'd better see Detective Curran in person. After their last encounter, he didn't think Curran would take him seriously over the phone.

Jason remembered the way to Curran's office without difficulty. Glancing into the sparsely furnished room, he saw the detective working over a form at his metal desk, his large fist gripping his pencil as if it were a prisoner trying to escape.

"Curran," Jason said, hoping the man would be in a better mood than he'd been the other night.

Curran glared up. "Oh, no!" he exclaimed, tossing his pencil onto the uncompleted form. "My favorite doctor!" He made an exaggerated expression of exasperation, then waved Jason into his office.

Jason pulled a metal-backed chair over to Curran's desk. The detective eyed him with obvious misgiving.

"There's been a new development," Jason said. "I thought you should know."

"I thought you were going back to doctoring."

Ignoring the cut, Jason went on. "Helene Brennquivist hasn't been at work all day."

"Maybe she's sick. Maybe she's tired. Maybe she's been sick and tired of you and all your questions."

Jason tried to hold on to his temper. "Personnel says she's extremely reliable. She'd never take a day off without calling. And when I tried her apartment, there was no answer."

Detective Curran gave Jason a disdainful look. "Have you considered the possibility that the attractive young lady might have taken a long weekend with a boyfriend?"

"I don't think so. Since I saw you I've learned she was having an affair with Hayes."

Curran sat up and for the first time gave Jason his full attention.

"I always felt she was covering for Hayes," Jason continued. "Now I know why. And I also believe she knows a lot more about his work than she's saying, and why his places were searched. I think Hayes made a major breakthrough and someone is after his notes—"

"If there was a breakthrough."

"I'm sure there was," Jason said. "And it adds to my suspicions about Hayes's death. It was too convenient."

"You're jumping to conclusions."

"Hayes said someone was trying to kill him," Jason said. "I think he made a major scientific discovery and was murdered because of it."

"Hold on!" Curran shouted, banging his fist on his desk. "The medical examiner determined that Dr. Alvin Hayes died of natural causes."

"An aneurysm, to be exact. But he was still being followed."

"He *thought* he was," Curran corrected, his voice rising in anger.

"I think he was too," Jason said with equal vehemence. "That would explain why someone ransacked his apartment and his—"

"We *know* why his apartment was tossed," Curran interrupted. "Only we found the drugs and the money first!"

"Hayes may have used cocaine." Jason was shouting now. "But he wasn't a dealer! And I think those drugs were planted, and—" He started to mention his conversation with Carol, then stopped. He wasn't ready to tell Curran that he had persisted in seeing the dancer. "In any case," he said more quietly, "I think the reason the lab was torn apart was that someone was searching for his lab books."

"What was that about a lab?" Curran's heavy-

lidded eyes opened wide and his face turned a mottled red.

Jason swallowed.

"Dammit!" Curran yelled. "You mean to tell me Hayes's lab was tossed and it wasn't reported? What do you people think you're doing?"

"The clinic was concerned about negative press," Jason said, forced to defend the decision he did not condone.

"When did this happen?"

"Friday night."

"What was taken?"

"Several data books and some bacterial cultures. But none of the valuable equipment. And it wasn't a robbery." Jason watched Curran's hound-dog face for some sign his concern for Helene was vindicated.

"Any damage, vandalism?" was all he said.

"Well, they turned the place upside down and dumped everything on the floor. So the lab was a mess. But the only deliberate destruction involved those, uh, animals."

"Good," Curran said. "Those monsters should have been destroyed. They made me sick. How were they killed?"

"Probably poisoned. Our pathology department is checking that out."

Detective Curran ran his thick fingers through his once-red hair. "You know something?" he asked rhetorically. "With the amount of cooperation I've gotten from you eggheads, I'm goddamned glad I turned this case over to Vice. They can have it. Maybe you'd like to go down the hall and rant and rage at them. Maybe they'll get a charge out of the fact that your mad scientist was humping his lab assistant as well as the exotic dancer—"

"Hayes and the dancer were no longer lovers."

"Oh, really?" Curran asked with a short, hollow laugh that ended in a belch. "Why don't you go over to the Vice department and leave me alone, doctor. I have a lot of genuine homicides to ponder."

Curran picked up his pencil and went back to his forms. Enraged, Jason returned to the ground floor and surrendered his visitor's pass. Then he went out to his car. Driving along Storrow Drive, with the Charles River lazily spread out on the right, Jason finally began to calm down. He was still convinced something had happened to Helene, but he decided that if the police weren't concerned, there was little he could do.

He pulled into the GHP parking lot and went back to his office. Claudia and Sally hadn't returned from their lunch break yet. A few patients were already waiting. Jason changed back to his white coat and called to check on Madaline Krammer's cardiac consult. Harry Sarnoff had agreed with Jason's appraisal, and Madaline was having an angiogram.

As soon as Sally returned, Jason went to work seeing his scheduled patients. He was on his third afternoon patient when Claudia ducked into the exam room.

"You have a visitor," she announced.

"Who?" Jason asked, tearing off a prescription.

"Our fearless leader. And she's foaming at the mouth. I thought I should warn you."

Jason handed the prescription to the patient, tossed his stethoscope around his neck, and walked down the corridor to his office. Shirley was standing by the window. The moment she heard Jason she turned to face him. She was without question furious.

"I certainly hope you have a good explanation, Dr. Howard," she said. "I just got a call from the police. They're on their way here to get a formal statement on why I didn't report the break-in of Hayes's lab. They said they heard about it from you—and they're threatening obstruction of justice."

"I'm sorry," said Jason. "It was an accident. I was at the police station. I didn't mean to mention it . . ."

"And just what the hell were you doing down at the station?"

"I wanted to see Curran," Jason said guiltily.

"Why?"

"There was some information I thought he should have."

"About the break-in?"

"No," Jason said, letting his hands fall to his sides. "Helene Brennquivist hasn't shown up today. I found out that she and Hayes were having an affair, and I guess I jumped to conclusions. The break-in just slipped out."

"I think it would be best if you stayed with doctoring," Shirley said, her voice softening a degree.

"That's what Curran said," sighed Jason.

"Well," Shirley said, reaching out and touching Jason's arm, "at least you didn't do it on purpose. For a while there I was wondering whose side you were on. I tell you, this Hayes affair has a life of its own. Every time I think the problem is contained, something else breaks."

"I'm sorry," Jason said sincerely. "I didn't mean to make things worse."

"It's okay. But remember—Hayes's death is already hurting this institution. Let's not compound our difficulties." She gave Jason's hand a squeeze, then walked to the door.

Jason went back to his patients, determined to leave the investigation to the police. It was nearly four when Claudia interrupted again.

"You have a call," she whispered.

"Who is it?" Jason asked nervously. The usual modus operandi was for Claudia to take messages and for Jason to return the calls at the end of the day. Unless, of course, it was an emergency. But Claudia didn't whisper when it was an emergency.

"Carol Donner," she said.

Jason hesitated, then said he'd take it in his office. Claudia followed, still whispering.

"Is that *the* Carol Donner?"

"Who is *the* Carol Donner?"

"The dancer in the Combat Zone," Claudia said.

"I wouldn't know," Jason said, entering his office. He closed the door on Claudia and picked up the phone. "Dr. Howard," he said.

"Jason, this is Carol Donner. I'm sorry to bother you."

"No bother." Her voice brought back the pleasant image of her sitting across from him at the Hampshire House. He heard a click. "Just a moment, Carol." He put the phone down, opened the door, and looked across the room at Claudia. With an irritated expression, he motioned for her to hang up.

"Sorry," Jason said, returning to the phone.

"I wouldn't call you unless I thought it might be important," Carol said. "But I came across a package in my locker at work. I'm a dancer at the Club Cabaret, by the way. . . ."

"Oh," Jason said vaguely.

"Anyway," Carol said, "I had to go in to the club today and I found it. Alvin had asked me to put it in my locker several weeks ago and I'd forgotten all about it."

"What's in it?"

"Bound ledgers, papers and correspondence. That type of stuff. There were no drugs, if that's what you were wondering."

"No," Jason said, "that's not what I was wondering. But I'm glad you called. The books might be important. I'd like to see them."

"Okay," Carol said. "I'll be at the club tonight. I'll have to think of some way to get them to you. My boss is giving me a lot of trouble about protection. Something weird is going on, which they won't tell me about, but I'm stuck with this goon following me around. I'd just as soon not involve you in that."

"Maybe I could come and pick it up?"

"No, I don't think that would be a good idea. I'll tell you what. If you give me your number, I'll call when I get home tonight."

Jason gave her the number.

"One other thing," Carol said. "Last night I realized there was something else I didn't tell you. About a month ago, Alvin said he was going to break up with Helene. He said he wanted her to concentrate on their work."

"Do you think he told her?"

"Haven't the slightest idea."

"Helene hasn't shown up for work today."

"No kidding!" Carol said. "That's strange. From what I'd heard, she was compulsive about work. Maybe she's the reason my boss is acting so crazy."

"How would your boss know about Helene Brennquivist?"

"He has a great informational network. He knows what's going on in the whole city."

Hanging up, Jason pondered the confusing inconsistencies between Carol's job and her intellectual sophistication. "Informational network" was a computer-age term—unexpected from an exotic dancer.

Going back to his patients, Jason studiously avoided Claudia's questioning gaze. He knew she was overwhelmingly curious, but he wasn't about to give her any satisfaction.

Toward the very end of the afternoon, Dr. Jerome Washington, a burly black physician who specialized in gastrointestinal disorders, interrupted Jason, asking for a quick consult.

"Sure," Jason said, taking him back to his office.

"Roger Wanamaker suggested I speak to you about this case." He took a bulky chart from under his arm and put it on the desk. "A few more like this and I'm going into the aluminum siding business."

Jason opened the chart. The patient was male, sixty years old.

"I did a physical on Mr. Lamborn twenty-three days ago," Jerome said. "The guy was a little overweight, but aren't we all? Otherwise I thought he was okay and told him so. Then, a week ago, he comes in looking like death warmed over. He'd dropped twenty pounds. I put him in the hospital, thinking he had a malignancy I'd missed. I gave him every test in the book. Nothing. Then three days ago he died. I put a lot of pressure on the family for an autopsy. And what did it show?"

"No malignancy."

"Right," Jerome said. "No malignancy—but every organ he had was totally degenerated. I told Roger and he said to see you, that you'd commiserate."

"Well, I've had some similar problems," Jason said. "So has Roger. To be truthful, I'm worried we're on the brink of some unknown medical disaster."

"What are we going to do?" Jerome asked. "I can't take too much of this kind of emotional abuse."

"I agree. With all the deaths I've had lately, I've been thinking of changing professions too. And I don't understand why we're not picking up symptoms on our physicals. I told Roger I'd call a meeting next week, but now I think we can't afford to wait." An image of Hayes's blood pumping over the dinner table flashed through Jason's mind. "Let's get together tomorrow afternoon. I'll have Claudia set it up, and I'll tell the secretaries to put together a list of all the physicals we've done over the last year and see what's happened to the patients."

"Sounds good to me," Jerome said. "Cases like this don't do much for a man's confidence."

After Jerome left, Jason went out to the central desk to make plans for the staff conference. He knew that a few people would have to put in some overtime, and he thanked providence for providing computers. There were a few groans when he explained what was needed, including rebooking all the afternoon patients, but Claudia took it on herself to be the ringleader. Jason was confident things would get done as well as the short time would permit.

At five-thirty, after seeing his last patient, Jason tried Helene's home number. Still no answer. Impulsively, he decided to stop by her apartment on his way home. He looked at the address he'd gotten from personnel and noted she lived in Cambridge on Concord Avenue. Then he recognized the address. It was the Craigie Arms apartment building.

What a coincidence, he thought. Before meeting Danielle he'd dated a girl at the Craigie Arms.

Descending to his car, Jason headed over to Cambridge. The traffic was terrible, but thanks to his familiarity with the area he had no trouble locating the address. He parked his car and went into the familiar lobby. Scanning the names, he found Brennquivist and pressed the buzzer. There was always the outside chance Helene wasn't picking up her phone, but would respond to the door. There was no answer. Jason looked at the tenant list, but Lucy Hagen's name was gone. After all, it had been fifteen years.

Instead, he reached for the super's buzzer and pressed it. A small speaker above the door buzzers crackled to life, and the gruff voice of Mr. Gratz grated out into the tiled foyer.

"There's no soliciting."

Jason quickly identified himself, admitting that Mr. Gratz might not remember him since it had been a few years. He said he was concerned about a colleague who was a tenant. Mr. Gratz didn't say anything, but the door buzzed open. Jason had to run a few steps to get it. Inside, Jason confronted the unmistakable odor, which he'd remembered for fifteen years. It was the smell of grilled onions. A metal door opened down the tiled hall and Mr. Gratz appeared dressed, as always, in a tank-top undershirt and soiled jeans. He sported a two-day growth of beard. He studied Jason's face, demanded his name again, then asked, "Didn't you used to date the Hagen girl in 2-J?"

Jason was impressed. The man certainly wouldn't win any beauty contests, but he apparently had a memory like a steel trap. Jason had gotten to know him because Lucy had chronic problems with her drains and Larry Gratz was in and out of her apartment.

"What can I do for you?" Larry asked.

Jason explained that Helene Brennquivist hadn't shown up for work and wasn't answering her phone. Jason said he was worried.

"I can't let you in her apartment."

"Oh, I understand," Jason said. "I just want to make sure everything is okay."

Gratz regarded him for a moment, grunted, then started toward the elevator. He pulled a ring of keys out of his pocket that looked adequate enough to open half the doors in Cambridge. They rode the elevator without speaking.

Helene's apartment was at the end of a long hall. Even before they got to the door, they could hear loud rock and roll.

"Sounds like she's having a party," Gratz said. He rang the bell for a full minute, but there was no response. Gratz put his ear to the door and rang again. "Can't even hear the door chimes," he said.

"Wonder no one's complained about the music."

Lifting a hairy fist, he pounded on the door. Finally he selected a key and turned the lock. As the door opened, the volume of the music increased dramatically. "Shit," Gratz said. Then he yelled, *"Hello!"* There was no answer.

The apartment had a small foyer with an arched opening to the left, but even from where he stood Jason recognized the unmistakable smell of death. He started to speak, but Gratz stopped him.

"You better wait here," Gratz said over the pounding music as he advanced toward the living room.

"Oh, *Christ!*" he shouted a second later. His eyes opened wide as his face contorted with horror. Jason looked between the arch and Larry's body. The room was a nightmare.

The super ran for the kitchen, his hand clasped over his mouth. Even with his medical training, Jason felt his own stomach turn over. Helene and another woman were side by side on the couch, naked, with their hands tied behind their back. Their bodies had been unspeakably mutilated. A large, stained kitchen knife was jammed into the coffee table.

Jason turned and looked into the kitchen. Larry was bent over the kitchen sink, heaving. Jason's first response was to help him, but he thought better of it. Instead, he went to the door to the hall and opened it, thankful for the fresh air. In a few minutes Larry stumbled past him.

"Why don't you go call the police," Jason said, allowing the door to close behind him. The relative quiet was refreshing. His nausea abated.

Thankful for something to do, Larry ran down the stairs. Jason leaned against the wall and tried not to think. He was trembling.

Two policemen arrived in short order. They were young and turned several shades of green when they looked into the living room. But they set about sealing off the scene and carefully questioning Jason and Gratz. With care not to disturb anything else, they finally pulled the plug on the stereo. More police arrived, including plainclothes detectives. Jason suggested Detective Curran might be interested in the case and someone called him. A police photographer arrived and began snapping shot after shot of the devastated apartment. Then the Cambridge medical examiner arrived.

Jason was waiting in the hall when Curran came lumbering toward Helene's apartment.

Seeing Jason, he paused only to shout, "What the hell are you doing here?"

Jason held his tongue, and Curran turned to the policeman standing by the door. "Where's the detective in charge?" he snapped, flashing his badge. The policeman jerked his thumb in the direction of the living room. Curran went in, leaving Jason in the hall.

The press appeared with their usual tangle of cameras and spiral notebooks. They tried to enter

Helene's apartment, but the uniformed policeman at the door restrained them. That reduced them to interviewing anybody in the area, including Jason. Jason told them he knew nothing, and they eventually left him alone.

After a while Curran reappeared. Even he looked a little green. He came over to Jason. He took a cigarette out of a crumpled pack and made a production out of finding a match. Finally, he looked at Jason.

"Don't tell me 'I told you so,'" he said.

"It wasn't just a rape murder, was it?" Jason asked quietly.

"That's not for me to say. Sure, it was a rape. What makes you think it was more?"

"The mutilation was done after death."

"Oh? Why do you say that, doctor?"

"Lack of blood. If the women had been alive, there would have been a lot of bleeding."

"I'm impressed," Curran said. "And while I hate to admit it, we don't think it was your ordinary loony. There's evidence I can't discuss but it looks like a professional job. A small-caliber weapon was involved."

"Then you agree Helene's death is tied to Hayes."

"Possibly," Curran said. "They told me you discovered the bodies."

"With the help of the superintendent."

"What brought you over here, doctor?"

Jason didn't answer immediately. "I'm not sure," he said finally. "As I told you, I had an uncomfortable feeling when Helene didn't show up for work."

Curran scratched his head, letting his attention wander around the hallway. He took a long drag on his cigarette, letting the smoke out through his nose. There was a crowd of police, reporters, and curious tenants. Two gurneys were lined up against the wall, waiting to take the bodies away.

"Maybe I won't turn the case over to Vice," Curran said at last. Then he wandered off.

Jason approached the policeman standing guard at the door to Helene's apartment. "I was wondering if I could go now."

"Hey, Rosati!" yelled the cop. The detective in charge, a thin, hollow-faced man with a shock of dark, unruly hair, appeared almost immediately.

"He wants to leave," said the cop, nodding at Jason.

"We got your name and address?" Rosati asked.

"Name, address, phone, social security, driver's license—everything."

"I suppose it's okay," Rosati said. "We'll be in touch."

Jason nodded, then walked down the hallway on shaky legs. When he emerged outside on Concord Avenue, he was surprised it had already gotten dark. The cold evening air was heavy with exhaust fumes. As one final slap in the face, Jason found a parking ticket under his windshield wiper. Irritated, he pulled it out, realizing he'd parked in a zone that required a Cambridge resident sticker.

It took much longer for him to return to GHP than

it had taken to drive to Helene's apartment. The traffic on Storrow Drive was backed up exiting at Fenway, so it was about seven-thirty P.M. when he finally parked and entered the building. Going up to his office, he found a large computer printout on his desk listing all the GHP patients who had received executive physicals in the last year, along with a notation of the patient's current physical status. *The secretaries did a great job,* Jason thought, putting the printout in his briefcase.

He went up to the floor for inpatient rounds. One of the nurses gave him the results of Madaline Krammer's arteriogram. All the coronary vessels showed significant, diffuse, nonfocal encroachment. When the results were compared with a similar study done six months previously, it showed significant deterioration. Harry Sarnoff, the consulting cardiologist, did not feel she was a candidate for surgery, and with her current low levels of both cholesterol and fatty acids, had little to suggest with regard to her management. To be one hundred percent certain, Jason ordered a cardiac surgery consult, then went in to see her.

As usual, Madaline was in the best of moods, minimizing her symptoms. Jason told her that he'd asked a surgeon to take a look at her, and promised to stop by the next day. He had the awful sense that the woman was not going to be around much longer. When he checked her ankles for edema, Jason noted some excoriations.

"Have you been scratching yourself?" he asked.

"A little," Madaline admitted, grasping the sheet and pulling it up as if she were embarrassed.

"Are your ankles itchy?"

"I think it's the heat in here. It's very dry, you know."

Jason didn't know. In fact, the air-conditioning system of the hospital kept the humidity at a constant, normal level.

With a horrible sense of déjà vu, Jason went back to the nurses' station and ordered a dermatology consult as well as a chemistry screen that included some forty automated tests. There had to be something he was missing.

The rest of rounds was equally depressing. It seemed all his patients were in decline. When he left the hospital he decided to take a run out to Shirley's. He felt like talking and she'd certainly made it clear she enjoyed seeing him. He also felt he should break the news of Helene's murder before she heard it from the press. He knew it was going to devastate her.

It took about twenty minutes before he pulled into her cobblestone driveway. He was pleased to see lights on.

"Jason! What a pleasant surprise," Shirley said, answering the bell. She was dressed in a red leotard with black tights and a white headband. "I was just on my way to aerobics."

"I should have called."

"Nonsense," Shirley said, grabbing his hand and

pulling him inside. "I'm always looking for an excuse not to exercise." She led him into the kitchen, where a mountain of reports and memoranda covered the table. Jason was reminded of what an enormous amount of work went into running an organization like GHP. As always, he was impressed by Shirley's skills.

After she brought him a drink, Jason asked if she'd heard the news.

"I don't know," Shirley said, pulling off her headband and shaking out her thick hair. "News about what?"

"Helene Brennquivist," Jason said. He let his voice trail off.

"Is this news I'm going to like?" Shirley asked, picking up her drink.

"I hardly think so," Jason said. "She and her roommate were murdered."

Shirley dropped her drink on the couch and then mechanically occupied herself cleaning up the mess. "What happened?" she asked after a long silence.

"It was a rape murder. At least ostensibly." He felt ill as he recalled the scene.

"How awful," Shirley said, clutching her hand to her chest.

"It was gruesome," agreed Jason.

"It's every woman's worst nightmare. When did it happen?"

"They seem to think it happened last night."

Shirley stared off into the middle distance. "I'd

better phone Bob Walthrow. This is only going to add to our PR woes."

Shirley heaved herself to her feet and walked shakily to the phone. Jason could hear the emotion in her voice as she explained what had happened.

"I don't envy you your job," he said when she hung up. He could see her eyes were bright with unshed tears.

"I feel the same about yours," she said. "Every time I see you after a patient dies, I'm glad I didn't go into medicine myself."

Although neither Shirley nor Jason was particularly hungry, they made a quick spaghetti dinner. Shirley tried to talk Jason into staying the night, but though he had found comfort being with her, helping him to endure the horror of Helene's death, he knew he couldn't stay. He had to be home for Carol's call. Pleading a load of unfinished work, he drove back to his apartment.

After a late jog and a shower, Jason sat down with the printouts of all patients who'd had GHP physicals in the last year. Feet on his desk, he went over the list carefully, noting that the number of physicals had been divided evenly among all the internists. Since the list had been printed in alphabetical order rather than chronologically, it took some time for Jason to realize that the poor predictive results were much more common in the last six months than in the beginning of the year. In fact, without graphing the material, it appeared that there had been a marked increase in unexpected deaths over the last few months.

Taking a pencil, Jason began writing down the unit numbers of the recent deaths. He was shocked by the number. Then he called the main operator at GHP and asked to be connected to Records. When he had one of the night secretaries on the line, he gave the list of unit numbers and asked if the outpatient charts could be pulled and put on his desk. The secretary told him there would be no problem at all.

Putting the computer printout back into his briefcase, Jason took down his Williams' *Textbook of Endocrinology* and turned to the chapters on growth hormone. Like so many other subjects, the more he read, the less he knew. Growth hormone and its relation to growth and sexual maturation were enormously complicated. So complicated, in fact, that he fell asleep, the heavy textbook pressing against his abdomen.

The phone shocked him awake—so abruptly that he knocked the book to the floor. He snatched up the receiver, expecting his service. It took another moment before he realized the caller was Carol Donner. Jason looked at the time—eleven minutes to three.

"I hope you weren't asleep," Carol said.

"No, no!" Jason lied. His legs were stiff from being propped up on the desk. "I've been waiting for your call. Where are you?"

"I'm at home," Carol said.

"Can I come get that package?"

"It's not here," Carol said. "To avoid problems, I gave it to a friend who works with me. Her name is Melody Andrews. She lives at 69 Revere Street on Beacon Hill." Carol gave him Melody's phone number. "She's expecting a call and should just be getting home. Let me know what you think of the material, and if there's any trouble, here's my number"—which she recited.

"Thanks," said Jason, writing everything down. He was surprised how disappointed he felt not to be seeing her.

"Take care," Carol said, hanging up.

Jason remained at his desk, still trying to fully wake up. As he did so, he realized he hadn't mentioned Helene's death to Carol. *Well, that might be a good excuse to call Carol back,* he reflected as he dialed her friend's number.

Melody Andrews answered her phone with a strong South Boston accent. She told Jason that she had the package, and he was welcome to come over and get it. She said she'd be up for another half hour or so.

Jason put on a sweater and down vest, left the house, walked down Pinckney Street, along West Cedar, and up Revere. Melody's building was on the left. He rang her bell, and she appeared at the door in pin curls. Jason didn't think anyone still used those things. Her face was tired and drawn.

Jason introduced himself. Melody merely nodded and handed over a parcel wrapped in brown paper and tied with string. It weighed about ten pounds. When Jason thanked her she just shrugged and said, "Sure."

Returning home, Jason pulled off his vest and sweater. Eagerly eyeing the package, he got scissors from the kitchen and cut the string. Then he carried the package into the den and placed it on his desk. Inside he found two ledgers filled with handwritten instructions, diagrams, and experimental data. One of the books had *Property of Gene, Inc.* printed on the cover; the other merely the word *Notebook.* In addition there was a large manila envelope filled with correspondence.

The first letters Jason read were from Gene, Inc., demanding that Hayes live up to his contractual agreements and return the Somatomedin protocol and the recombinant E. coli strain of bacteria that he'd illegally removed from their laboratory. As Jason continued reading, it was apparent that Hayes had a significant difference of opinion concerning the ownership of the procedure and the strain, and that he was in the process of patenting the same. Jason also found a number of letters from an attorney by the name of Samuel Schwartz. Half of them involved the application for the patent on the Somatomedin-producing E. coli and the rest dealt with the formation of a corporation. It seemed that Alvin Hayes owned fifty-one percent of the stock, while his children shared the other forty-nine percent along with Samuel Schwartz.

So much for the correspondence, Jason thought. He returned the letters to the manila envelope. Next he took up the ledger books. The one that had "Gene, Inc." on the cover seemed to be the protocol referred to in the correspondence. As Jason flipped through it, he realized that it detailed the creation of the recombinant strain of bacteria to produce Somatomedin. From his reading, he knew that Somatomedins were growth factors produced by the liver cells in response to the presence of growth hormone.

Putting the first book aside, Jason picked up the second. The experiments outlined were incomplete, but they concerned the production of a monoclonal antibody to a specific protein. The protein was not named, but Jason found a diagram of its amino-acid sequence. Most of the material was beyond his comprehension, but it was clear from the crossing out of large sections and the scribbling in the margins that the work was not progressing well and that at the time of the last entry, Hayes had obviously not created the antibody he'd desired.

Stretching, Jason got up from his desk. He was disappointed. He had hoped the package from Carol would offer a clearer picture of Hayes's breakthrough, but except for the documentation of the controversy between Hayes and Gene, Inc., Jason knew little more than he had before opening the package. He did have the protocol for producing the Somatomedin E. coli strain, but that hardly seemed a major discovery, and all the other lab book outlined was failure.

Exhausted, Jason turned out the lights and went to bed. It had been a long, terrible day.

11.

Nightmares involving gross permutations of the terrible scene in Helene's apartment drove Jason out of bed before the sun paled the eastern sky. He put on coffee and as he waited for it to filter through his machine, he picked up his paper and read about the double murder. There was nothing new. As he'd expected, the emphasis was on the rape. Putting the Gene, Inc., ledger in his briefcase, Jason started out for the hospital.

At least there was no traffic at that early hour as he drove to the GHP, and he had his choice of parking places. Even the surgeons who usually arrived at such an uncivilized hour were not there yet.

When he arrived at GHP, he went directly to his office. As he'd requested, his desk was piled with charts. He took off his jacket and began to go through them. Keeping in mind these were patients who had died within a month of getting a fairly clean bill of health from doctors who'd completed the most extensive physicals GHP had to offer, Jason searched for commonalities. Nothing caught his eye.

He compared EKGs and the levels of cholesterol, fatty acids, immunoglobulins, and blood counts. No common group of compounds, elements, or enzymes varied from the normal in any predictable pattern. The only shared trait was most of the patients' deaths occurred within a month of having the physical. More upsetting, Jason noticed, was that in the last three months the number of deaths increased dramatically.

Reading the twenty-sixth chart, one correlation suddenly occurred to Jason. Although the patients did not share physical symptoms, their charts showed a predominance of high-risk social habits. They were overweight, smoked heavily, used drugs, drank too much, and failed to exercise, or combined any and all of these unhealthy practices; they were men and women who were eventually destined to have severe medical problems. The shocking fact was that they deteriorated so quickly. And why the sudden upswing in deaths? People weren't indulging in vices more than they were a year ago. Maybe it was a kind of statistical equalizing: they'd been lucky and now the numbers were catching up to them. But that didn't make a whole lot of sense, for there seemed to be too many deaths. Jason was not an experienced statistician, so he decided to ask a better mathematician than he was to look at the numbers.

When he knew he wouldn't be waking the patients, Jason left his office and made rounds. Nothing had changed. Back in his office and before he saw the first scheduled patient, he called Pathology and inquired about the dead animals from Hayes's lab, and waited several minutes while the technician looked for the report.

"Here it is," the woman said. "They all died of strychnine poisoning."

Jason hung up and called Margaret Danforth at the city morgue. A technician answered, since Margaret was busy doing an autopsy. Jason asked if the toxicology on Gerald Farr revealed anything interesting.

"Toxicology was negative," the tech said.

"One more question. Would strychnine have shown up?"

"Just a moment," the technician said.

In the background Jason could hear the woman shouting to the medical examiner. She returned to the phone. "Dr. Danforth said yes, strychnine would have shown up if it had been present."

"Thank you," Jason said.

He hung up the phone, then stood up. At the window, he examined the developing day. He could see the traffic snarled on the Riverway from his window. The sky was light but overcast. It was early November. Not a pretty month for Boston. Jason felt restless and anxious and disconsolate. He thought about the parcel from Carol and wondered if he should turn it over to Curran. Yet for what purpose? They weren't even investigating Hayes except as a drug pusher.

Walking back to the desk Jason took out his phone

directory and looked up the phone number of Gene, Inc. He noted the company was located on Pioneer Street in east Cambridge next to the MIT campus. Impulsively, he sat down and dialed the number. The line was answered by a woman receptionist with an English accent. Jason asked for the head of the company.

"You mean Dr. Leonard Dawen, the president?"

"Dr. Dawen will be fine," Jason said. He heard the extension ring. It was picked up by a secretary.

"Dr. Dawen's office."

"I'd like to speak to Dr. Dawen."

"Who may I say is calling?"

"Dr. Jason Howard."

"May I tell him what this is in reference to?"

"It's about a lab book I have. Tell Dr. Dawen I'm from the Good Health Plan and was a friend of the late Alvin Hayes."

"Just a moment, please," the secretary said in a voice that sounded like a recording.

Jason opened the center drawer to his desk and toyed with his collection of pencils. There was a click on the phone, then a powerful voice came over the line, "This is Leonard Dawen!"

Jason explained who he was and then described the lab book.

"May I ask how it came into your possession, sir?"

"I don't think that's important. The fact is I have it." He was not about to implicate Carol.

"That book is our property," Dr. Dawen said. His

voice was calm but with a commanding and threatening undercurrent.

"I'll be happy to turn the book over in exchange for some information about Dr. Hayes. Do you think we might meet?"

"When?"

"As soon as possible," Jason said. "I could get over just before lunch."

"Will you have the book with you?"

"I will indeed."

For the rest of the morning Jason had trouble concentrating on the steady stream of patients. He was pleased Sally hadn't scheduled him through lunch. The minute he finished his last exam, he hurried out to his car.

Reaching Cambridge, Jason threaded his way past MIT and among the new East Cambridge corporate skyscrapers, some with dramatically modern architecture that contrasted sharply with the older and more traditional New England brick structures. Making a final turn on Pioneer Street, Jason found Gene, Inc., housed in a startlingly modern building of polished black granite. Unlike its neighbors, the structure was only six floors high. Its windows were narrow slits alternating with circles of bronze mirrored glass. It had a solid, powerful look, like a castle in a science fiction movie.

Jason got out of his car with his briefcase and gazed up at the striking façade. After reading so much about recombinant DNA and seeing Hayes's grossly deformed zoo, Jason was afraid he was about to enter a house of horrors. The front entrance was circular, defined by radiating spikes of granite, giving the illusion of a giant eye, the black doors being the pupil. The lobby was also black granite: walls, floor, even ceiling. In the center of the reception area was a dramatically illuminated modern sculpture of the double helix DNA molecule opening like a zipper.

Jason approached an attractive Korean woman sitting behind a glass wall and in front of a control panel that looked like something out of the *Starship Enterprise.* She wore a tiny earpiece along with a small microphone that snaked around from behind her neck. She greeted Jason by name and told him he was expected in the fourth-floor conference room. Her voice had a metallic sound as she spoke into the microphone.

The minute the receptionist stopped speaking, one of the granite panels opened, revealing an elevator. As he thanked her, Jason suddenly fancied that she was a lifelike robot. Smiling, he boarded the elevator and looked for the floor buttons. The door closed behind him. There was no floor-selector panel, but the elevator started upward.

When the doors reopened, Jason found himself in a doorless black foyer. He assumed the entire building was controlled from a central location, perhaps by the receptionist downstairs. To his left a granite panel slid open. Within the doorway stood a man with coarse features, impeccably dressed in a dark pinstripe suit, white shirt, and red paisley tie.

"Dr. Howard, I'm Leonard Dawen," the man said, motioning Jason into the room. He didn't offer to shake hands. His voice had the same commanding quality Jason remembered from the phone conversation. Compared to the tomblike austerity of the rest of the building, the conference room looked more like a wood-paneled library and seemed positively cozy until you looked at the fourth wall, which was glass. It looked out on what appeared to be a large ultramodern lab. There was another man in the room, an Oriental, wearing a white zippered jumpsuit. Dawen introduced the man as Mr. Hong, a Gene, Inc., engineer. After they were all seated around a small conference table, Dawen said, "I assume you have the lab book. . . ."

Jason opened his briefcase and handed the ledger to Dawen, who handed it to Hong. The engineer began studying it page by page. A heavy silence ensued.

Jason looked back and forth between the two men. He'd expected things to be a bit more cordial. After all, he was doing them a favor.

He turned and peered through the glass wall. The floor of the room beyond was a story below. Much of the area was filled with stainless steel vats, reminding Jason of a visit he'd once made to a brewery. He guessed they were the incubators for the culture of the recombinant bacteria. There was a lot of other equipment and complicated piping. People in white jumpsuits with white hoods were moving about checking gauges, making adjustments.

Hong closed the lab book with a snap. "It seems complete," he said.

"That's a nice surprise," Dr. Dawen said. Turning to Jason he said, "I hope you realize everything in this book is confidential."

"Don't worry," Jason said, forcing a smile. "I didn't understand much of it. What I'm interested in is Dr. Hayes. Just before he died he said he'd made a major discovery. I'm curious to know if what is described in those pages would be considered as such."

Dawen and Hong exchanged glances. "It's more of a commercial breakthrough," Hong said. "There's no new technology here."

"That's what I suspected. Hayes was so distraught I couldn't tell if he was entirely rational. But, if he made a major breakthrough, I'd hate to have it lost to humanity."

Dawen's blunt features softened for the first time since Jason had arrived.

Jason continued, directing his attention to the engineer. "Any idea what Hayes could have been talking about?"

"Unfortunately, no. Hayes was always rather secretive." Dawen folded his hands on the table and looked directly at Jason. "We were afraid you were going to extort us with this material—make us pay to get it back," he said, touching the cover of the lab book. "You have to understand that Dr. Hayes had been giving us a rather difficult time."

"What was Dr. Hayes's role here?" Jason asked.

"We hired him to produce a recombinant strain of bacteria," Dawen explained. "We wanted to produce a certain growth factor in commercial quantities."

Jason guessed that was the Somatomedin.

"We agreed to pay him a flat fee for the project, as well as letting him use the Gene, Inc., facilities for his own research. We have some very unique equipment."

"Any idea what his own research involved?" Jason asked.

Hong spoke up. "He spent most of his time isolating growth-factor proteins. Some of them exist in such minute quantities that the most sophisticated equipment is required to isolate them."

"Would the isolation of one of these growth factors be considered a major scientific discovery?" Jason asked.

"I can't see how," Hong replied. "Even if they've never been isolated, we know their effects."

Another dead end, Jason thought wearily.

"There's just one thing I remember that might be significant," Hong said, pinching the bridge of his nose. "About three months ago Hayes got very excited about some side effect. He said it was ironic."

Jason straightened. There was that word again. "Any idea what caused his excitement?" he asked.

Hong shook his head. "No," he said, "but after

that we didn't see him for a time. When we did see him, he said he'd been to the Coast. Then he set up an elaborate extraction process on some material he'd brought back with him. I don't know if it worked, but then he abruptly switched to monoclonal antibody technology. At that point his excitement seemed to die."

The words "monoclonal antibody" reminded Jason of the second lab book, and he wondered if he shouldn't have brought it after all. Maybe Mr. Hong could have made more out of it than he had.

"Did Dr. Hayes leave any other research material here?" Jason asked.

"Nothing significant," Leonard Dawen answered. "And we checked carefully, because he'd walked off with our lab book and the cultures. In fact, we were suing Dr. Hayes. We never anticipated he would try and contend he owned the strains that we'd hired him to produce."

"Did you get your cultures back?" Jason asked.

"We did."

"Where did you find them?"

"Let's say we looked in the right place," Dawen said evasively. "But even though we have the strain, we still appreciate getting the protocol book back. On behalf of the company, I'd like to thank you. I hope we have helped you in some small way."

"Perhaps," Jason said vaguely. He had an idea he'd inadvertently found out who had searched Hayes's lab and apartment. But why would the scientists from Gene, Inc., want to kill the animals? He wondered if the huge animals had been treated with Gene, Inc.'s, Somatomedin. "I appreciate your time," he said to Dawen. "You have an impressive setup here."

"Thank you. Things are going well. We plan to have recombinant strains of farm animals soon."

"You mean like pigs and cows?"

"That's right. Genetically we can produce leaner pigs, cows that produce more milk, and chickens that have more protein, just to give you a few examples."

"Fascinating," Jason said without enthusiasm. How far away could they be from genetically engineering people? He shivered again, seeing Hayes's outsized rats and mice, especially those with supernumerary eyes.

Back in the car, Jason glanced at his watch. He still had an hour before the staff meeting being held to go over recent patient deaths, so he decided to visit Samuel Schwartz, Hayes's attorney.

Starting the car, Jason backed out of the Gene, Inc., parking lot and worked his way over to Memorial Drive. He crossed the Charles River, stopping at Philip's Drug Store on Charles Circle. Double-parking with his emergency light blinking, he ran into the store and looked up Schwartz's address. Ten minutes later he was in the lawyer's waiting room, flipping the pages of an outdated *Newsweek*.

Samuel Schwartz was an enormously obese man

with a glistening bald head. He motioned Jason into his office as if he were directing traffic. Settling himself into his chair and adjusting his wire-rimmed glasses, he studied Jason, who had seated himself in front of the massive mahogany partner's desk.

"So you are a friend of the late Alvin Hayes. . . ."

"We were more colleagues than friends."

"Whatever," Schwartz said with another wave of his chubby hand. "So what can I do for you?"

Jason retold Hayes's story of a purported breakthrough. He explained that he was trying to figure out what Hayes had been working on and had come across correspondence from Samuel Schwartz.

"He was a client. So what?"

"No need to be defensive."

"I'm not defensive. I'm just bitter. I did a lot of work for that bum and I'm going to have to write it all off."

"He never paid?"

"Never. He conned me into working for stock in his new company."

"Stock?"

Samuel Schwartz laughed without humor. "Unfortunately, now that Hayes is dead, the stock is worthless. It might have been worthless even if he had lived. I should have my head examined."

"Was Hayes's corporation going to sell a service or a product?" Jason asked.

"A product. Hayes told me he was on the verge of developing the most valuable health product ever known. And I believed him. I figured a guy who'd been on the cover of *Time* had to have something on the ball."

"Any idea what this product was?" Jason asked, trying to keep the excitement out of his voice.

"Not the foggiest. Hayes wouldn't tell me."

"Do you know if it involved monoclonal antibodies?" Jason asked, unwilling to give up.

Schwartz laughed again. "I wouldn't know a monoclonal antibody if I walked into it."

"Malignancies?" Jason was only fishing, but he hoped he could jog the lawyer's memory. "Could the product have involved a cancer treatment?"

The obese man shrugged— "I don't know. Possibly."

"Hayes told someone that his discovery would enhance their beauty. Does that mean anything to you?"

"Listen, Dr. Howard. Hayes told me nothing about the product. I was just setting up the corporation."

"You were also applying for a patent."

"The patent had nothing to do with the corporation. That was to be in Hayes's name."

Jason's beeper startled both men. He watched the tiny screen. The word "urgent" blinked twice, followed by a number at the GHP hospital. "Would it be possible to use your phone?" Jason asked.

Schwartz pushed it across the desk. "Be my guest, doctor."

The call was from Madaline Krammer's floor. She'd arrested and they were giving her CPR. Jason said he'd be right there. Thanking Samuel Schwartz, Jason ran from the lawyer's office and impatiently waited for the elevator.

When he got to Madaline's room, he saw an all too familiar scene. The patient was unresponsive. Her heart refused to respond to anything, including external pacing. Jason insisted they continue life support while his mind went over various drugs and treatments, but after an hour of frantic activity, even he was forced to give up and he reluctantly called a halt to the proceedings.

Jason remained at Madaline's bedside after everyone else had left. She'd been an old friend, one of the first patients he'd treated in his private practice. One of the nurses had covered her face with a sheet. Madaline's nose poked it up like a miniature snow-covered mountain. Gently, Jason turned it back. Even though she had been only in her early sixties, he couldn't get over how old she looked. Since she'd entered the hospital, her face had lost all its cheerful plumpness and taken on the skeletal cast of those nearing death.

Needing some time by himself, Jason retreated to his office, avoiding both Claudia and Sally, who each had a hundred urgent questions about the upcoming conference and the problems of rescheduling so many patients. Jason locked his door and settled himself at his desk. As such an old patient, Madaline's passing seemed like the severing of one more connection to Jason's former life. Jason felt poignantly alone, fearful, yet relieved, that Danielle's memory was receding.

Jason's phone rang, but he ignored it. He looked over his desk, which was a mass of stacked hospital charts of deceased patients, including Hayes's. Involuntarily, Jason's mind went back to the Hayes affair. It was frustrating that the package from Carol, which had held such hope, had added so little information. It did give a bit more credence to the idea Hayes had made a discovery that at least he thought was stupendous. Jason cursed Hayes's secrecy.

Leaning back, Jason put his hands behind his head and stared up at the ceiling. He was running out of ideas about Hayes. But then he remembered the Oriental engineer's comment that Hayes had brought something back from the Coast, presumably Seattle. It must have been a sample of something because Hayes had subjected it to a complicated extraction process. From Hong's comments, it seemed to Jason that Hayes had probably been isolating some kind of growth factor which would stimulate growth, or differentiation, or maturation, or all three.

Jason came forward with a thump. Remembering that Carol had said Hayes had visited a colleague at the University of Washington, Jason suddenly entertained the idea that Hayes had obtained some kind of sample from the man.

All at once, Jason decided he'd go to Seattle, provided, of course, Carol would go along. She might.

After all, she'd be the key to finding this friend. Besides, a few days away sounded extremely therapeutic to Jason. With a little time left before the staff meeting, Jason decided to stop by and see Shirley.

Shirley's secretary at first insisted that her boss was too busy to see Jason, but he convinced her to at least announce his presence. A moment later he was ushered inside. Shirley was on the phone. Jason took a seat, gradually catching the drift of the conversation. She was dealing with a union leader, handling the person with impressive ease. Absently she ran her fingers through her thick hair. It was a wonderfully feminine gesture, reminding Jason that underneath the professional surface was a very attractive woman, complicated but lovely.

Shirley hung up and smiled. "This is a treat," she said. "You *are* filled with surprises these days, aren't you, Jason? I suppose you're here to apologize for not having spent more time with me last night."

Jason laughed. Her directness was disarming. "Maybe so. But there's something else. I'm thinking of taking a few days off. I lost another patient this morning and I think I need some time away."

Shirley clicked her tongue in sympathy. "Was it expected?"

"I guess so. At least over the last few days. But when I'd admitted her I had no idea she was terminal."

Shirley sighed. "I don't know how you deal with this sort of thing."

"It's never easy," Jason agreed. "But what's made it particularly hard lately is the frequency."

Shirley's phone rang, but she buzzed her secretary to take a message.

"Anyway," Jason said, "I've decided to take a few days off."

"I think it's a good idea," Shirley said. "I wouldn't mind doing the same if these damned union negotiations conclude. Where are you planning to go?"

"I'm not sure," Jason lied. The trip to Seattle was such a long shot that he was ashamed to mention it.

"I have some friends who own a resort in the British Virgin Islands. I could give them a call," Shirley offered.

"No, thanks. I'm not a sun person. What's happened about the Brennquivist tragedy? Much fallout?"

"Don't remind me," Shirley said. "To tell you the truth, I couldn't face it. Bob Walthrow is handling that."

"I had nightmares all night," admitted Jason.

"Not surprising," Shirley said.

"Well, I've got a meeting," Jason said, getting to his feet.

"Would you have time for dinner tonight?" Shirley asked. "Maybe we can cheer each other up."

"Sure. What time?"

"Let's say around eight."

"Eight it is," Jason said, heading for the door. As he left, Shirley called after him.

"I'm really sorry about your patient."

* * *

The staff meeting was better attended than Jason had expected, given such short notice. Fourteen of the sixteen internists were there, and several had brought along their nurses. It seemed obvious they all recognized they were facing a serious problem.

Jason started with the statistics that he'd extracted from the computer printout listing all patients who'd died within a month of a complete physical. He pointed out that the number of deaths had increased in the last three months, and said he was trying to check up on all GHP clients who'd had executive physicals in the last sixty days.

"Were the physicals evenly distributed among us?" Roger Wanamaker asked.

Jason nodded.

A number of the doctors spoke out, making it clear they feared the start of a nationwide epidemic. No one could understand the connection with the physicals, and why the deaths were not being anticipated. The acting chief of cardiology, Dr. Judith Rolander, tried to take much of the blame on herself, admitting that in most of the cases she'd reviewed, the EKG done during the physical did not predict the imminent problems, even when she was armed with hindsight.

The conversation then switched to stress testing as the main key to predicting catastrophic cardiac events. There were many opinions on this issue; all were duly discussed. Upon recommendation from the floor, an ad hoc committee was formed to look into specific ways to alter their stress testing in hopes of increasing its prognostic value.

Jerome Washington then took the floor. Getting heavily on his feet, he said, "I think we're overlooking the significance of unhealthy lifestyles. That's one factor that all these patients seem to share."

There were a few joking references to Jerome's weight and his affection for cigars. "All right, you guys," he said. "You know patients should do what we say and not what we do." Everyone laughed. "Seriously," he continued. "We all know the dangers of poor diet, heavy smoking, excess alcohol and lack of exercise. Such social factors have far more predictive value than a mild EKG abnormality."

"Jerome is right," Jason said. "The poor risk-factor profile was the only negative commonality I could find."

By a vote, it was decided to form a second committee to investigate risk-factor contribution to the current problem and come up with specific recommendations.

Harry Sarnoff, the current month's consulting cardiologist, raised his hand, and Jason recognized him. When he got to his feet, he began to talk about noticing an increase in morbidity and mortality for his inpatients. Jason interrupted him.

"Excuse me, Harry," Jason said. "I can appreciate your concern, and frankly I've had experience apparently similar to yours. However, this current meeting involves the problem with the outpatient executive physicals. We can schedule a second meeting if the staff desires to discuss any potential inpatient problem. They very well may be related."

Harry threw up his hands, and reluctantly sat back down.

Jason then encouraged the staff to be sure to autopsy any patients who met unexpected deaths if the medical examiner didn't take them. Jason then told the audience that the results from the medical examiner's office on his patients suggested that the people were suffering multisystem disease including extensive cardiovascular problems. Of course, that fact only undermined the concern that their conditions had not been picked up on either resting or exercise EKGs. Jason added that Pathology thought there was an autoimmune component.

After the meeting broke up, the doctors gravitated to smaller groups to discuss the problem. Jason collected his printout and searched for Roger Wanamaker. He was in an animated conversation with Jerome.

"May I interrupt?" Jason asked. The two men separated to allow Jason to join them. "I'm about to leave town for a few days."

Roger and Jerome exchanged glances. Roger spoke: "Seems like a poor time to be leaving."

"I need it," Jason said without elaborating. "But I have five patients in house. Would either of you gentlemen be willing to cover? I'll admit right up front that they're all pretty sick."

"Wouldn't much matter," Roger said. "I've been in here night and day trying to keep my own half dozen alive. I'll be happy to cover."

With that problem solved, Jason went into his office and called Carol Donner, thinking late afternoon would be a good time to catch her. The phone rang a long time and he was about to give up when she answered, out of breath. She told him she'd been in the bath.

"I want to see you tonight," Jason said.

"Oh," Carol said noncommittally. She hesitated. "That might be difficult." Then she added angrily, "Why didn't you tell me about Helene Brennquivist last night? I read in the paper that you were the one who found the bodies."

"I'm sorry," Jason said defensively. "To be perfectly honest, you woke me last night and all I could think about was the package."

"Did you get it?" Carol asked, her voice softening.

"I did," Jason said. "Thank you."

"And . . . ?"

"The material wasn't as enlightening as I'd hoped."

"I'm surprised," said Carol. "The ledgers must have been important or Alvin wouldn't have asked me to keep them. But that's beside the point. What an awful thing about Helene. My boss is so distressed he won't let me go anywhere without one of the club bouncers. He's outside the building at this very moment."

"It's important that I see you alone," Jason said.

"I don't know if I can. This behemoth takes orders from my boss, not me. And I don't want any trouble."

"Well, call me the minute you get home," Jason said. "Promise! We'll think of something."

"It'll be late again," Carol warned.

"That doesn't matter. It's important."

"All right," Carol agreed before hanging up.

Jason made one more call, to United Airlines, and checked on service from Boston to Seattle. He learned there was a daily flight at four P.M.

Gathering his stethoscope, Jason left his office and headed for the hospital to make rounds. He knew he needed to thoroughly update his charts if Roger was going to cover. None of his patients was doing very well, and Jason was disturbed to find that another patient had developed advanced cataracts. Troubled, he arranged an ophthalmology consult. This time he was certain he hadn't noticed the problem on admission. How could the cataracts have progressed so far so fast?

At home, he changed into jogging clothes and ran a good hour, trying to sort out his thoughts. By the time he showered, changed, and drove over to Shirley's, he was in a better mood.

Shirley outdid herself with the dinner, and Jason began to think she'd fit into the Superwoman category. She'd worked all day running a multimillion-dollar company and conducting crucial union negotiations, yet somehow she'd gotten home, put together a fabulous feast of roast duck with fresh pasta and artichoke. And on top of that she'd dressed herself in a black silk chemise that would have been appropriate for the opera. Jason felt embarrassed that he'd put on jeans and a rugby shirt over a turtleneck after his shower.

"You wore what you wanted and so did I," Shirley said with a laugh. She gave him a Kir Royale and told him to wash the radicchio and the arugula for their salad. She checked the duck and said it was about done. To Jason, it smelled heavenly.

They ate in the dining room, sitting at opposite ends of a long table with six empty chairs on either side. Every time Jason poured more wine, he had to get up and walk several steps. Shirley thought it was amusing.

As they ate, Jason described the staff meeting and added that all the doctors were going to intensify the quality of their stress testing. Shirley was pleased, reminding Jason that the executive physical was an important part of GHP's sales pitch to corporate clients. She told Jason that there would be a new emphasis on preventive medicine for executive customers.

Later, over coffee, she said, "Michael Curran came by this afternoon."

"Really," said Jason. "I'm sure that was unpleasant. What did he want?"

"Background material on the Brennquivist woman. We gave him everything we had. He even interviewed the woman in personnel who'd hired her."

"Did he mention if they had any suspects?"

"He didn't say," Shirley said. "I just hope it's all over."

"I wish I'd gotten to talk with Helene again. I still think she was covering for Hayes."

"Do you still think he discovered something?"

"Absolutely." Jason went on to describe the lab ledgers and his visit to Gene, Inc., and to Samuel Schwartz. He told Shirley that Schwartz had set up a corporation for Hayes that was to market the new discovery, whatever it was.

"Didn't the lawyer know what the product was?"

"Nope. Apparently Hayes trusted no one."

"But he would have needed seed capital. He would have had to trust *someone* if he was planning to manufacture and distribute."

"Maybe so," Jason admitted. "But I can't find anyone he told—at least not yet. Unfortunately, Helene was the best bet."

"Are you still looking?"

"I guess so," he admitted. "Does that sound stupid?"

"Not stupid," Shirley said, "just disturbing. It would be a tragedy if an important discovery were lost, but I definitely think it's time to put the Hayes affair to rest. I hope you're taking time off to relax, not to continue this wild-goose chase."

"Now why would you suggest that?" Jason asked, surprised at his own transparency.

"Because you don't give up easily." She moved over and put her hand on his shoulder. "Why don't you go to the Caribbean? Maybe I could get away over the weekend and join you. . . ."

Jason experienced an excitement he'd not felt since Danielle's death. The idea of the hot sun and cool, clear water sounded wonderful, especially if Shirley were there too. But then he hesitated. He didn't know if he was ready for the emotional commitment that would entail. And, more important, he'd promised himself he'd visit Seattle.

"I want to go out to the West Coast," he said finally. "There's an old friend out there I'd like to see."

"That sounds innocent enough. But the Caribbean sounds better to me."

"Maybe soon." He gave Shirley's arm a squeeze. "How about a cognac?"

As Shirley got up to get the Courvoisier, Jason studied her figure with increasing interest.

When Carol called at two-thirty in the morning, Jason was wide awake. He'd been so worried that she might forget, he hadn't been able to sleep.

"I'm exhausted, Jason," Carol announced, instead of saying hello.

"I'm sorry, but I must see you," he said. "I can be over in ten minutes."

"I don't think that would be a good idea. As I told you this afternoon, I'm not alone. There's someone outside watching my building. Why do you have to see me tonight? Maybe we can work something out tomorrow."

Jason thought about asking her on the phone to go to Seattle, but decided he'd have a better chance convincing her in person. It was a bit out of the ordinary asking a young woman to accompany him to Seattle after only two meetings.

"Is this bodyguard alone?"

"Yes. But what difference does that make? The guy's built like an ox."

"There's an alley in back of your building. I could come up the fire escape."

"The fire escape! This is crazy! What on earth is so important that you have to see me tonight?"

"If I told you, I wouldn't have to see you."

"Well, I'm not crazy about men coming to my apartment at night."

Oh, sure, Jason thought. "Look," he said aloud, "I'll tell you this much I've been trying to figure out what Hayes could have discovered and I'm down to my last idea. I need your help."

"That's quite a line, Dr. Jason Howard."

"It's true. You're the only one who can help me."

Carol laughed. "When you put it that way, who could refuse? All right, come along. But you're coming at your own risk. I have to warn you, I don't have much control over Atlas outside."

"My disability insurance is all paid up."

"I live at . . ." Carol began.

"I know where you live," Jason interrupted. "In

fact, I've already had a run-in with Bruno, if that's the charming fellow guarding your door."

"You've met Bruno?" Carol asked incredulously.

"Lovely man. Such a wonderful conversationalist."

"Let me warn you, then," Carol said. "It was Bruno who walked me home."

"Luckily he's pretty easy to spot. Watch out your back window. I don't want to be stranded on your fire escape."

"This is really insane," Carol said.

Jason changed into a dark slacks and sweater. He'd be visible enough on the fire escape without wearing light colors. He donned running shoes and went down to his car. Driving along Beacon Street, he kept an eye out for Bruno. He went left on Gloucester Street and left again on Commonwealth. When he crossed Marlborough, he slowed. He knew there was no chance to find a parking place, so he pulled in at the nearest hydrant. He left the doors unlocked; if need be the firemen could run the hoses right through the car.

Getting out of his car, Jason peered down the alleyway between Beacon and Marlborough streets. Intermittent lights formed pools of illumination. There were lots of dark areas, and trees threw spider-weblike shadows. Jason could vividly remember his last attempted flight from Bruno down the same alley.

Marshaling his courage, Jason started into the alley as tense as a sprinter waiting for the starting gun. A sudden movement to his left made him gasp. It was a rat the size of a small cat, and Jason felt the hairs on the back of his neck spring up. He kept walking, happy to see no sign of Bruno. It was so quiet he could hear his breathing.

Arriving at Carol's building, he noted the familiar light in the fourth-floor window before taking a good look at the fire escape. Unfortunately, it had one of those ladder mechanisms that have to be lowered from the first floor. Jason glanced around for something to stand on. The only thing available was a trash can, and that meant turning it over and dumping it. Despite the fact it would make a lot of noise, he realized he had no choice. But he shuddered as the metal clanged against the pavement and a number of beer cans clattered down the street.

Holding his breath, he looked up. No lights had come on. Satisfied, he climbed up on the garbage can and got hold of the lowest rung of the raised ladder.

"Hey!" someone yelled. Jason's head turned and he saw a familiar bulky figure coming down the alley on the run, his thick arms pumping, his breaths coming in puffs like a steam engine. At that moment Bruno looked like a fullback for the Washington Redskins.

"Shit," Jason said. With all his strength he pulled himself up on the ladder, half expecting it to drop under his weight. Luckily it didn't. Hand over hand, he lifted himself until he could put his foot on the first rung and scamper up to the first floor.

"Hey, you goddamned little pervert!" Bruno was yelling. "You get the hell down here!"

Jason hesitated. He could hold the man off by stepping on his fingers if he tried to come up, but that wouldn't get him in to see Carol. And somebody would call the police if there were enough ruckus. Jason decided to take the chance. He ran up the next two flights of the fire escape, arriving at Carol's window. She was looking out and raised the sash the second she spotted him. Before she could speak, Jason gasped, "Your neo-Nazi is on his way up. Do you think he has a gun?" Jason found himself standing in a large kitchen.

"I don't know."

"He's going to be here in a moment," Jason said, slamming down the window and locking it. That was going to delay Bruno just about ten seconds.

"Maybe I should talk to him," Carol suggested.

"Will he listen?"

"I'm not sure. He's kinda bullheaded. . . ."

"That's my impression," Jason said. "And I know he's not fond of me. I think I need something like a baseball bat."

"You can't hit him, Jason."

"I don't want to, but I don't think Bruno wants to sit down and talk this over. I need something to threaten him with to keep him away from me."

"I have a fire poker."

"Get it." Jason turned the light out in the kitchen. Putting his nose to the glass, he could see Bruno struggling to pull himself onto the first ladder. He was strong but he was also bulky. Carol returned with the fire poker. Jason hefted it. With a little luck he might be able to convince the guy to listen.

"I knew this was a bad idea," Carol said.

Jason glanced around the room and noticed that the floor was old-fashioned linoleum. He looked at the door leading from the kitchen to the rest of the apartment. It was thick and solid, with a lock and key. At one point the room had been something other than a kitchen.

"Carol, would you mind if I made a mess? I mean, I'll be happy to pay to have it cleaned up."

"What are you talking about?"

"Do you have a big can of vegetable oil?"

"I suppose."

"Can I have it?"

Perplexed, Carol opened the pantry door and lifted out a gallon can of imported Italian olive oil.

"Perfect," Jason said. After another quick check out the window, he hurriedly pulled the two chairs and table out of the kitchen. Carol watched him with growing confusion.

"Okay, out," Jason ordered. Carol stepped into the hall.

Jason uncorked the olive oil and began pouring the contents over the floor in wide, sweeping movements. As he closed and locked the door, he heard banging on the kitchen window, followed by the crash of glass.

He wedged the kitchen table between the door and the opposite hall.

"Come on," he said, taking Carol's hand. In his other he still held the poker. He led her to the front door of the apartment, which was adequately secured with double latches and a metal-pole police lock. In the kitchen they heard a tremendous crash. Bruno had fallen down for the first time.

"That was ingenious," laughed Carol.

"When you're one hundred and sixty pounds, you have to compensate." Jason's heart was still racing. "Anyway, I have no idea how long Bruno will be entertained in there, so this has to be fast. I need you. The last chance I have of reconstructing Alvin Hayes's discovery is to go to Seattle and try to find out what he did there. Apparently, he . . ."

There was another crash followed by a volley of swear words, some of which were appropriately in Italian.

"He's going to be in a foul mood," Jason said as he undid the locks on the front door.

"So you want me to go to Seattle with you. That's what this is all about?"

"I knew you'd understand. Hayes brought back a biological sample from there, which he processed at Gene, Inc. I have to find out what it was. The best bet is the man he saw out at the University of Washington."

"The man whose name I can't remember."

"But you saw him and could recognize him?"

"Probably."

"I know it's presumptuous to ask you to come," Jason said. "But I really do believe Hayes made some sort of breakthrough. And considering his previous track record, it has to be significant."

"And you really think going to Seattle might solve it?"

"It's a long shot. But the only one left."

The door to the kitchen rattled and they heard Bruno begin a steady pounding.

"I think I've overstayed my welcome," Jason said. "Bruno won't hurt you, will he?"

"Heavens, no. My boss would skin him alive. That's why he's so rabid now. He thinks I'm in danger."

"Carol, would you come with me to Seattle?" Jason asked while removing the pole to the police lock.

"When would you want to go?" Carol asked, vacillating.

"Late today. We wouldn't stay long. Would it be possible for you to get off on short notice?"

"I have in the past. I just say I want to go home. Besides, after Helene's murder my boss might be relieved to have me out of town."

"Then say you'll go?" Jason pleaded.

"All right." Carol gave him one of her heartwarming smiles. "Why not?"

"There's a flight to Seattle at four this afternoon. We'll meet at the gate. I'll get the tickets. How does that sound?"

"Insane," Carol said, "but fun."

"See you there." Jason ran down the stairs to his car, fearful that Bruno might have reversed direction and gone back out the window.

12.

Jason woke early and called Roger to brief him on his patients. He wasn't going to the hospital today. He had another trip he wanted to take before meeting Carol for the four o'clock flight to Seattle. He packed quickly, being careful to take clothes for rainy, chilly weather, and called a cab to the airport, getting there just in time to store his bag in a locker and take the ten o'clock Eastern shuttle to La Guardia. At La Guardia he rented a car and drove to Leonia, New Jersey. It was probably even less of a possibility than Seattle, but Jason was going to see Hayes's former wife. He was not about to leave even the smallest stone unturned.

Leonia turned out to be a surprisingly sleepy little town that belied its proximity to New York. Within ten minutes of the George Washington Bridge, he found himself on a wide street lined with one-story commercial establishments fronted by angled parking. It could have been Main Street, USA. Instead, it was called Broad Avenue. There was a drugstore, a hardware store, a bakery, and even a luncheonette.

It looked like a movie set from the fifties. Jason went into the luncheonette, ordered a vanilla malted, and used the phone directory. There was a Louise Hayes on Park Avenue. While he drank his malted, Jason debated the wisdom of calling or just dropping by. He opted for the latter.

Park Avenue bisected Broad and rose up the hillside that bordered Leonia on the east. After Pauline Boulevard, it arched to the north. That was where Jason found Louise Hayes's house. It was a modest, dark-brown, shingled structure, much in need of repair. The grass in the front yard had gone to seed.

Jason rang the bell. The door was opened by a smiling, middle-aged woman in a faded red housedress. She had stringy brown hair, and a little girl of five or six, a thumb buried to the second knuckle in her mouth, clung to her thigh.

"Mrs. Hayes?" Jason asked. The woman was a far cry from Hayes's two other girlfriends.

"Yes."

"I'm Dr. Jason Howard, a colleague of your late husband." He'd not rehearsed what he was going to say.

"Yes?" Mrs. Hayes repeated, reflexly pushing the young girl behind her.

"I'd like to talk to you if you have a moment." Jason took out his wallet and handed over his driver's license with its photo and his GHP staff identity card. "I went to medical school with your husband," he added for good measure.

Louise looked at the cards and handed them back. "Would you like to come in?"

"Thank you."

The interior of the house also looked in need of work. The furniture was worn and the carpet was threadbare. Children's toys littered the floor. Louise hastily cleared a spot on the couch and motioned for Jason to sit down.

"Can I offer you something? Coffee, tea?"

"Coffee would be nice," he said. The woman seemed anxious, and he thought the activity would calm her. She went into the kitchen, where Jason could hear the sound of running water. The little girl had hung behind, regarding Jason with large brown eyes. When Jason smiled at her, she fled into the kitchen.

Jason gazed around the room. It was dark and cheerless, with a few mail-order prints on the walls. Louise returned with her daughter in tow. She gave Jason a mug of coffee and placed sugar and cream on the small coffee table. Jason helped himself to both.

Louise sat down across from Jason. "I'm sorry if I didn't seem hospitable at first," she said. "I don't have many visitors asking about Alvin."

"I understand," Jason said. He looked at her more carefully. Underneath the frowsy exterior, Jason could see the shadow of an attractive woman. Hayes had good taste, that was for sure. "I'm sorry to barge in like this, but Alvin had spoken of you. Since I was in the area I thought I'd drop by." He thought a few untruths might help.

"Did he?" Louise said indifferently.

Jason decided to be careful. He wasn't there to dredge up painful emotions.

"The reason I wanted to talk to you," he said, "is that your husband told me he'd made an important scientific discovery." Jason went on to explain the circumstances of Alvin Hayes's death, and how he, Jason, had made it a personal crusade to try to find out if her husband had indeed made a scientific breakthrough. He explained that it would be a tragedy if Alvin had come across something that could help mankind, only to have it lost. Louise nodded, but when Jason asked if she had any idea of what the discovery could have been, she said she didn't.

"You and Alvin didn't speak much?"

"No. Only about the children and financial matters."

"How are your children?" Jason asked, remembering Hayes's concern about his son.

"They are both fine, thank you."

"Two?"

"Yes," Louise said. "Lucy here"—she patted her daughter's head—"and John is in school."

"I thought you had three children."

Jason saw the woman's eyes film over. After an uncomfortable silence she said, "Well . . . there is another. Alvin Junior. He's severely retarded. He lives at a school in Boston."

"I'm sorry."

"It's all right. You'd think I'd have adjusted by now, but I guess I never will. I guess it was the reason Alvin and I got divorced—I couldn't deal with it."

"Where exactly is Alvin Junior?" Jason asked, knowing he was probing a painful area.

"At the Hartford School."

"How is he doing?" Jason knew of the Hartford School. It was an institution acquired by GHP when the corporation purchased an associated acute-care proprietary hospital. Jason also knew the school was for sale. It was a money-loser for GHP.

"Fine, I guess," Louise said. "I'm afraid I don't visit too often. It breaks my heart."

"I understand," Jason said, wondering if this was the son Hayes had been referring to the night he died. "Would it be possible for us to call and inquire how the boy is doing?"

"I suppose," Louise said, not reacting to the extraordinary nature of the question. She got stiffly to her feet and, with her daughter still clinging to her, went to the telephone and called the school. She asked for the pre-teen dormitory and, when they answered, talked for a while about her son's condition. When she hung up, she said, "They feel he's doing as well as can be expected. The only new problem is some arthritis, which has interfered with his physical therapy."

"Has he been there long?"

"Just since Alvin went to work for GHP. Being able to place Alvin Junior at Hartford was one of the reasons he accepted the job."

"And your other son? You say he's fine."

"Couldn't be better," Louise said with obvious pride. "He's in the third grade and considered one of the brightest in the class."

"That's wonderful," Jason said, trying to think back to the night Hayes died. Alvin had said that someone wanted him and his son dead. That it was too late for him but maybe not for his son. What on earth had he meant? Jason had assumed one of his sons had been physically sick, but apparently that was not the case.

"More coffee?" Louise asked.

"No, thank you," Jason said. "There's just one more thing I wanted to ask. At the time of his death, Alvin was involved in setting up a corporation. Your children were to be stockholders. Did you know anything at all about that?"

"Not a thing."

"Oh, well," Jason said. "Thanks for the coffee. If there's anything I can do for you in Boston, like look in on Alvin Junior, don't hesitate to call." He got up and the little girl buried her head in Louise's skirt.

"I hope Alvin didn't suffer," she said.

"No, he didn't," Jason lied. He could still remember the look of agony on Alvin's face.

They were at the door when Louise suddenly said, "Oh, there's one thing I didn't tell you. A few days after Alvin died, someone broke in here. Luckily we were out."

"Was anything taken?" Jason wondered if it could have been Gene, Inc.

"No," Louise said. "They probably saw the usual mess and just moved on." She smiled. "But they seemed to have searched through everything. Even the children's bookcases."

As Jason drove out of Leonia, New Jersey, and made his way back to the George Washington Bridge, he thought about his meeting with Louise Hayes. He should have been more discouraged than he was. After all, he'd learned nothing of importance to have justified the trip. But he realized there had been more to his wanting to go. He'd been genuinely curious about Hayes's wife. Having had his own wife rudely taken away from him, Jason couldn't understand why someone like Hayes would split up voluntarily. But Jason had never experienced the trauma of a retarded child.

Jason was able to catch the two o'clock afternoon shuttle back to Boston. He tried to read on the plane, but couldn't concentrate. He began to worry that Carol wouldn't meet him at the Boston airport, or, worse yet, that she'd show up with Bruno.

Unfortunately, the two o'clock shuttle that was supposed to land in Boston at two-forty didn't even leave La Guardia until two-thirty. By the time Jason got off the plane it was three-fifteen. He got his luggage from the locker and ran from the Eastern terminal over to United.

There was a long line at the ticket window, and Jason couldn't imagine what the airline agents were doing to make each transaction so lengthy. It was now twenty to four and no sign of Carol Donner.

At last it was Jason's turn. He tossed over his American Express card, asking for two round-trip tickets to Seattle for the flight leaving at four, with open returns.

At least with Jason the agent was efficient. Within three minutes Jason had the tickets and boarding cards and was running for Gate 19. It was now five minutes to four. The flight was in the final stages of boarding. Arriving at Gate 19, Jason breathlessly asked if anyone had asked for him. When the girl at the desk said no, he quickly described Carol and asked if the agent had seen her.

"She's very attractive," he added.

"I'm sure she is," smiled the agent. "Unfortunately, I haven't noticed her. But if you are planning to go to Seattle you'd better board."

Jason watched the second hand sweep around the face of the wall clock behind the check-in counter. The agent was busy counting the tickets. Another agent made the final announcement for the departure to Seattle. It was two minutes before four.

With his carry-on bag draped over his shoulder, Jason looked up the concourse toward the terminal proper. At the point he was about to give up all hope, he saw her. She was running in his direction. Jason should have been elated. The only problem was that a few steps behind her was the impressive hulk of Bruno. Farther down the hall was a policeman, lounging at the point where bags were picked up from the X-ray machine. Jason made a mental note: that would be his direction of flight if the need arose.

With her own carry-on shoulder bag, Carol was having some difficulty running. Bruno made no attempt to assist her. Carol came directly up to Jason. Jason saw the expression on Bruno's broad face go from vexation to confusion to anger.

"Did I make it?" she panted.

The agent was now at the door to the jetway, kicking out the doorstop.

"What the hell are *you* doing here, creep?" Bruno shouted, looking up at the destination sign. He turned accusingly on Carol. "You said you were going home, Carol."

"Come on," Carol urged, grasping Jason's arm and pulling him toward the jetway.

Jason stumbled backward, his eyes on Bruno's pudgy face, which had turned an unattractive shade of red. The veins in his temple swelled to the size of cigars.

"Just a moment!" Carol called to the agent. The agent nodded and shouted something down the jetway. Jason watched Bruno until the very last second. He saw him lumber over to a bank of telephones.

"You people like to cut it close," the agent said, ripping off a part of each boarding card. Jason finally turned to face ahead, at last convinced that Bruno had decided not to cause a scene. Carol was still pulling Jason's arm as they descended the jetway. They had to wait while the jetway operator pounded on the side of the plane to get the cabin attendant inside to reopen the already sealed aircraft. "This is about as close as you can make it," he said, frowning.

Once they were seated, Carol apologized for being late. "I'm furious," she said, jamming her carry-on under the seat ahead of her. "I appreciate Arthur's concern for my well-being, but this is ridiculous."

"Who's Arthur?"

"He's my boss," Carol said disgustedly. "He told me if I left now he might actually fire me. I think I'll quit when we get back."

"Would you be able to do that?" Jason asked, wondering just what Carol's work involved besides dancing. It was his understanding that women like Carol lost control of their lives.

"I was planning on stopping soon anyway," said Carol.

The plane lurched as it was towed backward out of the gate.

"You do know what kind of work I do?" Carol asked.

"Well, sort of," Jason said vaguely.

"You've never mentioned it," Carol said. "Most people bring it up."

"I figured it was your business," Jason said. Who was he to judge?

"You're a little strange," Carol said, "likable but strange."

"I thought I was pretty normal," Jason said.

"Ha!" Carol said playfully.

There was a good bit of air traffic and they waited for over twenty minutes before they lifted off the ground and headed west.

"I didn't think we were going to make it," Jason said, finally beginning to relax.

"I'm sorry," Carol said again. "I tried to lose Bruno, but he stuck like glue. I didn't want him to know I wasn't heading back to Indiana. But what could I do?"

"It doesn't matter," Jason said, although in the back of his mind it disturbed him that anyone but Shirley knew where he was going. He'd meant it to be a secret. At the same time he couldn't figure out how it would make any difference.

Taking notes on a yellow pad, Jason began quizzing Carol as to Hayes's schedule on each of his two trips to Seattle. The first visit was the more interesting. They'd stayed at the Mayfair Hotel and among other things had visited a club called the Totem, similar to the Cabaret in Boston. He asked her what it was like.

"It was okay," Carol said, "nothing special. But it didn't have the excitement of the Club Cabaret. Seattle seems a bit conservative."

Jason nodded, wondering why Hayes would waste

his time at a place like that when he was traveling with Carol. "Did Alvin talk to anyone there?" he asked.

"Yes. Arthur arranged for him to speak to the owner."

"Your boss did? Did Alvin know your boss?"

"They were friends. That was how I met Alvin."

Jason recalled the rumors about Alvin's taste for discos and the like. Apparently they'd been true. But the idea of a world-famous molecular biologist being chummy with a man who managed a topless bar seemed ludicrous.

"Do you know what Alvin spoke to this man about?"

"No, I don't," Carol said. "They didn't talk very long. I was busy watching the dancers. They were quite good."

"And you visited the University of Washington, correct?"

"That's right. We did that the first day."

"And you think you can find the man Alvin saw there?" Jason asked, just to be sure.

"I think so. He was a tall, good-looking fellow."

"And then what?"

"We went up into the mountains."

"And that was vacation time?"

"I suppose."

"Did Alvin meet anyone up there?"

"No one in particular. But he talked to a lot of people."

Jason settled back after the cocktail service. He

thought about what Carol had told him, believing the most critical event was the visit to the University of Washington. But the visit to the club was also curious and deserved to be checked out.

"One other thing," Carol said. "On the second trip we had to spend some time looking for dry ice."

"Dry ice? What on earth for?"

"I didn't know and Alvin didn't tell me. Alvin had a cooler and he wanted it full of dry ice."

Perhaps to transport the specimen, Jason thought. *This sounds promising.*

When they touched down in Seattle, they dutifully changed their watches to Pacific Coast time. Jason looked out the airplane window. True to expectations, it was raining. He could see the drops in the darkened pools of water on the runway. Soon, even the window was streaked with moisture.

They rented a car and once they were clear of the airport traffic, Jason said, "In case it helps your memory, I thought we'd stay at the same hotel you did last time. Separate rooms, of course."

Carol turned to eye him in the half-light of the car. Jason wanted it very clear this trip was all business.

Two cars behind Jason and Carol was a dark blue Ford Taurus. Behind the wheel was a middle-aged man dressed in a turtleneck sweater, suede jacket, and checked slacks. He'd gotten a call only about five hours earlier to meet the United flight from Boston. He was supposed to spot a forty-five-year-old doctor who'd be arriving with a beautiful young woman. The names were Howard and Donner, and he was to keep them under surveillance. The operation had been easier than he'd expected. He'd confirmed their identity simply by coming up behind them at the Avis counter.

Now all he had to do was keep them in sight. Supposedly he'd be contacted by somebody who'd be coming from Miami. For this he was being paid his usual fifty dollars an hour plus expenses. He wondered if it were some kind of domestic problem.

The hotel was elegant. Judging from Hayes's usual disheveled appearance, Jason wouldn't have expected the man to have such expensive tastes. They got separate rooms, but Carol insisted they open the connecting door. "Let's not be prudish," she said. Jason didn't know how to take that.

Since they'd barely touched the airplane food, Jason suggested they have dinner before heading out to the Totem Club. Carol changed, and as they entered the dining room, Jason was pleased at how young and lovely she looked. The maître d' even checked her ID when Jason ordered a bottle of California chardonnay. The episode thrilled Carol, who complained of looking as if she were already over the hill at age twenty-five.

By ten P.M., one o'clock East Coast time, they were ready to leave for the Totem Club. Jason was already beginning to feel sleepy, but Carol felt fine. To avoid difficulty, they left the rental car in the hotel parking lot and took a taxi. Carol admitted she had trouble finding the place with Hayes.

The Totem Club was outside of the downtown area of Seattle, on the border of a pleasant residential neighborhood. There was none of the sordid color of the Boston Combat Zone. The club was surrounded by a large asphalt parking area that wasn't even littered, and there were no street people panhandling. It looked like any restaurant or bar, except for several ersatz totem poles flanking the entrance. When Jason got out of the car, he could feel the beat of the rock music. They ran through the rain to the entrance.

Inside, the club seemed much more conservative than the Cabaret. The first thing Jason noticed was that the crowd consisted mostly of couples rather than the heavy-drinking men who lined the runway in Boston. There was even a small dance floor. The only real similarity was the configuration of the bar, which was also U-shaped with a runway for the dancers in the center.

"They don't dance topless here," Carol whispered.

They were shown to a booth on the first level, away from the bar. There was another level behind them. A waitress placed a cardboard coaster in front of each and asked for their drink order.

After they'd been served, Jason asked if Carol saw the owner. At first she didn't, but after a quarter hour she grasped Jason's arm and leaned across the table.

"There he is." She pointed to a young man, probably in his early thirties, dressed in a tuxedo with a red tie and cummerbund. He had olive skin and thick blue-black hair.

"Do you remember his name?"

She shook her head.

Jason eased out from the booth and walked toward the owner, who had a friendly, boyish face. As Jason came up to him, he laughed and patted the back of a man sitting at the bar.

"Excuse me," Jason said. "I'm Dr. Jason Howard. From Boston." The owner turned to him. He wore a plastic smile.

"I'm Sebastion Frahn," the owner said. "Welcome to the Totem."

"Could I speak to you for a moment?"

The man's smile waned. "What's on your mind?"

"It will take a minute or two to explain."

"I'm awfully busy. Maybe later."

Unprepared for such a quick brush-off, Jason stood for a moment watching Frahn move among his customers. His smile had immediately returned.

"Any luck?" Carol asked when Jason returned to their booth and sat down again.

"None. Three thousand miles and the guy won't talk to me."

"People have to be careful in this business. Let me try."

Without waiting for Jason's reply, she slid from the booth. Jason watched her gracefully make her way over to the owner. She touched his arm and spoke briefly. Jason saw him nod, then gaze in his direction. The man nodded again and moved off. Carol returned.

"He'll be over in a minute."

"What did you say?"

"He remembered me," Carol said simply.

Jason wondered what that meant. "Did he remember Hayes?"

"Oh, yes," Carol said. "No problem."

Sure enough, within ten minutes Sebastion Frahn made a swing around the room and stopped at their table.

"Sorry to have been so curt. I didn't know you people were friends."

"That's all right," Jason said. He didn't know exactly what the man meant, but it sounded cordial.

"What can I do for you?"

"Carol says you remember Dr. Hayes."

Sebastion turned to Carol. "Was that the man you were here with last time?" he asked.

Carol nodded.

"Sure I remember him. He was a friend of Arthur Koehler."

"Do you think you could tell me what you talked about? It might be important."

"Jason worked with Alvin," Carol interjected.

"I don't have any problem at all telling you what we discussed. The man wanted to go salmon fishing."

"Fishing!" Jason exclaimed.

"Yup. He said he wanted to catch some big chums but he didn't want to drive too far. I told him to go to Cedar Falls."

"Was that all?" Jason asked, his heart sinking.

"We talked about the Seattle Supersonics for a few minutes."

"Thank you," Jason said. "I appreciate your time."

"Not at all," Sebastion said with a smile. "Well, got to circulate." He stood up, shook hands, and told them to come back again. Then he moved off.

"I can't believe it," Jason said. "Every time I think I have a lead, it turns out to be a joke. Fishing!"

At Carol's request they stayed for another half hour to watch the show, and by the time they got back to the hotel, Jason was totally exhausted. By East Coast time it was four o'clock Thursday morning. Jason got ready for bed and climbed between the sheets with relief. He'd been disappointed by the results of his visit to the Totem Club, but there was still the University of Washington. He was about to drop off to sleep when there was a soft knock on the connecting door. It was Carol. She said she was starving and couldn't sleep. Could they order room service? Feeling obliged to be a good sport, Jason agreed. They ordered a split of champagne and a plate of smoked salmon.

Carol sat on the edge of Jason's bed in a terrycloth robe, eating salmon and crackers. She described her childhood growing up outside of Bloomington, Indiana. Jason had never heard her talk so much. She'd lived on a farm and had to milk cows before going to school in the morning. Jason could see her doing that. She had that freshness about her that suggested such a life. What he had trouble with was relating that former life to her current one. He wanted to know how things got on the wrong track, but he was afraid to ask. Besides, exhaustion took over and try as he might, he could not keep his eyes open. He fell asleep and Carol, after covering him with a blanket, returned to her own room.

13.

Awakening with a start, Jason checked his watch, which said five A.M. That meant eight in Boston, the time he usually left for the hospital. He opened the drapes and looked out on a crystal-clear day. In the distance a ferry was making its way across Puget Sound toward Seattle, leaving a sparkling wake.

After showering, Jason knocked on the adjoining door. There was no answer. He knocked again. Finally he opened it a crack, allowing a swath of bright sunlight to fall into the cool, darkened room. Carol was still fast asleep, clutching her pillow. Jason watched her for a moment. She looked angelically lovely. Silently, he closed the door so as to not waken her.

He went back to his bed, dialed room service, and ordered fresh orange juice, coffee, and croissants for two. Then he called GHP and paged Roger Wanamaker.

"Everything okay?"

"Not quite," Roger admitted. "Marge Todd threw

a big embolus last night. She went into a coma and died. Respiratory arrest."

"My God," Jason said.

"Sorry to be the bearer of sad tidings," Roger said. "Try to enjoy yourself."

"I'll give you a call in a day or so," Jason said.

Another death. Except for one young woman with hepatitis, he was beginning to think the only way his patients could leave the hospital was feetfirst. He wondered if he should fly directly back to Boston. Yet Roger was right. There was nothing he could do, and he might as well see the Hayes business through, even though he wasn't very optimistic.

Two hours later Carol knocked at the door and came in, her hair still wet from the shower. "Top of the morning," she said in her cheerful voice. Jason ordered fresh coffee.

"Guess we're lucky," he said, pointing out at the bright sunlight.

"Don't be so sure. The weather around here can change mighty quickly."

While Carol breakfasted, Jason had another cup of coffee.

"Hope I didn't talk your ear off last night," Carol said.

"Don't be silly. I'm sorry I fell asleep."

"What about you, doctor?" Carol asked, putting jam on a croissant. "You haven't told me much about yourself." She didn't mention that Hayes had told her a good deal about him.

"Not much to tell."

Carol raised her eyebrows. When she saw his smile, she laughed. "For a second I thought you were serious."

Jason told Carol about his boyhood in Los Angeles, his education at Berkeley and Harvard Medical School, and his residency at Massachusetts General. Without meaning to, he found himself describing Danielle and the awful November night when she'd been killed. No one had ever drawn him out the way Carol did, not even Patrick, the psychiatrist he'd seen after Danielle's death. Jason even heard himself describing his current depression over his increased patient mortality and then Roger's news that morning about Marge Todd's death.

"I'm flattered that you've told me this," Carol said sincerely. She hadn't expected such openness and trust. "You've had a lot of emotional pain."

"Life can be like that," Jason said with a sigh. "I don't know why I've bored you with all this."

"It hasn't been boring," Carol said. "I think you've made an extraordinary adjustment. I think it was difficult yet very positive that you changed your work and living environment."

"Do you?" Jason asked. He hadn't remembered saying that. He hadn't expected to be so personal with Carol, but now that he'd done so, he felt better.

Enjoying their time together, it wasn't until ten-thirty that they emerged from their respective rooms dressed for the day. Jason asked the bellman to bring their car to the front entrance, and they took the elevator down to the lobby. True to Carol's prediction, when they emerged from the hotel the sky had darkened and a steady rain was falling.

With the help of an Avis map and Carol's memory, they drove out to the University of Washington's Medical School. Carol pointed out the research building Hayes had visited. They went in the front entrance and were immediately challenged by a uniformed security man. They had no University of Washington identity badges.

"I'm a doctor from Boston," Jason said, removing his wallet to show his ID.

"Hey, man, I don't care where you're from. No badge, no entry. Simple as that. If you want to come in here, you have to go to Central Administration."

Seeing it was fruitless to argue, they went to Central Administration. En route, Jason asked how Hayes had handled security.

"He called his friend beforehand," Carol said. "The man met us in the parking lot."

The woman at Central Administration was friendly and accommodating, and even showed Carol a faculty book to see if she could pick out Hayes's friend. But faces weren't enough, and Carol couldn't identify him. Instead, armed with security badges, they returned to the research building.

Carol led Jason up to the fifth floor. The corridor

was crowded with spare equipment, and the walls were in need of fresh paint. There was a pungent chemical smell, akin to formaldehyde.

"Here's the lab," Carol said, stopping by an open doorway. The names to the left of the door were Duncan Sechler, MD, PhD; and Rhett Shannon, MD, PhD. The department was, as Jason might have guessed, molecular genetics.

"Which name?" Jason asked.

"I don't know," Carol said, going up to a young technician and asking if either of the doctors was in.

"Both. They're in the animal room." He pointed over his shoulder, then turned as Carol walked by so he could catch the view from the rear. Jason was surprised by his blatancy.

The door to the animal room had a large glass panel. Inside were two men in white coats drawing blood from a monkey.

"It was the tall one with the gray hair," Carol said, pointing. Jason moved closer to the window. The man Carol indicated was handsome and athletic appearing, of approximately Jason's age. His hair was a uniform silver color that gave him a particularly distinguished look. The other man, in contrast, was almost bald. What hair he had was combed over the top of his head in a vain attempt to cover the thinning spot.

"Will he remember you?"

"Possibly. We only met for a moment before I went off to the Psychology Department."

They waited until the doctors finished their task and emerged from the animal room. The tall gray-haired man was carrying the vial of blood.

"Excuse me," Jason said. "Could I possibly have a moment of your time?"

The man glanced at Jason's badge. "Are you a drug rep?"

"Heavens, no." Jason smiled. "I'm Dr. Jason Howard and this is Miss Carol Donner."

"What can I do for you?"

"I'll see you in a minute, Duncan," interrupted the balding man.

"Okay," Duncan said. "I'll run the blood immediately." Then, turning to Jason, he said, "Sorry."

"Quite all right. I wanted to talk to you about an old acquaintance."

"Oh?"

"Alvin Hayes. Do you remember him visiting you here?"

"Sure," Duncan said, turning to Carol. "And weren't you with him?"

Carol nodded. "You have a good memory."

"I was shocked to hear he'd died. What a loss."

"Carol said Hayes came to ask you something important," Jason said. "Could you tell me what it was about?"

Duncan looked upset, glancing nervously around at the technicians.

"I'm not sure I want to talk about it."

"I'm sorry to hear that. Was it business or a personal matter?"

"Maybe you'd better come into my office."

Jason had trouble containing his excitement. It finally sounded as if he'd stumbled onto something significant.

After entering the office, Duncan closed the door. There were two metal-backed chairs. Removing stacks of journals, he motioned for Jason and Carol to sit.

"To answer your question," he said, "Hayes came to see me for personal reasons, not business."

"We've come three thousand miles just to talk with you," Jason said. He wasn't going to give up so easily, but it wasn't sounding encouraging.

"If you'd called, I could have saved you the trip." Some of Duncan's friendliness had disappeared from his voice.

"Maybe I should tell you why we are so interested," Jason said. He explained the mystery of Hayes's possible discovery and his own futile attempts to figure out what it might have been.

"You think Hayes came to me for help in his research?" Duncan asked.

"That's what I'd hoped."

Duncan gave a short, unpleasant laugh. He looked at Jason out of the corner of his eye. "You wouldn't be a narc, would you?"

Jason was confused.

"All right, I'll tell you what Hayes wanted. A place to buy marijuana. He said he was terrified to fly with the stuff and couldn't bring any with him. As a favor, I set him up with a kid on campus."

Jason was stunned. His excitement dwindled like air seeping out of a balloon, leaving him deflated.

"I'm sorry to have taken your time. . . ."

"Not at all."

Carol and Jason walked out of the research building, surrendering their visitor's badges to the security guard. Carol was smiling slyly.

"It isn't so funny, you know," Jason said as they got into the car.

"But it is," Carol said. "You just can't see it right at this moment."

"We might as well go home," he said gloomily.

"Oh, no! You dragged me all the way out here, and we're not leaving until you see the mountains. It's only a short drive."

"Let me think about it," Jason told her moodily.

Carol prevailed. They went back to the hotel, got their belongings, and before Jason knew it, they were on a freeway heading out of town. She insisted on driving. Soon the suburbs gave way to misty green forest, and the rolling hills became mountains. The rain stopped and Jason could see snowcapped peaks in the distance. The scenery was so beautiful he forgot his disappointment.

"It gets even prettier," Carol said as they left the freeway, heading toward Cedar Falls. She remembered the route now and happily pointed out the sights. Taking an even smaller road, Carol drove along the Cedar River.

It was a nature fairyland, with deep forests, craggy rocks, distant mountains, and rushing rivers. As dusk fell, Carol turned off the road and bumped across a crushed stone driveway, coming to a halt in front of a picturesque mountain lodge constructed like an enormous five-story log cabin. Smoke curled up lazily from a huge fieldstone chimney. A sign over the steps leading to the porch said SALMON INN.

"Is this where you and Alvin stayed?" Jason asked, peering through the windshield. There was a huge porch with raw pine furniture.

"This is it." Carol reached around to get her bag from the back seat.

They got out of the car. There was a chill to the air and the pungent smell of woodsmoke. Jason heard a distant sound of rushing water.

"The river's on the other side of the lodge," Carol said, mounting the steps. "Just a little way up there's a cute waterfall. You'll see it tomorrow."

Jason followed her, suddenly wondering what the hell he was doing. The trip had been a mistake; he belonged back in Boston with his critically ill patients. Yet here he was in the Cascade Mountains with a girl he had no business admiring.

The interior of the inn was every bit as charming as the exterior. The central room was a large, two-story affair dominated by a gargantuan fireplace. It was furnished with chintz, animal heads, and scattered bearskin rugs. There were several people reading in front of the fire and a family playing Scrabble.

A few heads turned as Jason and Carol approached the registration desk.

"Do you people have a reservation?" asked the man behind the desk.

Jason wondered if the man was joking. The place was immense, it was in the middle of nowhere, it was early November, and it wasn't a weekend. He couldn't imagine the demand would be very high.

"No reservations," Carol said. "Is that a problem?"

"Let me see," said the man, bending over his book.

"How many rooms are there in the hotel?" Jason asked, still bemused.

"Forty-two and six suites," the receptionist said without looking up.

"Is there a shoe convention in town?"

The man laughed. "It's always full this time of year. The salmon are running."

Jason had heard of the Pacific salmon and how they'd mysteriously return to the particular freshwater breeding grounds that had spawned them. But he'd thought the phenomenon occurred in the spring.

"You're in luck," the receptionist said. "We have a room, but you might have to move tomorrow night. How many nights are you planning to stay?"

Carol looked at Jason. Jason felt a rush of anxiety—only one room! He didn't know what to say. He started to stammer.

"Three nights," Carol said.

"Fine. And how will you settle your bill?"

There was a pause.

"Credit card," Jason said, fumbling for his wallet. He couldn't believe what was happening.

As they followed the bellboy down the second-floor hallway, Jason wondered how he'd gotten himself into this. He hoped there would at least be twin beds. Much as he admired Carol's looks, he wasn't prepared for an affair with an exotic dancer who did God knows what else on the side.

"You people have a wonderful view," the bellboy said.

Jason went in, but his eyes shifted immediately to the sleeping arrangements, not the windows. He was relieved to see separate beds.

When the boy left, Jason finally went over to admire the dramatic vista. The Cedar River, which at that point widened to what appeared to be a small lake, was bordered by tall evergreens that glowed a dark purple in the fading light. Immediately below was a lawn that sloped down to the water's edge. Extending out into the river was a maze of docks used to moor twenty to thirty rowboats. On racks, out of the water, were canoes. Four large rubber boats with outboard motors were tied to the end of a dock. Jason could tell there was a significant current in the river despite its placid appearance, since all four of the rubber boats had their sterns pointed downriver, their bowlines taut.

"Well, what do you think?" Carol said, clapping her hands. "Isn't it cozy?"

The room was papered with a flower print. The

floor was broad-planked pine with scattered rag rugs. The beds were covered with comforters printed to appear like quilts.

"It's wonderful," Jason said. He glanced into the bathroom, hoping for robes. "You seem to be the tour director. What now?"

"I vote for dinner immediately. I'm starved. And I think the dining room only serves until seven. People turn in early here."

The restaurant had a curved, windowed wall facing the river. In the center of the wall were double doors leading to a wide porch. Jason guessed that in the summer the porch was used for dining. There were steps from the porch down to the lawn, and at the docks the lights had come on, illuminating the water.

About half of the two dozen tables in the room were filled. Most of the people were already on their coffee. It seemed to Jason that everyone stopped talking the moment he and Carol appeared.

"Why do I feel we're on display?" Jason whispered.

"Because you're anxious about sleeping in the same room with a young woman whom you barely know," Carol whispered. "I think you feel defensive and a little guilty and unsure of what's expected of you."

Jason's lower jaw slowly sank. He tried to look into Carol's warmly liquid eyes to comprehend what was in there. He knew he was blushing. How on earth could a girl who danced half nude be so perceptive? Jason had always prided himself on his ability to evaluate people: after all, it was his job. As a physician, he had to have a sense of his patients' inner dynamics. Yet why did he feel there was something about Carol that didn't fit?

Glancing at Jason's red face, Carol laughed. "Why don't you just relax and enjoy yourself. Let down your hair, doctor—I'm certainly not going to bite."

"Okay," Jason said. "I'll do just that."

They dined on salmon, which was offered in bewilderingly tempting varieties. After great deliberation, they both had it baked in a pastry shell. For authenticity, they sampled a Washington State chardonnay which Jason found surprisingly good. At one point he heard himself laughing aloud. It had been a long time since he'd felt so free. It was at that point they both realized they were alone in the dining room.

Later that night when Jason was in bed, looking up at the dark ceiling, he again felt confused. It had been a comedy of sorts getting to bed, juggling towels as coverups, flipping a coin to see who used the bathroom first, and having to get out of bed to turn out the light. Jason had never remembered feeling quite so body conscious. Jason rolled over. In the darkness, he could just make out the outline of Carol's form. She was on her side. He could hear the faint sound of her rhythmical breathing against the background sound of the distant waterfall. She was obviously asleep. Jason envied her honest acceptance of herself and her untroubled slumber. But what confused Jason was not the inconsistencies of Carol's personality, but rather the fact that he was enjoying himself. And it was Carol who was making it happen.

14.

Weatherwise, their luck held. When they opened the drapes in the morning, the river sparkled with the brilliance of a million gemstones. The minute they finished breakfast, Carol announced they were going on a hike.

With box lunches from the hotel, they walked up the Cedar River on a well-marked trail alive with birds and small animals. About a quarter of a mile from the lodge they came upon the waterfall Carol had mentioned. It was a series of rocky ledges, each about five feet high. They joined several other tourists on a wooden viewing platform and watched in awed silence as the wild water cascaded downward. Just below them, a magnificent rainbow-colored fish, three to four feet long, broke the turbulent surface of the water, and in defiance of gravity leaped up the face of the first ledge. Within seconds it had leaped again, clearing the second ledge by a wide margin.

"My God," Jason exclaimed. He'd remembered reading that salmon were capable of running through rapids against the current, but he had no idea that they could navigate such high falls. Jason and Carol stayed mesmerized as several other salmon leaped. He could only marvel at the physical stamina the fish were displaying. The genetically determined urge to procreate was a powerful force.

"It's unbelievable," he said as a particularly large fish began to swim the watery gauntlet.

"Alvin was fascinated too," Carol said.

Jason could well imagine, especially with Hayes's interest in developmental and growth hormones.

"Come on," Carol said, taking Jason's hand. "There's more."

They continued up the trail, which left the river's edge for a quarter of a mile, taking them deep into a forest. When the trail returned to the river, the Cedar had widened into another small lake like the one in front of the Salmon Inn. It was about a quarter of a mile across and a mile long, and its surface was dotted with fishermen.

A cabin much like a miniature Salmon Inn lay nestled in a stand of large pines. In front of it at the water's edge was a short dock with half a dozen rowboats. Carol took Jason up the flagstone walk and through the front door.

The cabin was a fishing concession run by the Salmon Inn. There was a long, glass-fronted counter to the right, presided over by a bearded man in a red-checkered wool shirt, red suspenders, faded trousers, and caulked boots. Jason guessed he was in his late sixties, and that he would have made a perfect department store Santa Claus. Arranged along the wall behind him was an enormous selection of fishing poles. Carol introduced Jason to the older man, whose name was Stooky Griffiths, saying that Alvin had enjoyed visiting with Stooky while she fished.

"Hey," Carol said suddenly. "How about trying your hand at some salmon fishing?"

"Not for me," Jason said. Hunting and fishing had never interested him.

"I think I'll try. Come on—be a sport."

"You go ahead," Jason urged. "I can entertain myself."

"Okay." She turned to Stooky and made arrangements for a pole and some bait, then tried once more to talk Jason into joining her, but he shook his head.

"Is this where you and Alvin fished?" he asked, looking out the window at the river.

"Nope," Carol said, collecting her gear. "Alvin was like you. He wouldn't join me. But I caught a big one. Right off the dock."

"Alvin didn't fish at all?" Jason asked, surprised.

"No," said Carol. "He just watched the fish."

"I thought Alvin told Sebastion Frahn he wanted to go fishing."

"What can I say? Once we got here, Alvin was content to wander around and observe. You know, the scientist."

Jason shook his head in confusion.

"I'll be on the dock," Carol said brightly. "If you change your mind, come on down. It's fun!"

Jason watched her run down the flagstone walk, wondering why Alvin would have made such elaborate inquiries about fishing and then never cast a line. It was weird.

Two men came into the cabin and made arrangements with Stooky for gear, bait, and a boat. Jason stepped outside onto the porch. There were several rocking chairs. Stooky had hung a bird feeder from the eaves and dozens of birds circled it. Jason watched for a while, then wandered down to join Carol. The water was crystal clear and he could see rocks and leaves on the bottom. Suddenly, a huge salmon flashed out of the dark emerald green of the deeper water and shot under the dock, heading for a shallow, shady area fifty feet away.

Looking after it, Jason noticed a disturbance on the surface of the water. Curious, he walked over along the shore. When he got close, he saw another large salmon lying on its side in a few feet of water, its tail flapping weakly. Jason tried pushing it with a stick into deeper water, but it didn't help. The fish was obviously ill. A few feet away he spotted another salmon lying immobile in just a few inches of water, and, still closer to shore, a dead fish being eaten by a large bird.

Jason walked back up the flagstone path. Stooky had come out of the cabin and was sitting in one of the rockers with a pipe stuck between his teeth.

Leaning on the rail, Jason asked him about the sick fish, wondering if there was some problem with pollution upriver.

"Nope," Stooky said. He took several puffs on his well-chewed pipe. "No pollution here. Them fish just spawned and now it's time for 'em to die."

"Oh, yeah," Jason said, suddenly remembering what he'd read about the salmon's life cycle. The fish pushed themselves to their limits to return to their spawning grounds, but once they laid their eggs and fertilized them, they died. No one knew exactly why. There had been theories about the physiological problems of going from saltwater to freshwater, but no one knew for certain. It was one of nature's mysteries.

Jason looked down at Carol. She was busy trying to cast her line out from the dock. Turning back to Stooky, he asked, "Do you by any chance remember talking with a doctor by the name of Alvin Hayes?"

"Nope."

"He was about my height," Jason continued. "Had long hair. Pale skin."

"I see a lot of people."

"I bet you do," Jason said. "But the man I'm talking about was with that girl." He pointed toward Carol. Jason guessed Stooky didn't see too many girls who looked like Carol Donner.

"The one on the dock?"

"That's right. She's a looker."

Smoke came out of Stooky's mouth in short puffs.

His eyes narrowed. "Could the fella you're talking about come from Boston?"

Jason nodded.

"I remember him," Stooky said. "But he didn't look like no doctor."

"He did research."

"Maybe that explains it. He was real strange. Paid me a hundred bucks to get him twenty-five salmon heads."

"Just the heads?"

"Yup. Gave me his telephone number back in Boston. Told me to call collect when I had 'em."

"Then he came back here to get them?" Jason asked, remembering Hayes and Carol had made two trips.

"Yup. Told me to clean 'em good and pack 'em in ice."

"Why did it take so long?" Jason asked. With all the fish available, it seemed twenty-five heads could have been collected in a single afternoon.

"He only wanted certain salmon," Stooky said. "They had to have just spawned—and spawning salmon don't take bait. You have to net 'em. Them people fishing out there are catching trout."

"A particular species of salmon?"

"Nope. They'd just had to have spawned."

"Did he say why he wanted those heads?"

"He didn't and I didn't ask," Stooky said. "He was payin' and I figured it was his business."

"And just fishheads—nothing else."

"Just fishheads."

Jason left the porch frustrated and mystified. The idea that Hayes had come three thousand miles for fishheads and marijuana seemed preposterous.

Carol spotted him at the edge of the dock and waved at him to join her.

"You have to try this, Jason," she said. "I almost caught a salmon."

"The salmon don't bite here," Jason said. "It must have been a trout."

Carol looked disappointed.

Jason studied her lovely, high-cheekboned face. If his original premise was correct, the salmon heads had to have been associated with Hayes's attempts to create a monoclonal antibody. But how could that help Carol's beauty as Hayes had told her? It didn't make any sense.

"I guess it doesn't matter whether it's trout or salmon," Carol said, turning her attention back to her fishing. "I'm having fun."

A circling hawk plunged down into the shallow water and tried to grasp one of the dying salmon with its talons, but the fish was too big and the bird let go and soared back into the sky. As Jason watched, the salmon stopped struggling in the water and died.

"I got one!" Carol cried as her pole arched over.

The excitement of the catch cleared Jason's mind. He helped Carol land a good-sized trout—a beautiful fish with steely black eyes. Jason felt sorry for it. After he'd gotten the hook out of its lower lip, he talked Carol into throwing it back into the water. It was gone in a flash.

For lunch they walked along the banks of the widened river to a rocky promontory. As they ate, they could not only see the entire expanse of the river, but the snow-capped peaks of the Cascade Mountains. It was breathtaking.

It was late afternoon when they started back to the Salmon Inn. As they passed the cabin they saw another large fish in its death throes. It was on its side, its glistening white belly visible.

"How sad," Carol said, gripping Jason's arm. "Why do they have to die?"

Jason didn't have any answers. The old cliché, "It's nature's way," occurred to him, but he didn't say it. For a few moments they watched the once magnificent salmon as several smaller fish darted over to feed on its living flesh.

"Ugh!" Carol said, giving Jason's arm a tug. They continued walking. To change the subject, Carol started talking about another diversion the hotel had to offer. It was white-water rafting. But Jason didn't hear. The horrid image of the tiny predators feeding from the dying larger fish had started the germ of an idea in Jason's mind. Suddenly, like a revelation, he had a sense of what Hayes had discovered. It wasn't ironic—it was terrifying.

The color drained from Jason's face and he stopped walking.

"What's the matter?" Carol asked.

Jason swallowed. His eyes stared, unblinking.

"Jason, what is it?"

"We have to get back to Boston," he said with urgency in his voice. He set off again at a fast pace, almost dragging Carol with him.

"What are you talking about?" she protested.

He didn't respond.

"Jason! What's going on?" She jerked him to a stop.

"I'm sorry," he said, as if waking from a trance. "I suddenly have an idea of what Alvin may have stumbled onto. We have to get back."

"What do you mean—tonight?"

"Right away."

"Now wait just a minute. There won't be any flights to Boston tonight. It's three hours later there. We can stay over and leave early in the morning if you insist."

Jason didn't reply.

"At least we can have dinner," Carol added irritably.

Jason allowed her to calm him down. *After all, who knows? I could be wrong,* he thought. Carol wanted to discuss it, but Jason told her she wouldn't understand.

"That's pretty patronizing."

"I'm sorry. I'll tell you all about it when I know for sure."

By the time he had showered and dressed, Jason

realized Carol was right. If they'd driven to Seattle, they'd have gotten to the airport around midnight Boston time. There wouldn't have been any flights until morning.

Descending to the dining room, they were escorted to a table directly in front of the doors leading to the veranda. Jason sat Carol facing the doors, saying she deserved the view. After they'd been given their menu, he apologized for acting so upset and gave her full credit for being right about not leaving immediately.

"I'm impressed you're willing to admit it," Carol said.

For variety, they ordered trout instead of salmon, and in place of the Washington state wine, they had a Napa Valley chardonnay. Outside, the evening slowly darkened into night and the lights went on at the docks.

Jason had trouble concentrating on the meal. He was beginning to realize that if his theory was correct, Hayes had been murdered and Helene had not been the victim of random violence. And if Hayes was right and someone was using his accidental and terrifying discovery, the result could be far worse than any epidemic.

While Jason's mind was churning, Carol was carrying on a conversation, but when she realized he was off someplace, she reached across and gripped his arm. "You are not eating," she said.

Jason looked absently at her hand on his arm, his

plate, and then Carol. "I'm preoccupied, I'm sorry."

"It doesn't matter. If you're not hungry, maybe we should go and find out about flights to Boston in the morning."

"We can wait until you're through eating," Jason said.

Carol tossed her napkin on the table. "I've had more than enough, thank you."

Jason looked for their waiter. His eyes roamed the room and then stopped. They became riveted on a man who had just entered the dining room and paused by the maître d's lectern. The man was slowly scanning the room, his eyes moving from table to table. He was dressed in a dark blue suit with a white shirt open at the collar. Even from the distance, Jason could tell the man wore a heavy gold necklace. He could see the sparkle from the overhead lights.

Jason studied the man. He looked familiar, but Jason couldn't place him. He was Hispanic, with dark hair and deeply tanned skin. He looked like a successful businessman. Suddenly, Jason remembered. He'd seen the face on that awful night when Hayes had died. The man had been outside the restaurant and then outside the Massachusetts General Hospital emergency room.

Just then the man spotted Jason, and Jason felt a sudden chill descend his spine. It was apparent the man recognized Jason because he immediately started forward, his right hand casually thrust into his jacket pocket. He walked deliberately, closing the distance quickly. Having just thought of Helen Brennquivist's murder, Jason panicked. His intuition told him what was coming, but he couldn't move. All he could do was look at Carol. He wanted to scream and tell her to run, but he couldn't. He was paralyzed. Out of the corner of his eye, he saw the man round the nearby table.

"Jason?" questioned Carol, tilting her head to one side.

The man was only steps away. Jason saw his hand come out of his pocket and the glint of metal as his hand covered the gun. The sight of the weapon finally galvanized Jason into action. In a sudden explosion of activity, he snatched the tablecloth from the table, sending the dishes, glasses, and silverware flying to the floor. Carol leaped to her feet with a scream.

Jason rushed the man, flinging the tablecloth over his head, pushing him backward into a neighboring table and knocking it over in a shower of china and glass. The people at the table screamed and tried to get away, but several were caught in the tangle of overturned chairs.

In the commotion, Jason grabbed Carol's hand and yanked her through the doors to the porch. Having managed to break his panic-filled paralysis, Jason was now a torrent of directed action. He knew who the Hispanic-looking businessman had been: the killer Hayes claimed was on his trail. Jason had no doubt his next targets were Carol and himself.

He pulled Carol down the front steps, intending to run around the hotel to the parking lot. But then he realized they'd never make it. They had a better chance running for one of the boats at the dock.

"Jason!" Carol yelled as he changed direction and dragged him down the lawn. "What's wrong with you?"

Behind them, Jason could hear the doors to the dining room crash open, and assumed they were being chased.

When they reached the dock, Carol tried to stop. "Come on, dammit," Jason shouted through gritted teeth. Looking back at the inn, he could see a figure run to the porch railing, then start down the stairs.

Carol tried to jerk her hand free, but Jason tightened his clasp and yanked her forward. "He wants to kill us!" he shouted. Stumbling ahead, they raced to the end of the dock, ignoring the rowboats. Jason shouted to Carol to help untie three of the rubber boats and push them off. They were already drifting downstream by the time their pursuer hit the dock. Jason helped Carol into the fourth boat and scrambled after her, pushing them away from the dock with his foot. They too drifted downstream, slowly at first, then gathering speed. Jason forced Carol to lie down, then covered her body with his own.

An innocent-sounding pop was immediately followed by a dull thud somewhere in the boat. Almost simultaneously there was the sound of escaping air. Jason groaned. The man was shooting at them with a silenced pistol. Another pop was followed by a ringing sound as a bullet ricocheted off the outboard motor, and another made a slapping sound in the water.

To Jason's relief, he realized the rubber boat was compartmentalized. Although a bullet had deflated one section, the boat wouldn't sink. A few more shots fell short, then Jason heard a thump of wood against the dock. Jason lifted his head cautiously and looked back. The man had pulled one of the canoes from the rack and was pushing it into the water.

Jason was again gripped with fear—the man could paddle much faster than they were drifting. Their only chance was to start the motor—an old-fashioned outboard with a pull cord. Jason shifted the gear lever to "start" and tugged the cord. The engine didn't even turn over. The killer had already boarded the canoe and was starting toward them. Jason pulled the cord again: nothing. Carol lifted her head and said nervously, "He's getting closer."

For the next fifteen seconds, Jason frantically jerked the starter cord over and over. He could see the silhouette of the oncoming canoe moving silently through the water. He checked to make sure the lever was at "start," then tried again without success. His eyes drifted to the gas tank, which he prayed was full. Its black cap appeared to be loose, so he tightened it. Just to its side was a button he guessed was to increase pressure in the tank. He pushed it a half dozen times, noticing that it became increasingly harder to depress. Looking up again, he saw the canoe was almost to them.

Grasping the starter cord again, Jason pulled with all his strength. The motor roared to life. Then he reached for the lever and pushed it to "reverse," as they were floating downstream backward. He jammed the throttle forward and threw himself back onto the bottom of the boat, pinning Carol beneath him. As expected, there were several more shots, two of which hit the rubber boat. When Jason dared to look out again, the gap had widened. In the darkness, he could barely see the canoe.

"Stay down," he commanded to Carol, while he checked the extent of the damage. A section of the right side of the bow was soft, as was a portion of the left gunwale. Otherwise the boat was intact. Moving back to the outboard, Jason cut the throttle, put the motor into "forward," then angled the tiller to head downstream, steering out to the center of the river. The last thing he wanted to do was hit rocks.

"Okay," he called to Carol. "It's safe to sit up."

Carol rose gingerly from the bottom of the boat and ran her fingers through her hair. "I really don't believe this," she shouted over the noise of the outboard. "Just what the hell are we going to do?"

"We'll head downriver until we see some lights. There's got to be plenty of places along here."

As they motored along, Jason wondered if it would be safe to stop at another dock. After all, their pursuer might get into his car and drive along the river. *Maybe there's a light on the opposite side,* he thought.

From the silhouettes of the trees lining the lakelike expanse of the river, Jason could gauge their speed. It seemed to be about a fast walk. He also had the feeling the river was again gradually narrowing, especially when it appeared that their speed was increasing. After a half hour, there were still no lights. Just a dark forest bordering a star-strewn, moonless sky.

"I don't see a thing," yelled Carol.

"It's okay," reassured Jason.

After traveling another quarter hour, the bordering trees closed in rather suddenly, suggesting the lakelike expanse was coming to an end. When the trees were closer, Jason realized he had misjudged their speed; they were moving much faster than he'd thought. Reaching back he cut the throttle. The small outboard whined down. As soon as the sound of the outboard fell, Jason heard another more ominous noise. It was the deep growling roar of white water.

"Oh, God," he said to himself, remembering the falls upriver from the Salmon Inn. He pushed the small outboard to the side and turned the boat around. Then he gave it full throttle. To his surprise and consternation, it slowed, but did not stop their rush downriver. Next he tried to angle the boat toward shore. Slowly, it moved laterally. But then all hell broke loose. The river narrowed to a rocky gorge, and Jason and Carol were unwittingly sucked into it.

Around the top edge of the rubber boat was a short rope secured at intervals by eyelets. Jason grabbed a hold on either side, spanning the craft with his outstretched arms. He yelled for Carol to do the same. She couldn't hear over the roar of the water, but when she saw what he was doing, she attempted to do the same. Unfortunately, she couldn't quite reach. She held on to one side and hooked a leg under one of the wooden seats. At that moment, they hit the first real turbulence, and the boat was tossed into the air like a cork. Water came into the boat in a blinding, drenching sheet. Jason sputtered. The darkness and water in his eyes made it all but impossible to see. He felt Carol's body hit up against his and he tried to anchor her with his leg. Then they thudded into a rock and the boat spun counterclockwise. Through all this violent activity, Jason kept seeing the image of the falls, knowing that at any second they could plummet to their death.

Jason and Carol clutched at the ropes in utter terror. They bounced from side to side and end to end, in rapid gyrations, completely at the mercy of the water. At every moment he thought they were going over. Water filled the cockpit. It was stingingly cold.

After what seemed like an eternity of hell, the water smoothed out. They were still spinning and careening downriver, but without the sudden violent upheavals. Jason glanced out. He could make out the sheer falls of rock on either side. He knew it wasn't over.

With a tremendous upward surge, the violent dubbing recommenced. Jason could feel his fingers begin to pain him; a combination of constant muscular contraction and the cold was having its effect. He gripped the rope holds with all his strength, trying to tighten his hold on Carol with his legs. The pain in his hands was so intense that for an instant he thought he'd have to let go.

Then, as suddenly as the nightmare began, it was over. Still spinning, the boat shot out onto relatively placid water. The thundering noise of the rapids lessened. The sides of the river fell away, opening up a clear view to the starry sky. Inside the boat there was a half foot of icy water, but Jason realized the outboard was chugging as smoothly as if nothing had happened.

With shaking hands, Jason straightened the boat and stopped its nauseating rotation. His fingers touched a button just inside the transom. He took a chance and pressed it; the water in the boat slowly receded.

Jason kept his eye on the silhouettes of the bordering trees. Ahead, the river bent sharply to the left, and as they rounded the point, they finally saw lights. Jason steered to shore.

As they approached, he could see several well-lit

buildings, docks, and a number of rubber boats like their own. He was still afraid the killer might have driven down to intercept them, but he knew they had to land. Jason pulled alongside the second dock and cut the engine.

"You sure know how to entertain a girl," Carol said through chattering teeth.

"I'm glad you still have your sense of humor," Jason said.

"Don't count on it lasting much longer. I want to know what in heaven's name is going on."

Jason stood up stiffly, holding on to the dock. He helped Carol out of the boat, got out himself, and tied the line to a cleat. The sound of country music drifted from one of the buildings.

"It must be a bar," said Jason. He took her hand. "We have to get warm before we get pneumonia." Jason led the way up the gravel path, but instead of going inside, he walked into the parking lot and began looking in the parked vehicles.

"Hold on," said Carol with irritation. "What are you doing now?"

"I'm looking for keys," Jason said. "We need a car."

"I don't believe this," said Carol, throwing up her hands. "I thought we were going to get warm. I don't know about you, but I'm going in that restaurant." Without waiting for a response, she started for the entrance.

Jason caught up to her and grabbed her arm. "I'm

afraid he'll be back—the man who was shooting at us."

"Then we'll call the police," Carol said. She pulled out of Jason's grasp and entered the restaurant.

The Hispanic was not in the restaurant, so, following Carol's suggestion, they called the police, who happened to be a local sheriff. The proprietor of the restaurant refused to believe that Jason and Carol had navigated Devil's Chute in the dark— "Nobody ain't done that before," he said. He found chef's smocks and oversized black and white checkered kitchen pants for them to change into, and a plastic garbage bag for their wet clothes. He also insisted they have steaming hot rum toddies, which finally stopped their shivering.

"Jason, you've got to tell me what's going on," Carol insisted as they waited for the sheriff. They sat at a table across from a Wurlitzer jukebox playing fifties music.

"I don't know for sure," Jason said. "But the man shooting at us was outside the restaurant where Alvin died. My guess is that Alvin was a victim of his own discovery, but if he hadn't died that night, the same man would have eventually killed him anyway. So Alvin was telling the truth when he said someone wanted him dead."

"This doesn't sound real," Carol said, trying to smooth her hair, which was drying in tangled ringlets.

"I know. Most conspiracies don't."

"What about Hayes's discovery?"

"I don't know for sure, but if my theory is right, it's almost too scary to contemplate. That's why I want to get back to Boston."

Just then the door opened and the sheriff, Marvin Arnold, walked in. He was a mountain of a man dressed in a wrinkled brown uniform that sported more buckles and straps than Jason had ever seen. More important to Jason was the .357 Magnum strapped to Marvin's oversized left thigh. That was the kind of cannon Jason wished he'd had back at the Salmon Inn.

Marvin had already heard about the commotion at the Salmon Inn, and had been there to check things out. What he hadn't heard about was any man with a gun, and no one had heard any gunshots. When Jason described what had happened, he could tell that Marvin regarded him with a good deal of skepticism. Marvin was surprised and impressed, however, when he heard that Jason and Carol had come down Devil's Chute by themselves in the dark. "Ain't a lot of people going to believe that," he said, shaking his massive head in admiration.

Marvin drove Jason and Carol back to the Salmon Inn, where Jason was surprised to find out there was a question of charges being filed against him, holding him responsible for the damages in the dining room. No one had seen any gun. And even more shocking, no one remembered an olive-complexioned man in a dark blue suit. But in the end, the management decided to drop the issue, saying they'd let their insurance take care of the damages. With that decided, Marvin tipped his hat, preparing to leave.

"What about protection?" asked Jason.

"From what?" asked Marvin. "Don't you think it is a little embarrassing that no one can corroborate your story? Listen, I think you people have caused enough trouble tonight. I think you should go up to your room and sleep this whole thing off."

"We need protection," said Jason. He tried to sound authoritative. "What do we do if the killer returns?"

"Look, friend, I can't sit here all night and hold your hand. I'm the only one on this shift and I got the whole damned county to keep my eye on. Lock yourself in your room and get some shut-eye."

With a final nod toward the manager, Marvin lumbered out the front door.

The manager in turn smiled condescendingly at Jason and went into his office.

"This is unreal," Jason said with a mixture of fear and irritation. "I can't believe nobody noticed the Hispanic guy." He went to the public phone booth and looked up private detective agencies. He found several in Seattle, but when he dialed he just got their answering machines. He left his name and the hotel number, but he didn't have much hope of reaching someone that night.

Emerging from the phone booth, he told Carol

that they were leaving immediately. She followed him up the stairs.

"It's nine-thirty at night," she protested, entering the room behind him.

"I don't care. We're leaving as fast as we can. Get your things together."

"Don't I have any say in the matter?"

"Nope. It was your decision to stay tonight and your decision to call the helpful local police. Now it's my turn. We're leaving."

For a minute, Carol stood in the center of the room watching Jason pack, then she decided he probably had a point. Ten minutes later, changed into their own clothes, they carried their luggage downstairs and checked out.

"I have to charge you for tonight," the man at the desk informed them.

Jason didn't bother to argue. Instead, he asked the man if he'd bring their car around to the front entrance. He tipped him five dollars and the clerk was happy to oblige.

Once in the car, Jason had hoped he'd feel less anxious and less vulnerable. Neither was the case. As he pulled out of the hotel parking lot and started down the dark mountain road, he quickly recognized how isolated they were. Fifteen minutes later, in the rearview mirror, he saw headlights appear. At first Jason tried to ignore them, but then it became apparent that they were relentlessly gaining on them despite Jason's gradual acceleration. The terror Jason had felt earlier crept back. His palms began to perspire.

"There's someone behind us," Jason said.

Carol twisted in the front seat and looked out the back. They rounded a curve and the headlights disappeared. But on the next straightaway they reappeared. They were closer. Carol faced forward. "I told you we should have stayed."

"That's helpful!" said Jason sarcastically.

He inched the accelerator closer to the floor. They were already going well over sixty on the curvy road. He tightened his grip on the steering wheel, then looked up at the rearview mirror. The car was close, its lights like eyes of a monster. He tried to think of what he could do, but he could think of nothing other than trying to outrun the car behind them. They came to another curve. Jason turned the wheel. He saw Carol's mouth open in a silent scream. He could feel the car start to jackknife. He braked, and they skidded first to one side and then to the other. Carol grabbed the dash to steady herself. Jason felt his seat belt tighten.

Fighting the car, Jason managed to keep it on the road. Behind him the pursuing car gained considerably. Now it was directly behind, its headlights filling Jason's car with unearthly light. In a panic, Jason floored the accelerator, pulling his car out of its careening course. They shot forward down a small hill. But the car behind stayed right with them, hounding them like a hunting dog at the heels of a deer.

Then to both Jason and Carol's bewilderment, their car filled with flashing red light. It took them a moment to realize that the light was coming from the top of the car behind them. When Jason recognized what it was, he slowed, watching in the rearview mirror. The car behind slowed proportionately. Ahead, at a turnout, Jason pulled off the road and stopped. Sweat stood out in little droplets along his hairline. His arms were trembling from his death grip on the steering wheel. Behind them, the other car stopped as well, its flashing light illuminating the surrounding trees. In the rearview mirror, Jason saw the door open, and Marvin Arnold stepped out. He had the safety strap off his .357 Magnum.

"Well, I'll be a pig's ass," he said, shining his flashlight into Jason's embarrassed face. "It's lover boy."

Furious, Jason shouted, "Why the hell didn't you turn on your blinker at the start?"

"Wanted to catch me a speeder." Marvin chuckled. "Didn't know I was chasing my favorite lunatic."

After an unsolicited lecture and a ticket for reckless driving, he let Jason and Carol continue. Jason was too angry to talk, and they drove in silence to the freeway, where Jason announced, "I think we should drive to Portland. God knows who may be waiting for us at the Seattle airport."

"Fine by me," Carol said, much too tired to argue.

They stopped for a couple hours' sleep at a motel near Portland, and at the first light of dawn, went on to the airport, where they boarded a flight to Chicago. From Chicago, they flew to Boston, touching down a little after five-thirty Saturday evening.

In the cab in front of Carol's apartment, Jason suddenly laughed. "I wouldn't even know how to apologize for what I've put you through."

Carol picked up her shoulder bag. "Well, at least it wasn't boring. Look, Jason, I don't mean to be sarcastic, or a nag, but please tell me what's going on."

"As soon as I'm sure," Jason said. "I promise. Really. Just do me one favor. Stay put tonight. Hopefully, no one knows we're back, but all hell might break loose if and when they find out."

"I don't plan on going anywhere, doctor." Carol sighed. "I've had it."

15.

Jason never even stopped at his apartment. As soon as Carol disappeared into her building, he told the cabdriver to drop him at his car and drove directly to GHP. He crossed immediately into the outpatient building. It was seven P.M. and the large waiting room was deserted. Jason went directly to his office, pulled off his jacket, and sat down at his computer terminal. GHP had spent a fortune on their computer system and was proud of it. Each station accessed the large mainframe where all patient data was entered. Although the individual charts were still the best source of patient information, most of the material could be obtained from the computer. Best of all, the sophisticated machinery could scan the entire patient base of GHP and graphically display the data on the screen, analyzed in almost any way one could wish.

Jason first called up the current survival curves. The graph that the computer drew was shaped like the steep slope of a mountain, starting high, then rounding and falling off. The graph compared the survival rate of GHP users by age. As one might expect, subscribers at the oldest end of the graph had the lowest survival rate. Over the past five years, although the median age of the GHP population had gradually increased, the survival curves stayed about the same.

Next, Jason asked the computer to print month-by-month graphs for the last half year. As he had feared, he saw the death rate rise for patients in their late fifties and early sixties, particularly during the last three months.

A sudden crash made him jump from his seat, but when he looked out in the hall he saw it was just the cleaning service.

Relieved, Jason returned to the computer. He wished he could separate the data on patients who had been given executive physicals, but he couldn't figure out how to do it. Instead, he had to be content with crude death rates. These graphs compared the percentages of deaths associated with age. This time the curve went the other way. It started low, then as the age increased the percentage of deaths went up. But then Jason asked the computer to print out a series of such graphs over the previous several months, month by month. The results were striking, particularly over the last two months. The death curves rose sharply starting at age fifty.

Jason sat at the computer terminal for another half hour, trying to coax the machine into separating out the executive physicals. What he expected he would see if he'd been able, was a rapid increase in death rates for people fifty and over who had high-risk factors such as smoking, alcohol abuse, poor diets, and lack of exercise. But the data was not available. It had not been programmed to be extracted en masse. Jason would have to take each individual name and laboriously obtain the data himself, but he didn't have time to do that. Besides, the crude death-rate curves were enough to corroborate his suspicions. He now knew he was right. But there was one more way to prove it. With enormous unease, he left his office and returned to his car.

Driving out the Riverway, Jason headed for Roslindale. The closer he got, the more nervous he became. He had no idea what he was about to confront, but he suspected it was not going to be pleasant. His destination was the Hartford School, the institution run by GHP for retarded children. If Alvin Hayes had been right about his own condition, he must have been right about his retarded son's.

The Hartford School backed onto the Arnold Arboretum, an idyllic setting of graceful wooded hills, fields, and ponds. Jason turned into the parking lot, which was all but deserted, and stopped within fifty feet of the front entrance. The handsome, Colonial-style building had a deceptively serene look that belied the personal family tragedies it housed. Severe retardation was a hard subject even for professionals to deal with. Jason vividly remembered examining some of the children on previous visits to the school. Physically many were perfectly formed, which only made their low IQs that much more disturbing.

The front door was closed and locked, so Jason rang the buzzer and waited. The door was opened by an overweight security guard in a soiled blue uniform.

"Can I help you?" he said, making it clear he had no wish to.

"I'm a doctor," Jason said. He tried to push by the security man, who stepped back to bar his way.

"Sorry—no visitors after six, doctor."

"I'm hardly a visitor," Jason said. He pulled out his wallet and produced his GHP identity card.

The guard didn't even look at the ID. "No visitors after six," he repeated, adding, "and no exceptions."

"But I . . ." Jason began. He stopped in midsentence. From the man's expression, he knew discussion was futile.

"Call in the morning, sir," the guard said, slamming the door.

Jason walked back down the front steps and gazed up at the five-story building. It was brick, with granite window casings. He wasn't about to give up. Assuming the guard was watching, Jason went back to his car and drove out the driveway. About a hundred yards down the road, he pulled over to the side. He got out, and with some difficulty made his way through the Arboretum back to the school.

He circled the building, staying in the shadows.

There were fire escapes on all sides but the front. They went right up to the roof. Unfortunately, as at Carol's building, none was at ground level, and Jason couldn't find anything to stand on to reach the first rung.

On the right side of the building, he spotted a flight of stairs that went down to a locked door. Feeling with his hands in the dark, he discovered the door had a central glass pane. He went back up the stairs and felt around the ground until he found a rock the size of a softball.

Holding his breath, Jason went back to the door and smashed the glass. In the quiet evening, the clatter seemed loud enough to wake the dead. Jason fled to the nearby trees and hid, watching the building. When no one appeared after fifteen minutes, he ventured out and returned to the door. Gingerly, he reached in and undid the latch. No alarm sounded.

For the next half hour Jason stumbled around a large basement he guessed was a storage area. He found a stepladder and debated taking it outside to use to reach a fire escape, but gave up that idea and continued feeling about blindly for a light. His hands finally touched a switch and he flicked it on.

He was in a maintenance room filled with lawnmowers, shovels, and other equipment. Next to the light switch was a door. Slowly, Jason eased it open. Beyond was a much larger furnace room that was dimly illuminated.

Moving quickly, Jason crossed the second room

and mounted a steep steel stairway. He opened the door at the top and immediately realized he had reached the front hall. From his previous visits he knew the stairs to the wards were to his right. On his left was an office where a middle-aged woman in a bulging white uniform was reading at a desk. Looking down toward the front entrance, Jason could see the guard's feet perched on a chair. The man's face was out of sight.

As quietly as possible, Jason slipped through the basement door and let it ease back into place. For a moment he was in full view of the woman in the office, but she didn't look up from her book. Forcing himself to move slowly, he silently crossed the hall and entered the stairwell. He breathed a sigh of relief when he was completely out of sight of both the woman and the guard. Taking the stairs on tiptoe two at a time, he headed for the third floor, where the ward for boys aged four to twelve was located.

The stairs were marble, and even though he tried to be quiet, his footsteps echoed in the otherwise silent, cavernous space. Above him was a skylight, which at that time looked like a black onyx set into the ceiling.

On the third floor, Jason carefully opened the stairwell door. He remembered there was a glassed-in nurses' office to the right at the end of a long hallway and noticed that although the corridor was dark, the office still blazed with light. A male attendant was, like the woman downstairs, busy reading.

Looking diagonally across the hall, Jason eyed the door to the ward. He noted it had a large central window with embedded wire. After one last check on the attendant, Jason tiptoed across the hall and let himself into the darkened room. Immediately, he was confronted by a musty smell. After waiting a moment to be sure the attendant hadn't been disturbed, he began searching for the light. To confirm his suspicions, he would have to turn it on even if it meant being caught.

The drab room was suddenly flooded with raw, white fluorescent light. The ward was some fifty feet long, with low iron beds lined up on either side, leaving a narrow aisle. There were windows, but they were high, near the ceiling. At the end of the room were tiled toilet facilities with a coiled hose for cleaning and a bolted door to the fire escape. Jason walked down the aisle looking at the nameplates attached to the ends of beds: Harrison, Lyons, Gessner. . . . The children, disturbed by the light, began to sit up, staring with wide, vacant, and unknowing eyes at the intruder.

Jason stopped, and a terrible sense of revulsion that expanded to terror gripped him. It was worse than he'd imagined. Slowly, his eyes went from one pitiful face to another of the unwanted creatures. Instead of looking like the children they were, they all looked like miniature senile centenarians with beady eyes, wrinkled dry skin, and thinned white hair, showing scaly patches of scalp. Jason spotted the name Hayes. Like the others, the child appeared prematurely aged. He'd lost most of his eyelashes and his lower lids hung down. In place of his pupils were the glass-white reflection of dense cataracts. Except for light perception, the child was blind.

Some of the children began getting out of their beds, balancing precariously on wasted limbs. Then, to Jason's horror they began to move toward him. One of them began to say feebly the word "*please*" over and over in a high-pitched, grating voice. Soon the others joined in a terrifying, unearthly chorus.

Jason backed up, afraid to be touched. Hayes's son got out of his bed and began to feel his way forward, his bony, uncoordinated little arms making helpless swirling motions in the air.

The mob of children backed Jason up against the ward door and began to tug at his clothes. Frightened and nauseated, Jason pushed open the ward door and retreated into the hall. After he closed the door, the children pressed their mummylike faces against the glass, still silently voicing the word "please."

"Hey, you!" Jason heard a rasping voice behind him.

Turning his head, he saw the attendant standing outside his office, waving his open book in astonishment. "What's goin' on?" the man yelled.

Jason ran across the hall to the stairwell, but he'd descended only a few steps before a second voice echoed up from below. "Kevin? What gives?"

Looking over the railing, Jason saw the guard down on the first-floor landing.

"Well, I'll be damned," the guard said, and charged up the stairs, club in hand.

Reversing direction, Jason returned to the third floor. The attendant was still standing in the doorway of his office, apparently too dumbfounded to move as Jason sprinted across the hall and back into the ward. Some of the children were wandering aimlessly about the room; others had collapsed back on their beds. Jason frantically beckoned them over, opened the door, and as the attendant and guard appeared, they were immediately surrounded by a swarm of boys.

They tried to shove their way through the crowd, but the children clung to them, shouting their eerie, monotonous chorus of *please.*

Reaching the emergency door at the opposite end of the room, Jason depressed its lever which, for safety's sake, was positioned six feet off the floor. At first the door wouldn't open. Obviously, it had not been used for years. Jason could see that paint had sealed it shut. Putting his shoulder against it, Jason finally got it to swing free. Stepping out into the dark night, he pushed several of the boys back into the ward before closing the heavy door.

Wasting no time, he clambered down the fire escape. There was no need to be quiet now. He was at the second level when the door above him opened. Once again he heard the shrieking of the children.

Then he felt the vibration of heavy boots on the fire escape.

Pulling out a pin caused the final ladder to descend with a deep thud, as it hit the asphalt of the parking lot below. Even before it had touched down, Jason was on it. The slight delay enabled the guard behind Jason to close the distance between them.

Once on the lawn, though, Jason's running ability soon left the beefy guard far behind, and by the time Jason reached his car, he had plenty of time to start the engine, put it in gear, and pull away. In his rearview mirror he could barely see the man just reaching the edge of the road, shaking his fist in the light of a street lamp.

Jason could barely control his disgust and fury at what he'd seen. He drove directly to Boston police headquarters and brazenly left his car in a no-parking zone in front of the building.

"I want to see Detective Curran," Jason told the officer at the desk, then identified himself.

The policeman calmly checked his watch, then called up to Homicide. He spoke for a minute, then covered the receiver with his hand. "Would anyone else do?"

"No. I want Curran. And now, please."

The policeman spoke into the phone a few minutes more, then hung up. "Detective Curran isn't available, sir."

"I think he'll talk with me. Even if he's off duty."

"That's not the problem," the policeman said. "Detective Curran is on a double homicide in Revere. He should be calling in within an hour or so. If you want, you can wait or leave your number. It's up to you, sir."

Jason thought for a moment. He'd been up most of the night, his nerves were shot, and the idea of a shower, a change of clothes, and food had a lot of appeal. Besides, once he got together with Curran, he would be busy for some time. He left his home number, asking that Curran call as soon as possible.

The United flight from Seattle had been delayed considerably, and by the time it landed at Logan, Juan Díaz was in a sour mood. He'd not screwed up an assignment so badly since he hit the wrong man in New York. That fiasco was excusable, but his current one was not. He'd been within a few seconds of popping both the doctor and the nightclub *puta* when Jason, an amateur, had outsmarted him. Juan had no excuse and had told the contact as much. He knew he had to redeem himself or else, and he looked forward to it eagerly. As soon as he got off the plane, he went to the phone. It was answered on the second ring.

Jason drove the short distance from the police station to Louisburg Square, trying to erase the horrible image of the prematurely aged children at the school. He didn't even want to think about Hayes and his discovery until he was safely in Curran's presence.

When he got to his building, he drove around the block a couple of times to make sure no one was watching it. Finally, convincing himself that the guard at the school had not looked at his ID, and hence had no idea who he was, Jason parked his car, carried his luggage up to his apartment, and turned on the lights. To his relief, the place was exactly as he'd left it. When he glanced out at the square, it seemed as peaceful as ever.

Jason was about to get into the shower when he remembered the one other person he should speak to besides the detective. He dialed Shirley. She finally answered on the eighth ring. Jason could hear animated voices in the background.

"Jason!" she exclaimed. "When did you get back from vacation?"

"I got in tonight."

"What's the matter?" she asked, picking up on the exhaustion and worry in his voice.

"Big trouble. I think I've figured out not only Hayes's discovery, but how it was being misused. It involves the GHP in a far worse way than you could ever imagine."

"Tell me."

"Not over the phone."

"Then come right over. I have guests here, but I'll get rid of them."

"I'm waiting to speak to Curran in Homicide."

"I see . . . you've already contacted him?"

"He's out on a case, but he should be calling shortly."

"Then why don't I come to your apartment? You've got me really terrified now."

"Welcome to the club," Jason said with a short, bitter laugh. "You might as well come over. You probably should be present when I talk to Curran."

"I'm on my way."

"Oh, one other thing. Do you remember who's currently medical director at the Hartford School?"

"Dr. Peterson, I believe," Shirley said. "I can find out for certain tomorrow."

"Wasn't Peterson closely involved in Hayes's clinical studies?" Jason asked, suddenly remembering that Peterson was the doctor who had done the physical on Hayes.

"I think so. Is it important?"

"I'm not sure," Jason said. "But if you're coming, hurry. Curran should be calling any minute."

Jason hung up and was again about to take his shower when he realized Carol too might be in danger. Picking up the phone again, he dialed her number.

"I want you to be sure to stay at home," he said the moment she answered. "I'm not fooling. Don't answer your door—don't go out."

"Now what is it?"

"The Hayes conspiracy is worse than anything I could imagine."

"You sound anxious, Jason."

In spite of himself, Jason smiled. Sometimes Carol could sound like a psychiatrist.

"I'm not anxious, I'm scared to death. But I'll be talking with the police shortly."

"Will you let me know what's going on?" Carol demanded.

"I promise." Jason hung up and finally went into the bathroom and turned on the shower.

16.

The buzzer sounded and Jason ran downstairs to see Shirley smiling at him through the glass side panel of his front door. He stepped back to let her in, admiring her usual impeccable dress. Tonight she was wearing a black leather miniskirt and a long, red suede jacket.

"Has Curran called?" she asked as they walked upstairs.

"Not yet," Jason said, carefully double-locking his apartment door.

"Now fill me in," Shirley said, slipping out of her jacket. Underneath she was wearing a soft cashmere sweater. She sat on the edge of Jason's sofa, her hands clasped in her lap, and waited.

"You're not going to like this," Jason said, sitting next to her.

"I've tried to prepare myself. Shoot."

"First let me give you a little background. If you don't understand the current research on aging, what I'm about to say may not make much sense.

"In the last few years, scientists like Hayes have

spent a lot of time trying to slow the aging process. Most of their work has focused on cells in cell cultures, although some work has been done with rats and mice. Most of the researchers have concluded that aging is a natural process with a genetic basis regulated by neuroendocrine, immune, and humoral factors."

"You've lost me already," Shirley admitted, lifting her hands in mock surrender.

"How about a drink, then?" Jason suggested, getting to his feet.

"What are you having?"

"A beer. But I have wine, hard stuff, you name it."

"A beer might be nice."

Jason went to the kitchen, opened the refrigerator, and took out two cold Coors.

"You doctors are all the same," Shirley complained, taking a sip. "You make everything sound complicated."

"It is complicated," Jason said, sitting back down. "Molecular genetics concerns the fundamental basis of life. Research in this area is scary, not just because scientists might accidentally create a new and deadly bacterium or virus. It is just as scary if it goes right, because we are playing with life itself. Hayes's tragedy was not that he failed; the problem was that he succeeded."

"What did he discover?"

"In a moment," Jason said, taking a long drink of beer and wiping his mouth with the back of his hand. "Let me put the story another way. We all reach puberty at about the same time, and if disease or accident doesn't intervene, we all age and die in about the same life-span."

Shirley nodded.

"Okay," Jason said, leaning toward her. "This happens because our bodies are genetically programmed to follow an internal timetable. As we develop, different genes are turned on while others are turned off. This is what fascinated Hayes. He had been studying the ways humoral signals from the brain control growth and sexual maturation. By isolating one after another of these humoral proteins, he discovered what they did to peripheral tissues. He was hoping to find out what caused cells to either start dividing or stop dividing."

"That much I do understand," Shirley said. "It's one of the reasons we hired him. We hoped he'd make a breakthrough in cancer treatment."

"Now let me digress a moment," Jason said. "There was another researcher by the name of Denckla, who was experimenting on ways to retard the aging process. He took out the pituitary glands of rats, and after replacing the necessary hormones, found that the rats had an increased life-span."

Jason stopped and looked expectantly at Shirley.

"Am I supposed to say something?" she asked.

"Doesn't Denckla's experiment suggest something to you?"

"Why don't you just tell me."

"Denckla deduced that not only does the pituitary secrete the hormones for growth and puberty, but it also secretes the hormone for aging. Denckla called it the death hormone."

Shirley laughed nervously. "That sounds cheerful."

"Well, I believe that while Hayes was researching growth factors, he stumbled onto Denckla's postulated death hormone," Jason said. "That was what he meant by an ironic discovery. While looking for growth stimulators, he finds a hormone that causes rapid aging and death."

"What would happen if this hormone were given to someone?" Shirley asked.

"If it were given in isolation, probably not much. The subject might experience some symptoms of aging, but the hormone would probably be metabolized and its effect limited. But Hayes wasn't studying the hormone in isolation. He realized that in the same way the secretion of the sex and growth hormone is triggered, there had to be a releasing factor for the death hormone. He was immediately drawn to the life cycle of salmon, which die within hours of spawning. I believe he collected salmon heads and isolated the death hormone's releasing factor from the brains. This was the free-lance work I think he did at Gene, Inc. Once he had isolated the releasing factor, he had Helene reproduce it in quantity by recombinant DNA techniques at his GHP lab."

"Why would Hayes want to produce it?"

"I believe he hoped to develop a monoclonal antibody that would prevent the secretion of the death hormone and halt the aging process." All at once Jason realized what Hayes meant about his discovery becoming a beauty aid. It would preserve youthful good looks, like Carol's.

"What would happen if the releasing factor were given to someone?"

"It would turn on the death gene, releasing the aging hormone just the way it is in salmon—with pretty much the same results. The subject would age and die in three or four weeks. And nobody would know why. And this brings me to the worst thing of all. I believe someone obtained the artificially created hormone Helene was producing at our lab and started giving it to our patients. Whoever it is must be insane—but that's what I think has been happening. Hayes caught on—probably when he visited his son—and was given the aging factor himself. If he hadn't died that night, I think he'd have been killed some other way." Jason shuddered.

"How did you find out?" Shirley whispered.

"I followed Hayes's experimental trail. When Helene was murdered I guessed that Hayes had been telling the truth both about his discovery and the fact that someone wanted him dead."

"But Helene was raped by an unknown intruder."

"Sure. But only to mislead the police as to the motive for her murder. I always felt she knew more than she was telling about Hayes's work. When I learned that she'd been having an affair with him, I was sure."

"But who would want to kill our patients?" Shirley asked desperately.

"A sociopath. The same kind of nut who puts cyanide in Tylenol. Tonight at the clinic I had the computer print out survival curves and death curves. The results were incredible. There's been a significant increase in the death rate at GHP for patients over fifty who are chronically ill or who have high-risk lifestyles." Suddenly Jason stopped. "Damn!"

"What's the matter?" Shirley asked, looking about nervously, as if the danger were just around the corner.

"I forgot something. I printed the curves month by month—I didn't look at them doctor by doctor."

"You think a physician's behind this?" Shirley asked incredulously.

"Must be. A doctor—or maybe a nurse. The releasing factor would be a polypeptide protein. It would have to be injected. If it was administered orally, the gastric juices would degrade it."

"Oh, my God." Shirley dropped her head into her hands. "And I thought we had troubles before." She took a breath and looked up. "Isn't there a chance you could be wrong, Jason? Maybe the computer made a mistake. God knows, data processing breaks down often enough. . . ."

Jason put his hand on her shoulder. He knew that

her hard-won empire was about to come crashing down. "I'm not wrong," he said gently. "I also did something else tonight. I saw Hayes's son at Hartford."

"And . . . ?"

"It's a horror. All the kids on his ward must have been given the releasing factor. Apparently it acts more slowly on prepubescent subjects, so the boys are still alive. There must be some kind of hormonal competition with growth hormone. But they all look one hundred years old."

Shirley shuddered.

"That's why I wanted to know the name of the current medical director."

"You think Peterson's responsible?"

"He'd have to be a prime suspect."

"Maybe we should go to the clinic and double-check the computer. We could even rerun your survival curves by doctor."

Before Jason could answer, the door buzzer shattered the silence and made them both jump. Jason got to his feet, his heart pounding.

Shirley dropped her drink on the table. "Who could that be?"

"I don't know." Jason had told Carol not to leave her apartment, and Curran would have called before coming over.

"What should we do?" Shirley asked urgently.

"I'm going downstairs and have a look."

"Is that such a good idea?"

"Got a better one?"

Shirley shook her head. "Just don't open the door."

"What do you think I am—crazy? Oh—and one thing I didn't tell you. Someone tried to kill me."

"No! Where?"

"In a remote country inn east of Seattle."

He unlocked his apartment door.

"Maybe you'd better not go down," Shirley said hurriedly.

"I've got to find out who it is." Jason went out to the railed landing and looked down at the front door. He could see a figure through one of the glass panels.

"Be careful," Shirley said.

Jason silently started down the stairs. The closer he got, the bigger the shadow of the individual in the foyer became. He was facing the nameplates and angrily hitting the buzzer. Suddenly he whirled around and pressed his face to the glass. For a moment, Jason's and the stranger's faces were only inches apart. There was no mistaking the massive face and tiny, closely set eyes. Their visitor was Bruno, the body-builder. Jason turned and fled back upstairs as the door rattled furiously behind him.

"Who is it?"

"A muscle-bound thug I know," Jason told her, double-locking his door, "and the only person who knew I went to Seattle." That point had just occurred to him with terrifying force. He ran into the den and snatched up the phone. "Damn!" he said after a minute. He dropped the receiver and tried the one in the bedroom. Again, there was no dial tone. "The phones are dead," he said with disbelief to Shirley, who had followed him, sensing his panic.

"What are we going to do?"

"We're leaving. I'm not getting trapped here." Rummaging in the hall closet, he found the key to the gate separating his building from the narrow alley that ran out to West Cedar Street. He opened the bedroom window, climbed onto the fire escape, and helped Shirley out after him. Single file, they descended to the small garden where the leafless white birches stood out like ghosts in the dark. Once in the alley, they ran to the gate, where Jason frantically fumbled to insert the key. When they emerged onto the narrow street, it was quiet and empty, the gloom pierced at intervals by the soft Beacon Hill gas lamps. Not a soul was stirring.

"Let's go!" Jason said, and started down West Cedar to Charles.

"My car is back on Louisburg Square," Shirley panted, struggling to match Jason's pace.

"So is mine. But obviously we can't go back. I have a friend whose car I can take."

On Charles Street there were a few pedestrians outside the 7-Eleven. Jason thought about calling the police from the store, but now that he was out of his apartment he felt less trapped. Besides, he wanted to check the GHP computer again before he spoke with Curran.

They walked down Chestnut Street, lined with its old Federal buildings. There were several people walking dogs, which made Jason feel safer. Just before Brimmer Street, Jason turned into a parking garage where he gave the attendant ten dollars and asked for the car that belonged to a friend. Luckily, the man recognized Jason and brought out a blue BMW.

"I think it would be a good idea to go to my place," Shirley said, sliding into the front seat. "We can call Curran from there and let him know where you are."

"First I want to go back to the clinic."

With almost no traffic, they reached the hospital in less than ten minutes. "I'll only be a minute," Jason said, pulling up to the entrance. "Do you want to come in or wait here?"

"Don't be silly," Shirley said, opening her side of the car. "I want to see these graphs myself."

They waved ID cards at the security guard and took the elevator, even though they were going up only one floor.

The cleaning service had left the clinic in pristine condition—magazines in racks, wastepaper baskets empty, and the floor glistening with fresh wax. Jason went directly into his office, sat down at his desk, and booted up his computer terminal.

"I'll call Curran," Shirley said, going out to the secretaries' station.

Jason gave a wave to indicate he'd heard her. He was already engrossed in data on the computer. First he called up the various clinic physicians' identification numbers. He was particularly interested in Peterson's. When he had all the numbers, he instructed the computer to separate the GHP patient population by doctor and then start drawing death curves on each group for the past two months, months that had shown the greatest changes when all the patients had been listed. He expected Peterson's patients to show either a higher or lower death rate, believing that a psychopath would experiment either significantly more or less with his own patients.

Shirley came back into the office and stood watching him enter the data.

"Your friend Curran's not back yet," she said. "He called in to the station and said he might be tied up a couple more hours."

Jason nodded. He was more interested in the emerging curves. It took about fifteen minutes to produce all the graphs. Jason separated the continuous sheets and lined them up.

"They all look the same," Shirley said, leaning on his shoulder.

"Just about," Jason admitted. "Even Peterson's. It doesn't rule out his involvement, but it doesn't help us either." Jason eyed the computer, trying to think of any other data that might be useful. He drew a blank.

"Well, that's all the bright ideas for the moment.

The police will have to take over from here."

"Let's go, then," Shirley said. "You look exhausted."

"I am," Jason admitted. Pushing himself out of the chair was an effort.

"Are these the graphs you produced earlier?" Shirley asked, pointing to the stack of printouts by the terminal.

Jason nodded.

"How about bringing them along? I'd like you to explain them to me."

Jason stuffed the papers into a large manila envelope.

"I gave Curran's office my phone number," Shirley said. "I think that's the best place to wait. Have you had a chance to eat anything?"

"Some dreadful airplane food, but that seems like days ago."

"I have a little leftover cold chicken."

"Sounds great."

When they got to the car, Jason asked Shirley if she'd mind driving so he could relax and think a little.

"Not at all," she said, taking his keys.

Jason climbed into the passenger side, tossing the envelope into the back seat. He fastened his seat belt, leaned back, and closed his eyes. He let his mind play over the various ways the clinic patients might have been given the releasing factor. Since it couldn't be administered orally, he wondered how the criminal could have injected the patients undergoing executive physicals. Blood was drawn for lab workups, but vacuum tubes provided no way to inject a substance. For inpatients it was a different story—they were always getting injections and intravenous fluids.

He had reached no plausible conclusion when Shirley drew up before her house. Jason staggered and almost fell as he got out of the car. The short rest had exaggerated his fatigue. He reached into the back seat for the envelope.

"Make yourself at home," Shirley said, leading him into the living room.

"First let's make sure Curran hasn't called."

"I'll check my service in a moment. Why don't you make yourself a drink while I rustle up that chicken."

Too tired to argue, Jason went over to the bar and poured some Dewar's over ice, then retreated to the couch. While he waited for Shirley, he again pondered the ways the releasing factor might have been administered. There weren't many possibilities. If it wasn't injected, it had to be through rectal suppositories or some other direct contact with a mucous membrane. Most of the patients having a complete executive physical got a barium enema, and Jason wondered if that was the answer.

He began sipping his Scotch as Shirley came in with a cold chicken and salad.

"Can I make you a drink?" Jason asked. Shirley

put the tray down on the coffee table. "Why not?" Then she added, "Don't move. I'll get it."

Jason watched her add a drop of vermouth to her vodka, and that was when he thought of eyedrops. All patients having executive physicals had complete eye exams, including eyedrops to dilate their pupils. If someone wished to introduce the death gene's releasing factor, the mucous membrane in the eye would absorb it perfectly. Even better, since the releasing factor could be secretly introduced to the regular eye medication, the fatal drops could be administered unwittingly by any innocent doctor or technician.

Jason felt his head begin to pound. Finding a plausible explanation of what might what have been the key to it all made the possibility of a psychopathic mass murderer suddenly real. Shirley returned from the bar, swirling her drink. For the moment, Jason decided to spare her this newest revelation.

"Any message from Curran?" he asked instead.

"Not yet," Shirley said, looking at him oddly. For a moment he wondered if she could read his mind.

"I have a question," she said hesitantly. "Isn't this supposed releasing factor for the death hormone part of a natural process?"

"Yes," Jason said. "That's why pathology hasn't been much help. All the victims, including Hayes, died of what are called natural causes. The releasing factor merely takes the gene activated at puberty and turns it on full force."

"You mean we start aging at puberty?" Shirley asked with dismay.

"That's the current theory," said Jason. "But obviously it is gradual, picking up speed only in later life, as the levels of growth hormone and sex hormones fall. The releasing factor apparently switches on the death hormone gene all at once, and in an adult without high titers of growth hormone to counter it, it causes rapid aging just like the salmon. My guess is about three weeks. The limiting factor seems to be the cardiovascular system. That's what apparently gives out first and causes death. But it could be other organ systems, as well."

"But aging is a natural process," she repeated.

"Aging is a part of life," agreed Jason. "Evolutionarily it is as important as growth. Yes, it is a natural process." Jason laughed hollowly. "Hayes certainly was right when he described his discovery as ironic. With all the work being done to slow aging down, his work on growth resulted in a way to speed it up."

"If aging and death have an evolutionary value," Shirley persisted, "perhaps they have a social one as well."

Jason looked at her with a growing sense of alarm. He wished he weren't so tired. His brain was sending danger signals he felt too exhausted to decode. Taking his silence as assent, Shirley continued. "Let me put it another way. Medicine in general is faced with the challenge of providing quality care at low cost. But because of increasing life-spans, hospitals are swamped with an elderly population that they keep alive at an enormous price, draining not just their economic resources, but the energy of the medical personnel as well. GHP, for example, did very well when it first started, because the bulk of the subscribers were young and healthy. Now, twenty years later, they are all older and require a great deal more health care. If aging were speeded up in certain circumstances, it might be best for both the patients and the hospitals.

"The important point," emphasized Shirley, "is that the old and infirm should age and die rapidly to avoid suffering as well as to avoid the over-utilization of expensive medical care."

As Jason's numb brain began to understand Shirley's reasoning, he felt himself becoming paralyzed with horror. Although he wanted to shout that what she was implying was legalized murder, he found himself sitting dumbly on the edge of the couch like a bird confronted by a poisonous snake and frozen with fear.

"Jason, do you have any idea how much it costs to keep people alive during their last months of life in a hospital?" Shirley said, again mistaking his silence for acquiescence. "Do you? If medicine didn't spend so much on the dying, it could do so much more to help the living. If GHP wasn't swamped with middle-aged patients destined to be ill because of their unhealthy lifestyles, think what we could do for the young. And aren't patients who fail to take care of themselves, like heavy smokers and drinkers, or people who use drugs, voluntarily speeding up their own demise? Is it so wrong to hasten their deaths so they don't burden the rest of society?"

Jason's mouth finally opened in protest, but he couldn't find the words to refute her. All he could do was shake his head in disbelief.

"I can't believe you won't accept the fact that medicine can no longer survive under the crushing burden of the chronic health problems presented by physically unfit people—those very patients who have spent thirty or forty years abusing the bodies God gave them."

"That's not for me or you to decide," Jason shouted at last.

"Even if the aging process is simply speeded up by a natural substance?"

"That's murder!" Jason stumbled to his feet. Shirley rose too, moving swiftly to the double doors leading to the dining room. "Come in, Mr. Díaz," she said, flinging them open. "I've done what I could."

Jason's mouth went dry as he turned to face the man he'd last seen at the Salmon Inn. Juan's darkly handsome face was alive with anticipation. He was carrying a small, German-made automatic muzzled with a cigar-sized silencer.

Jason backed up clumsily until his back struck the far wall. His eyes went from the gun to the killer's strikingly handsome face, to Shirley, who eyed him as calmly as if she were in a board meeting.

"No tablecloth this time," Díaz said, grinning to show movie-star-perfect white teeth. He advanced on Jason, putting the muzzle of the gun six inches from Jason's head. "Good-bye," he said with a friendly flick of his head.

17.

"Mr. Díaz," Shirley said.

"Yes," Juan answered without taking his eyes off Jason.

"Don't shoot him unless he forces you to. It will be better to deal with him the way we did with Mr. Hayes. I'll bring you the material from the clinic tomorrow."

Jason breathed out. He hadn't realized he was holding his breath.

The smile vanished from Juan's face. His nostrils flared; he was disappointed and angry. "I think it would be much safer if I killed him right now, Miss Montgomery."

"I don't care what you think—and I'm paying you. Now let's get him into the cellar. And no rough stuff—I know what I'm doing."

Juan moved the pistol so the cold metal touched Jason's temple. Jason knew the man was hoping for the slightest excuse to shoot; he remained perfectly still, petrified by fear.

"Come on!" called Shirley from the front hall.

"Go!" said Juan, pulling the gun back from Jason's head.

Jason walked stiffly, his arms pressed against his sides. Juan fell in behind, occasionally touching Jason's back with the gun.

Shirley opened a door under the staircase across from the front entrance. Jason could see a flight of steps leading to the basement.

As Jason approached, he tried to catch Shirley's eye, but she turned away. He stepped through the door and started down, Juan directly behind him.

"Doctors amaze me," said Shirley, turning on the cellar light and closing the door behind her. "They think medicine is just a question of helping the sick. The truth is unless something is done about the chronically unhealthy, there won't be money or manpower to help those who can actually recover."

Looking at her calm, pretty face, the perfect clothes, Jason couldn't believe it was the same woman he'd always admired.

She interrupted herself to direct Juan down a long narrow hallway to a heavy oak door. Squeezing by Juan and Jason, she unlocked it and flicked on the light, illuminating a large square room. Jason was pushed inside, where he saw an open doorway to the left, a workbench, and another heavy closed door to the right. Then the light went out, the door slammed, and total darkness surrounded him.

For a few minutes, Jason stood still, immobilized by shock and lack of vision. He could hear small sounds; water coursing through pipes, the heating system kicking on, and footsteps above his head. The darkness remained absolute: he could not even tell if his eyes were open or closed.

When Jason was finally able to move, he stepped back to the door through which he'd entered. He grabbed the door knob and tried to turn it. He pulled on the door. There was no doubt it was secure. Running his hands around the jamb, he felt for hinges. He gave that up when he remembered the door opened into the hall.

Leaving the door, Jason worked his way laterally, taking baby steps and gingerly sliding his hands along the wall. He came to the corner and turned ninety degrees. He continued moving step by miniature step until he felt the doorway of the open door. Carefully reaching inside, he felt for a wall switch. On the left side, about chest height, he found one. He threw the switch. Nothing happened.

Advancing into the side room, he began to feel the walls, trying to ascertain the dimensions. His fingers hit on a metal object on the wall whose front was glass. Feeling down at waist height he touched a sink. Over to the right was a toilet. The room was only about five by seven.

Returning to the main room, Jason continued his slow circuit. He encountered a second small room with a closed door just beyond the bathroom. When he opened the door, his nose told him it was a cedar closet. Inside he felt several garment bags filled with clothes.

Back in the main room, Jason came to another

corner, and he turned again. Within a dozen small steps, he gently hit against the workbench, which stuck out about three feet into the room. Skirting the end of the bench, he felt beneath it, finding cabinets. The workbench, he estimated, was about ten to fifteen feet long. Beyond the workbench, he returned to the wall, encountering shelving with what felt like paint cans. Beyond the shelving was another corner.

In the middle of the fourth wall, Jason came to another heavy door that was tightly closed and secured. He could feel a lock, but it needed a key. There were no hinges. Continuing his circuit, Jason came to the fourth corner. After a few minutes, he was back at the entrance.

Getting down on his hands and knees, Jason felt the floor. It was poured concrete. Standing up again, he tried to think of what else he could do. He had no good ideas. Suddenly, he felt an overwhelming sense of mortal fear like he was being smothered. He'd never suffered from claustrophobia, but it descended on him with crushing severity. "HELP!" he shouted, only to have his voice echo back to his ears. Losing control, he groped madly for the entrance door and pounded on it with closed fists. "PLEASE!" he shouted. He pounded until he became aware of pain in his hands. He stopped abruptly with a wince and clutched his bruised hands to his chest. Leaning forward, Jason touched the door with his forehead. Then the tears came.

Jason could not remember crying since he'd been

a child. Even after Danielle's death. And all those years of denying that emotion came out as he crouched in the blackness of Shirley's basement. He lost complete control and slowly sank to the floor, where he curled up in front of the door like an imprisoned dog, choking on his own tears.

The ferocity of Jason's emotional reaction surprised him. And after ten minutes of sobbing, he began to regain his composure. He was embarrassed at himself, having always believed he had more self-control. Finally, he sat up with his back against the door. In the darkness, he wiped his tears from his damp cheeks.

Instead of surrendering to utter despair, he thought about the room he was in. He tried to guess the dimensions and picture the location of things he'd encountered on his exploratory circuit. He began to wonder if there were any other light switches. Getting to his feet, he slowly returned to the second locked door that was to his right. When he got there, he felt along the walls on both sides, but there was no light switch.

Striking out across the room, he returned to the bathroom. He tried the switch in there several more times. Then he felt for the fixture, thinking he could exchange the bulb provided he could locate the lights in the ceiling of the main room. But there was no fixture, either as part of the medicine cabinet or as part of the ceiling. Discouraged, Jason returned to the large room.

"Ahhh!" cried Jason, as he walked directly into a

lolly column, hitting his nose against the six-inch diameter metal surface. Momentarily off balance, he felt his nose already beginning to swell. There was a bony ridge along the right side: he'd broken it. Once more, tears involuntarily filled his eyes, but this time it was from reflex, not emotion. When he recovered enough to proceed, Jason had become disoriented. Reverting to baby steps, he moved until he encountered a wall. Only then was he able to find the workbench.

Bending down, Jason began opening the cabinets, then carefully exploring each with his hands. Each cabinet was about four feet wide and contained a single removable shelf. He found more cans of what he thought was paint, but no tools whatsoever. Standing up, Jason leaned over the workbench and felt the wall above it. There was some narrow shelving to the right with small jars and boxes. Moving to the central part, Jason felt the wall again, hoping to encounter a pegboard or the like with screwdrivers, hammers and chisels. Instead, his hand encountered a glass bowl facing away from him. Curious as to what it was, Jason felt around it, ascertaining that the glass bowl was secured to a metal box. Pipes entered the metal box. Jason realized it was the electric meter.

Moving down to the left end of the workbench, Jason again felt the wall. There was more shelving containing plastic and ceramic flower pots, but there were no tools.

Discouraged, Jason wondered what else he could

do. He thought about finding something to stand on so that he could explore the walls close to the ceiling in case there was a blacked-out window. Then his mind went back to the electric meter. Climbing up on the workbench, he located the meter and traced the wires to a second rectangular metal box. Feeling the surface, Jason immediately encountered a hinged metal ring. Giving it a slight tug, Jason opened the box.

Inside was the service panel for the house. Slowly he reached inside, hoping he was not about to touch a live wire. Instead, his fingers touched the low row of circuit breaker switches.

For the next five minutes Jason thought about how to make use of his discovery. Getting off the bench, he opened the door to the cabinet underneath and removed its contents, storing the cans in the two side cabinets. Then he removed the single shelf, which luckily was not nailed down, and climbed in. He had plenty of room.

He got out, climbed back on the workbench and, one by one, threw all the circuit breakers. Then he closed the service panel, scrambled into the empty cabinet, pulled the door shut behind him, and prayed. If they'd already gone to bed, the lack of power wouldn't bother them.

After what Jason guessed was another five minutes, he heard a door opening. Then he heard voices, and through a crack in the cabinet door saw a line of flickering light. Then there was the sound of a key in the entrance door and it swung open. His eye to the crack, he could plainly see two figures. One was holding a flashlight which slowly swung around the room.

"He's hiding," said Juan.

"I don't need you to tell me that," said Shirley with irritation.

"Where is your fuse box?" asked Juan.

The flashlight swung around above the workbench.

"You stay here," said Juan. He started into the room, coming between Jason and the light which Shirley must have been holding. Jason suspected Juan's hands were busy with his gun.

Jason leaned against the back wall of the cabinet and lifted his feet. As soon as he heard the circuit breakers being turned back on, Jason kicked the cabinet doors with all the force and power his runner's legs could muster. The doors caught Juan Díaz entirely by surprise, hitting him in the groin. He gasped with pain and staggered back against the cedar closet.

Jason lost no time. He crawled out and raced across the room, catching the door before Shirley had a chance to close it. He hit it with full force, running directly into Shirley and knocking the two of them onto the floor. Shirley cried as her head hit the concrete. The flashlight rolled out of her hand.

Scrambling to his feet, Jason raced down the hallway toward the stairs, thankful that this area of the house again had lights. He grabbed the banister and used it to catapult himself up the first steps. That was when he heard the dull pop. Simultaneously he felt a pain in his thigh and his right leg crumbled beneath him. Pulling himself upright, he hopped up the rest of the stairs. He was almost at the foyer; he could not give up.

His right leg dragging, Jason struggled over to the front door. Below, he heard someone start up the stairs.

The dead bolt opened and Jason stumbled out into the raw November night. He knew he'd been shot. He could feel the blood from his bullet wound running down his leg into his shoe.

Jason only got as far as the center of the driveway when Juan caught up to him and knocked him to the cobblestones with the butt of his pistol. Jason fell to his hands and knees. Before he could rise, Juan kicked him over onto his back. Once again, the pistol was pointed directly at Jason's head.

Suddenly, both men were bathed in brilliant light. Keeping the gun on Jason, Juan tried to shield his eyes from the glare of two high-beam headlights. A second later, there was the sound of car doors opening, followed by the ominous sound of shotguns being cocked. Juan backed up several steps like a cornered animal.

"Hold it, Díaz," called a voice unfamiliar to Jason. It was thick with a South Boston accent. "Don't do anything stupid. We don't want trouble with you or Miami. All we want you to do is walk to your car nice and easy and leave. Can you do that?"

Juan nodded. His left hand was still vainly trying to shield his eyes from the light.

"Then do it!" commanded the voice.

After taking two or three uncertain steps backward, Juan turned and fled to his car. He started the engine, gunned it, then roared out of the driveway.

Jason rolled onto his stomach. As soon as Juan left, Carol Donner ran out of the circle of light and dropped to her knees in front of him.

"My God, you're hurt!" A large bloodstain had formed on Jason's thigh.

"I suppose," said Jason vaguely. Too much had happened too quickly. "But it doesn't hurt too much," he added.

Another figure emerged from the glare; Bruno came up hefting a pump-action Winchester shotgun.

"Oh, no!" said Jason, trying to sit up.

"Don't worry," said Carol. "He knows you're a friend now."

At that moment, Shirley appeared on her front porch. Her clothing was disheveled and her hair spiked up like a punk rocker. For a second, she took in the scene. Then she stepped back and slammed the door. Locks were heard being engaged.

"We have to get him to a hospital," said Carol, pointing to Jason.

A second body-builder appeared. Gingerly they picked Jason up.

"I don't believe this," said Jason.

Jason found himself carried behind the glare of the lights. The vehicle turned out to be a white stretch Lincoln with a "V"-shaped TV antenna on the rear deck. The two muscle men eased Jason into the back seat where a man with dark glasses, slicked-back hair, and an unlit cigar was waiting. It was Arthur Koehler, Carol's boss. Carol jumped in after Jason and introduced him to Arthur. The muscle men got in the front seat and started the limo.

"Am I glad to see you two," said Jason. "But what in God's name brought you here?" Jason winced as the car bumped out of the driveway.

"Your voice," explained Carol. "That last time you called, I knew you were in trouble again."

"But how did you know I was here in Brookline?"

"Bruno followed you," said Carol. "After you called, I called my lovable boss here." Carol slapped Arthur's leg.

Arthur said, "Cut it out!" It had been his voice that had terrified Juan Díaz.

"I asked Arthur if he would protect you and he said he would under one condition. I have to dance for at least another two months or until he finds a replacement."

"Yeah, but she got me down to one month," complained Arthur.

"I'm very grateful," said Jason. "Are you really going to stop dancing, Carol?"

"She's a goddamn brat," said Arthur.

"I'm amazed," said Jason. "I didn't think girls like you could stop whenever you wanted."

"What are you talking about?" asked Carol indignantly.

"I'll tell you what he means," laughed Arthur, reaching forward and returning Carol's slap on the thigh. "He thinks you're a goddamn hooker." Arthur collapsed into paroxysms of laughter that changed to coughing. Carol had to pound him on the back several times before he got control of himself. "I used to have more fits like that when I lit these things," said Arthur, holding up his cigar. Then he looked at Jason in the half-light of the car. "You think I would have let her go to Seattle if she were a prostitute? Be reasonable, man."

"I'm sorry," Jason said. "I just thought . . ."

"You thought because I was dancing at the club I was a hooker," said Carol with somewhat less indignation. "Well, I suppose that's not entirely unfair. A couple of them are. But most aren't. For me, it was a great opportunity. My family name isn't Donner. It's Kikonen. We're Finnish and we've always had a healthier attitude to nudity than you Americans."

"And she's my wife's sister's kid," said Arthur. "So I gave her a job."

"You two are related?" asked Jason, amazed.

"We don't like to admit it," said Arthur, starting to laugh again.

"Come on," Carol said.

But Arthur continued, saying, "We hate the idea of any of our people going to Harvard. It hurts our image."

"You're going to Harvard?" asked Jason, turning to Carol.

"For my doctorate. The dancing covers my tuition."

"I guess I should have known Alvin would never have lived with your average exotic dancer," said Jason. "In any case, I'm grateful to you both. God knows what would have happened if you hadn't come along. I know the police will take care of Shirley Montgomery, but I wish you hadn't let Juan go."

"Don't worry," said Arthur with a wave of his cigar. "Carol told me what happened in Seattle. He won't be around for long. But I don't want trouble with my people in Miami. We'll deal with Juan through channels or I can give you enough information for the Miami police to pick him up. They'll have enough stuff on him down there to put him away. Believe me."

Jason looked at Carol. "I don't know how I can make it up to you."

"I have a few ideas," she said brightly.

Arthur had another laughing fit. When he was finally under control, Bruno lowered the glass to the front compartment.

"Hey, pervert," he called with a chuckle. "Where do you want us to take you? GHP emergency?"

"Hell, no," said Jason. "For the moment, I'm a little down on prepaid health care. Take me to Mass General."

EPILOGUE

Jason had never enjoyed ill health, as the saying goes, but currently he was loving it. He'd been hospitalized for three days following surgery on the wound in his leg. The pain had lessened significantly and the nursing staff at General was superbly competent and attentive. Several of them even remembered Jason as a resident.

But the best part of his hospitalization was that Carol spent most of each day with him, reading out loud, regaling him with funny stories, or just sitting in companionable silence.

"When you're all better," she said on the second day as she rearranged flowers that had come from Claudia and Sally, "I think we should go back to the Salmon Inn."

"What on earth for?" Jason said. After their experience, he couldn't imagine wanting to revisit the place.

"I'd like to try Devil's Chute again," Carol said cheerfully. "But this time in daylight."

"You're kidding!"

"Really. I bet it's a gas when the sun's shining."

A soft cough made them turn to the doorway. Detective Curran's disheveled bulk looked distinctly out of place in the hospital. His large hands were clutching a khaki rain hat that looked as if it had been run over by a truck.

"I hope I'm not bothering you, Dr. Howard," he said with uncharacteristic politeness.

Jason guessed that Curran was as intimidated by the hospital as Jason had been by the police station.

"Not at all," Jason said, pushing himself up to a sitting position. "Come in. Sit down."

Carol pulled a chair away from the wall and positioned it next to the bed. Curran lowered himself into it, still clutching the hat.

"How's the leg coming?" he asked.

"Fine," Jason said. "Mostly muscle injury. Not going to be a problem at all."

"I'm glad."

"Candy?" Carol asked, extending a box of chocolates that the GHP secretaries had sent.

Curran examined them carefully, chose a chocolate-covered cherry, and plopped it whole into his mouth. Swallowing, he said, "I thought you'd like to know how the case is developing."

"Absolutely," Jason said. Carol went around to the other side of the bed and sat on the edge.

"First of all, they picked Juan up in Miami. He has a sheet a mile long. You name it. He's one of Castro's gifts to America. We're going to try to get him extradited to Massachusetts for Brennquivist's and Lund's murders, but it'll be tough. Seems four or five other states want the creep for similar capers, including Florida."

"Can't say I feel very sorry for him," Jason said.

"The guy's a psychopath," Curran agreed.

"What about GHP?" Jason asked. "Have you been able to prove that the releasing factor for the death gene was introduced into the eyedrops used by the ophthalmological office?"

"We're working closely with the DA's office on it," Curran said. "It's turning out to be quite a story."

"How much do you feel will be made public?"

"At this point we aren't certain. Some will have to come out. The Hartford School's closed and the parents of those kids aren't blind. Furthermore, as the DA points out, there's a slew of local families with million-dollar lawsuits to file against the GHP. Shirley and her crew are finished."

"Shirley . . ." Jason said wistfully. "You know, there was a time, if I hadn't met Carol, I might have gotten involved with the lady."

Carol shook a playful fist at him.

"I guess I owe you an apology, doctor," Curran said. "At first I thought you were just a pain in the ass. But it turns out you're responsible for busting the deadliest conspiracy I've ever heard of."

"It was mostly luck," Jason said. "If I hadn't been with Hayes the night he died, we doctors would have thought we were battling some new epidemic."

"This guy Hayes must have been a smart cookie," Curran said.

"A genius," Carol said.

"You know what bugs me the most?" Curran said. "Until the end Hayes thought he was working on a discovery to help mankind. Probably thought he'd be a hero, like Salk. Nobel prizes and all that. Save the world. I'm not a scientist, but it seems to me Hayes's whole field of research is pretty damned scary. You know what I mean?"

"I know exactly what you mean," Jason said. "Medical science has always assumed its research would save lives and reduce suffering. But now science has awesome potential. Things can go either way."

"As I understand it," Curran said, "Hayes found a drug that makes people age and die in a couple of weeks—and he wasn't even looking for it. Makes me think you eggheads are out of control. Am I wrong?"

"I agree," Jason said. "Maybe we're getting too smart for our own good. It's like eating the forbidden fruit all over again."

"Yeah, and we're going to get kicked right out of paradise," Curran added. "Incidentally, doesn't Uncle Sam have watchdogs overseeing guys like Hayes?"

"They don't have a very good record on this sort of thing," Jason explained. "Too many conflicts of interest. Besides, both doctors and laymen tend to believe all medical research is inherently good."

"Wonderful," snorted Curran. "It's like a car barreling down the freeway at a hundred miles an hour with no driver."

"That's probably the best analogy I've ever heard," Jason said.

"Oh, well." The detective shrugged his huge shoulders. "At least we can deal with GHP. Formal indictments are coming down soon. Of course, the whole pack is out on bail. But the case has broken wide open, with all the principals stabbing each other in the back and trying to plea bargain. Seems that friend Hayes originally approached some guy by the name of Ingelbrook."

"Ingelnook. He's one of the GHP vice presidents," Jason said. "I think he's in finance."

"Must be," Curran said. "Apparently Hayes approached him for seed capital to front a company."

"I know," Jason said.

The detective looked hard at him. "Did you, now? And just how did you know about that, Dr. Howard?"

"It's unimportant. Go on."

"Anyway," Curran said, "Hayes must have told Ingelnook that he was about to develop some kind of elixir of youth."

"That would have been an antibody to the death-hormone releasing factor," Jason said.

"Hold it a minute," Curran said. "Maybe you should be telling me this stuff rather than vice versa."

"I'm sorry," Jason said. "It's all finally making sense to me. Please—go on."

"Ingelnook must have liked the death hormone better than the elixir of youth," Curran continued. "For some time he'd been racking his brains about lowering costs at GHP to keep them competitive. So far the conspiracy only involves six people, but there may be more. They've been responsible for eliminating a lot of patients they thought were going to use more than their fair share of medical services. Nice, huh?"

"So they killed them," Carol said with horror.

"Well, they kept telling themselves that the process was natural," Curran said.

"Some excuse for murder—we're all going to die anyway," Jason commented bitterly. The faces of some of his recently deceased patients rose to haunt him.

"In any case, it's the end of GHP," Curran said. "The criminal charges notwithstanding, malpractice claims are through the roof. GHP is already filing for Chapter Eleven. So I think you'll be looking for a job."

"Looks like it." Then, looking up at Carol, Jason added, "Carol's finishing her studies in clinical psychology. We thought we'd open an office together. I think I want to get back to private practice. No more corporations for a while."

"That sounds cozy," Curran said. "Then I can get my head and my ticker fixed at the same place."

"You can be our first patient."

Robin Cook
Godplayer £3.99

In Boston Memorial Hospital the incidences of sudden surgical death have reached epidemic proportions. Post-operative patients are dying without reason. Pathologist Robert Seifert has found a pattern among the victims. They're homosexual or mentally defective or terminally ill. Somebody has the knowledge and access to kill them. Maybe Seifert knows who it is . . . but he is hospitalised for minor surgery and becomes the next victim. If a sane surgeon holds the power of life and death, just how insane does he have to be to start playing God?

Robin Cook

Fever £3.99

Charles Martel is a doctor turned researcher: his wife died of cancer and he wanted to know why. His world is shattered a second time when his daughter is sick with fever. Suddenly he's a man against odds: against doctors who want to treat his daughter's leukaemia the wrong way; against the research institute that puts profits before ethics; against a recycling plant that's dumping cancer-inducing benzene in the rivers. For a man whose daughter's life is on the line, these are odds enough to turn a responsible citizen into a criminal.

'Scalpel-edged tension' DAILY EXPRESS

Coma £3.99

Why did the two patients who underwent routine minor surgery in Boston's greatest hospital never regain consciousness? Up against the scorn of the medics and the hostility of the establishment, one girl medical student starts to probe the coma cases steadily – and uncovers something unbelievably hideous . . .

Robin Cook

Outbreak £4.50

His most harrowing medical horror yet

Dr Marissa Blumenthal is a recently qualified member of Atlanta's renowned Centre for Disease Control, yet to put her skills to the test in the field.

But when a mysterious viral outbreak occurs in Los Angeles, she has no time for self-doubt, finding herself plunged into a desperate race to contain a lethal virus for which there is no known cure.

Then further outbreaks occur across the States, all seemingly unconnected except for one bizarre similarity: the victims are always only the doctors and patients of clinics offering low-cost medical care.

In the face of her superiors' fury and colleagues' scepticism, Marissa begins to investigate, her evidence pointing more and more at a ruthless and sinister organisation sworn to achieve a horrific goal no matter what the cost in human life – including Marissa's.

Outbreak is Robin Cook at his hair-raising best. A fiendishly compelling and all too plausible chiller guaranteed to echo in the mind long after the last page is turned.

All Pan books are available at your local bookshop or newsagent, or can be ordered direct from the publisher. Indicate the number of copies required and fill in the form below.

Send to: **CS Department, Pan Books Ltd., P.O. Box 40, Basingstoke, Hants. RG21 2YT.**

or phone: 0256 469551 (Ansaphone), quoting title, author and Credit Card number.

Please enclose a remittance* to the value of the cover price plus: 60p for the first book plus 30p per copy for each additional book ordered to a maximum charge of £2.40 to cover postage and packing.

*Payment may be made in sterling by UK personal cheque, postal order, sterling draft or international money order, made payable to Pan Books Ltd.

Alternatively by Barclaycard/Access:

Card No. | | | | | | | | | | | | | | | | |

____

Signature:

Applicable only in the UK and Republic of Ireland.

While every effort is made to keep prices low, it is sometimes necessary to increase prices at short notice. Pan Books reserve the right to show on covers and charge new retail prices which may differ from those advertised in the text or elsewhere.

NAME AND ADDRESS IN BLOCK LETTERS PLEASE:

....

Name _______________________________

Address _______________________________

____

____

____

3/87